Mike Huss

WHY OH WHY COULDN'T YOU HAVE BURNT THE BLOODY PLACE DOWN?

*For Sam,
Don't go getting any ideas!
Gt Uncle Mike
(aka Jack!)*

Limited Special Edition. No. 7 of 25 Paperbacks

Mike was born in London and raised happily in Surbiton. He left the grammar school at 18 and joined the regular army straight from school. He volunteered to serve in Aden (now Yemen) so as to join his fiancée who had already been posted there. She gave him the ring back on the night he got there and his subsequent adventures in a war for two years can be read in the first book in this trilogy, *It must have been the compo*. This, second book relates our hero Jack's adventures for 6 months in a brutal training regime to become an officer following his recommendation for a commission in Aden. Subsequent service in the Depot (the now notorious Deepcut!), the Junior Leaders' Regiment and a tank depot followed. A varied career with a N. Ireland Training Board, a group training association, as Personnel Director and Tribunal Advocate resulted in writing the Dear Doctor employment law column in the Sunday Times for 10 years. This is his second venture into fiction with a third in the trilogy to follow.

Mother Nature, Father Time and the Grim Reaper all combine to interfere with the best-laid plans of mice and men and which often therefore 'gang aglee!' Two men, Tony Sutcliffe and Peter Done stood by me when what seemed like the whole world was against me. For five years, I suffered the tortures of the dammed (plus serious ill health!) while the legal process dragged on and on, but these two stood by me, supported me even when the evidence seemed entirely against me and, when the evidence of the other side justifiably fell apart, saw that their faith in me had been justified.

One of them is, alas, no longer with us but I hope he will be able to read the heavenly edition (top of the 100 best reads when cloud resting) and receive my thanks. To the other one, Peter, don't you dare catch the Heavenly Express, Platform 131/2, Piccadilly, before I can thank you – thank you. Because those three troublemakers mentioned above could interfere and leave neither around to read it (I hope they don't! They've already done so with Tony). I have had to place this dedication at the start of Book 2, instead of 3, where it more properly belongs. For the full details, my reader, you will have to wait 'til Book 3 when all will become clear.

Mike Huss

WHY OH WHY COULDN'T YOU HAVE BURNT THE BLOODY PLACE DOWN?

AUSTIN MACAULEY PUBLISHERS™
LONDON · CAMBRIDGE · NEW YORK · SHARJAH

Copyright © Mike Huss 2022

The right of Mike Huss to be identified as author of this work has been asserted by the author in accordance with section 77 and 78 of the Copyright, Designs and Patents Act 1988.

All rights reserved. No part of this publication may be reproduced, stored in a retrieval system, or transmitted in any form or by any means, electronic, mechanical, photocopying, recording, or otherwise, without the prior permission of the publishers.

Any person who commits any unauthorised act in relation to this publication may be liable to criminal prosecution and civil claims for damages.

This is a work of fiction. Names, characters, businesses, places, events, locales, and incidents are either the products of the author's imagination or used in a fictitious manner. Any resemblance to actual persons, living or dead, or actual events is purely coincidental.

A CIP catalogue record for this title is available from the British Library.

ISBN 9781528959704 (Paperback)
ISBN 9781528967143 (ePub e-book)

www.austinmacauley.com

First Published 2022
Austin Macauley Publishers Ltd®
1 Canada Square
Canary Wharf
London
E14 5AA

Once again, I must thank Austin Macauley for their invaluable assistance in producing this book – thank you.

Chapter 1

The sign said 'Welcome', but the atmosphere said anything but that. *Let's see just how welcoming this place is then*, thought Jack. He had seen a Rolls Royce drive away with its passenger, presumably upset by his treatment (see Book 1 'It must have been the compo' for the full story). He started the engine and drove slowly down to the Guardroom. The Duty NCO stepped out and indicated where he should park. Jack parked as indicated and returned to the NCO, a Welsh Guards Staff or Colour Sergeant by his rank badges and reported in by quoting his rank and serial number. Looking him carefully up and down the NCO said,

"Park your car in the garage labelled for Officer Cadets, then find spider Kohima; you are in bed 5, Room 1 and you will find an instructions envelope with your name on it which you are to read immediately. Clear, Sir?"

"Yes, Staff," Jack replied – he knew that all NCOs, without exception, under the rank of WOII were to be addressed as 'Staff' and WOIIs and above were to be addressed as 'Sir'. The NCO gave Jack a sharp look but said no more and gestured for him to get on with it. The car park, an old drill shed, was clearly marked as being the one for Officer Cadets but there was an old Morris Minor blocking the entrance. The driver was nowhere to be seen. Jack was just about to get out when a man walked out of the Shed and, seeing Jack, just shrugged his shoulders. Winding the window down Jack called out,

"What's the problem?"

"Some daft bugger has left a brand-new Ford Mustang right in the way into the Shed and I can't get my car in," he said, indicating the Morris Minor. Jack got out and went for a look himself. Looking into the Drill Shed, there was a clear driveway through the shed and cars were clearly supposed to be parked at angles off the central drive. A brand-new Mustang, hood down, with just 50 miles on the clock had been left right in the entrance. There was no sign of an owner. Clearly they couldn't stay there all day and asking the Duty NCO for help would not create a good first impression. Looking more closely at the Mustang, Jack saw that the keys had been left in the ignition. Problem solved. Jumping in and moving it into a parking bay was only the work of a few moments. Clearly some idle sod had left it for someone else to park it up. Jack was not pleased. So the question was what to do with the keys? He was tempted to lose them completely but there was a witness, the other Cadet, so Jack simply opened the boot of the Mustang and dropped them in there. It turned out that the car belonged to the son of a minor Arab state's sheik's son who was used to being waited on hand and foot. He was about to receive a rude awakening and not just the loss of his car keys!

Later on, when they were allowed out for a specific purpose, the Mustang would not start; the battery had gone flat, he must have left something on to drain it flat was the general consensus. The Cadet, Officer Cadet 'Horsey' Fawaz, disappeared in a taxi and returned in a brand-new Mini Cooper. Having learned nothing, he left it blocking the entrance in the same spot as he had left the Mustang. This time the other Cadets, including Jack, were not so complacent and when 'Horsey' did come to go out in it, it was to find it parked between two uprights of the shed. The gap between the uprights was only two inches longer than the Mini and no number of reversing and forwarding was going to get it out – it had been carried/bounced sideways into the gap by a few Cadets and the only way to get it out was to bounce it out. Since no one was willing to help, the car stayed there for the next six months and for all Jack knew, it is still there.

Jack parked his car a few spaces down from the Mustang by the sidewall and made his way to the Kohima spider, an old wooden hut which had been rendered with a light gravel in an endeavour to modernise its appearance, and into Room 1 and found bed 5. In addition to the bed number being prominently displayed at the head of the bed, so was the Officer Cadet's name, in Jack's case, Officer Cadet Hughes John. The large room, capable of holding 16 beds, had room dividers so that the first miniature room had two bed spaces, the second space had four and the third one also had four, making ten in total, as it was to turn out that composed No 1 Section of Kohima platoon.

So large was the printing of the names that Jack could easily read the name on the next bed to his. It read 'Officer Cadet Mohammed Mohammed'. Jack experienced an intense feeling of shock, the like of which he had never experienced before. It couldn't be, could it? Jack had left Aden in November the previous year; Britain had pulled out in April this year i.e., a month ago so could it be possible that the terrorist he had shot at, twice, just for the minor offence of throwing a hand grenade at Jack, was now going to be sleeping in the next bed to Jack for the next six months? An awful lot of Arabs named their sons after the great Prophet, so it was possible that it was a different Mohammed Mohammed and that hope lasted precisely three minutes until the Mohammed Mohammed walked, or more precisely staggered, through the door with a mountain of luggage and kit. Jack knew immediately he saw him that it was 'his' Mohammed. The question was, did Mohammed know that Jack was his target of long ago? Whilst Jack had had the advantage of seeing Mohammed 'full faced' in the streetlights, Mohammed had been looking at a figure in shadow spitting bullets at him from a sub-machine gun. Jack decided to say nothing and see what happened. Knowing nothing of how Mons operated, he didn't feel he could ask to be moved without having to say why and then how confidential would their history remain. Definitely nothing for now.

Chapter 2

Making introductions took a while as they were more or less repeated as each member of the Section arrived. Eventually, all 10 were present in Jack's room and the other two rooms totalled 20 more, so the Rolls Royce passenger was not from their platoon. Four were serving soldiers, three were from overseas and the remaining three were straight from civilian life. The Permanent Staff Member allocated to this platoon was Sergeant Dewey from the Light Infantry. Always to be addressed as 'Staff', he was not long in calling all the serving soldiers in the platoon, 10 in all, to his office at the end of the spider. Not designed to hold 11 people, it was a bit of a crush and already hot. The temperature rapidly climbed. The 'welcome' speech was quite short. Dewey made it clear that for the next ten days, they would be going through the admin process, issues of uniforms, kit, medical inspections, injections and the like before starting their training proper on the week Monday. He then went around the group asking for their name and military experience to date. Jack was not particularly pleased to be told that as a Staff Clerk with three and a half years of service, he would undoubtedly find the going physically hard, as he was not used to the physical side of Army life as were the seven infanteers amongst their number. Jack took exception to this. He was pretty fit, partly from all the physical exercise jobs the CSM at the holding company had had him doing and partly because Jack had heard through the grapevine how hard the physical side of Mons was, so he had been going for three-mile runs whenever the opportunity presented itself so that he should be fit for anything Mons could throw at him. In fact, as Jack was to find out that was a lot, a lot more than he could ever have imagined and Dewey was indeed right, Jack would find it excruciatingly difficult but so would all the infanteers, so demanding was the physical side of Mons. It was also to be mentally challenging as, as they were becoming tired on the physical side, so the pressure was increased and the mental challenge to keep going got harder and harder to try and determine their limits.

Dewey explained some of this to them. He made it clear that in only six months, they would become commissioned officers, those that passed, and they would be ordering and leading platoons of very fit soldiers so that on route marches, forced marches and similar, one-minute, they would be at the front of the platoon and then drop back to the back to chase up stragglers and then back up to the front to guide and push on the soldiers there so that they would need to be fitter than any of their men because they would be travelling far further than the platoon by virtue of their keeping control of it so that Mons would make sure they were fit enough, physically and mentally to cope. They would indeed be tired staggering into bed shattered in the early hours if they were lucky – on many nights, they would have no sleep at all.

He went on to explain that they would function as sections initially and after that as a platoon. Those Officer Cadets from civilian life would not only have to learn all the basic soldiering skills with which they, trained soldiers, were all already acquainted but the officer-like training as well. As trained soldiers, they would have a head start but that would avail them not a lot since they would have to act as mentors, trainers and tutors to the civvies to keep them up to speed with the trained soldiers. The overseas Cadets were largely, at this stage, an unknown quantity. One was an American Marine 2nd Lieutenant who was going to go through the Mons training with them to assess it against the Marine training he had just completed as would the 2nd Lieutenant from the South African Army and the same for the Rhodesian Army one. The remaining seven were largely unknown although it was known that one of them was the son of a Sheikh of one of the Trucial Oman states, one had been a soldier in the National Liberation Front (NLF) which had fought Britain for the last two years or so in Aden, so he would apparently have had practical experience of fighting a guerrilla war. None of you seven have had such experience so it might be we can learn something from him.

"Excuse me, Staff, would that be Mohammed Mohammed?"

"In future, you will not speak until I have given you permission to do so, but I will let it go on this occasion, as you have not been told that. Clear?"

"Yes, Staff," said Jack.

"As it happens, yes you are right, he fought against us. How did you know it was him?" This told Jack that at least his documentation had not arrived, or if it had it hadn't been read, or Dewey would have known that Jack at least had served in a war zone.

Debating whether to tell Dewey or not in front of the other nine, Jack decided that discretion was the better part of valour and he just said, "I guessed, Staff, but may I have a private interview with you fairly soon?" Jack felt all the eyes on him – something he would rather not have happened, but he did not want his situation to leak out in an inappropriate moment or manner. Dewey took a long time looking at Jack and then he said,

"See me after this meeting."

"Yes, Staff."

Dewey spent quite some time explaining what they could expect and what would be expected of them – some of it would turn out to be true but on the whole, it would be much harder than he said. He did not say that there would be almost no training to be an officer, just a higher standard of all the basic drills, fitness, weapons handling, map reading, physical treks and infantry skills of defence, attack, reconnaissance and working with armour and helicopters. It was a huge amount to get through in just six months and, if previous courses were anything to go by, about 25% would drop out either by not reaching the standard required after six, twelve and 24 weeks or by the individual opting to leave, either back to their unit or civilian life. In fact, the Marine dropped out after 6 weeks, the South African at 12 weeks and the Rhodesian after 20. Each of them thought that the British Army training would be a lot easier than their own training they had only just completed before travelling to Mons, but it turned out that their perceptions were wrong and Mons was hard, hard, hard.

Dewey completed the meeting by wishing them all good luck and then offered to sell them extra kit that they would find useful like extra boots. He made it clear that high standards of turnout would be expected at all times and trying to keep the DMS (rubber-soled boots) shiny when they were still wet from the previous time they were worn was nigh on impossible. (He would, of course be the one inspecting them most of the time so he could absolutely guarantee that they would not pass inspection!) He also had ammunition boots (steel-toe and heel-tipped) which would only be worn for the passing out parades but which would be thrown around the room and damaged, particularly by chipping of the heel and toe caps which was pretty well impossible to repair for during inspections and therefore, a spare undamaged pair kept in their personal locker was highly desirable. Jack bought two pairs of DMS boots and one pair of ammo boots – he had no intention of letting Dewey find out that he already had highly polished ammo boots from his Army Cadet Force days. At £5 per pair, they were expensive but as they were highly polished, it would save an awful lot of work and grief. He also bought a complete set of webbing, belt, anklets, ammo pouches and small pack as these too would be inspected at awkward times and the cleanliness would not always be good.

Jack remained behind as all the others left and was not expecting the attack Dewey served on him.

"I hope this is not some whining bleat, Mr, who are you? Complainants receive short thrift at Mons and soon find themselves RTU'd (Returned to Unit), so what is it?" Jack had always believed that attack was the best form of defence so he moved to the attack straight away.

"It's Mr Hughes, Staff. I believe you should know that Mr Mohammed tried to kill me in Aden and I tried to kill him in return. I did kill one of his mates. You should know that he is not the only one to have experience of warfare, I did too on several occasions – we were soldiers first and clerks or whatever second." Dewey just stood there with his mouth open for several seconds before gathering himself together and saying,

"Tell me about it." Jack gave a brief description of the two events when he had been ambushed by Mohammed and when he had shot the terrorist who was in the process of throwing a hand grenade at the Officers' Mess which Jack was guarding. Dewey asked how he identified Mohammed and Jack had to explain going to the MP offices and identifying him from the photograph books. He added that Mohammed had probably not got a good look at him because at first he had been driving the car and when Mohammed had looked back around the corner of the wall, Jack had been turning away and realising Mohammed had reappeared had fired immediately from the hip and the fire from the muzzle would have hidden Jack. Dewey continued to stare at Jack for several seconds before speaking. When he did, it was not what Jack expected but it was typical Army.

"It's a pity you didn't fucking kill him or he you, then we wouldn't have this problem. We are going to have to teach you to shoot straight so next time you kill the bastard. I will pass this upwards (the typical reaction of an NCO when faced with a problem; a far cry from running the Army or Petty Officers running the Navy as was their frequent claim; the reality was that when the shit hit the fan, the first thing an NCO did was to look to an Officer for help). In the meantime, don't talk about Aden; if you have to admit that you have been in the Middle East, say it was Libya or Bahrain, anywhere but Aden. I'll get back to you as soon as I can but in the meantime (with a smile on his face), search your bed for grenades every night before going to bed; the last thing we want is to have to teach the drill for funerals so soon in the course." And with that, Jack was thrown out. *Lot of sympathy and care there,* he thought, probably black humour but he didn't know Dewey well enough yet.

Chapter 3

The first week or so was a mirror image of the Recruit Intake Wing when he had joined the Royal Army Service Corps in Bordon. This time there was much more kit issued and measurements for the Service Dress (SD) were properly done. It seemed very wasteful to hand in a perfectly good SD uniform only to be issued with a new one; the new one would fit much better when it returned from tailoring but it would only be worn about three or four times in the six months, twice for actual passing out parades of senior companies and one practice for the final one and, of course the final passing-out parade – an expensive exercise as they handed it in after their passing out parade as they would, henceforth, wear real officer's SD – which they would order early on for delivery in their last week at Mons. Since about 25% would drop out; it was an expensive system but unavoidable given the amount of time and work necessary to produce a couple of SDs, Mess Kit, handmade Mess Wellingtons, shoes, Side Cap, Service Cap, No 1 Uniform Cap and No 1 Dress Uniform, overcoat, raincoat, Sam Brown, swagger stick, ties, shirts, cap badges, collar dogs, etc. It cost a fortune which the grant from the Army did nowhere near cover.

Again, like Bordon, they had medicals, medicals, medicals; so many injections that when they had a drink, they leaked everywhere. In between, they started basic training – easy enough for the ex-rankers but hard for the ex-civilians as the instructors pushed on at a fair rate. The overseas Cadets were a problem as most of their English was quite poor and a screamed left turn by a Drill Instructor could result in a left turn by the ex-rankers, a right turn by the civvies and a variety of waltzes by the overseas lot – of whom Mohammed was one. His English was so poor as to be non-existent for anything other than the simplest words which suited Jack no end as conversations between the two of them were very limited. Jack's mentoring ended up with Jack showing Mo – it was shortened since the full word was too close to the Muslim Prophet's name; not in the name itself but the rich, ripe language of an irate Drill Instructor, when driven to distraction by Mo's inability to carry out the simplest of commands, did come over a bit like disrespect of the Prophet – that a change to Mo was simple and safe. Indeed so much demonstrating did Jack do that he was almost cleaning all of Mo's kit himself – so much so that Jack started to get suspicious that Mo's 'not understand' was just a way of getting Jack to do the work.

Another problem with Mo and some of the other overseas Cadets was that they were very small. Mo could not have been much more than 5'1"/5'2" tall. With Jack and some of the others being well over 6' tall, exercises on the parallel bars were fun because the bars had to be hoisted to the maximum, something approaching 7'6", which the overseas Cadets could not reach even by jumping and therefore, Mo and a couple of the other short Cadets had to be lifted up so that they could hang on. Pull-ups to chest high was quite hard work especially when the call was for 20 of them at a time. You'd think that Mo would have no trouble as he only had six or seven stones to lift; Jack weighed 14 St. 4 lb. at that time so he was effectively lifting twice the weight Mo was except Mo could not pull himself up once, let alone 20 times. Even the PT instructors' direst threats had no effect – he probably didn't understand what was being threatened anyway – but the funniest was when the exercise on the bars was over and the Cadets dropped down. For Jack and the other tall ones, it was only a short drop but for Mo and one of the others it was too high and they were too frightened to drop! Consequently, they had to be lifted down as well as up! They might not have been strong enough to pull up but by Christ, they were strong enough to hold on to avoid the fall! Jack, as Mo's allocated mentor, was the one who had to lift him up and back down again. Lifting six stones up and down (actually down was quite easy because all he did was squeeze Mo's chest, Mo let go of the bar and Jack let go of Mo, so not so hard going down just up) but the up, six stones to full arms reach was hard work and extra to what the others were doing. By the end of the first week, Mo was able to do five pull-ups. Jack was easily able to do the 20 and lift Mo up and Mo was starting to let go albeit still supported by Jack to get down. They were, following so much exercise in the day, already going to bed – usually in the early hours of the morning – physically and mentally tired and it was going to get worse!

On their second Saturday at lunchtime, they were assembled at noon to be spoken to by the Company Sergeant Major (CSM). It was the first time they had seen him and his Highlander uniform, complete with kilt, caused a bit of a stir amongst some of the overseas Cadets who had not seen a man in a skirt before. He was properly square like a CSM looked like in Commando comics and other such magazines displayed them as, square chin, square shoulders, square chest, square eyeballs, anything you cared to look at was square. And of course, he used the hoary old intro, "You will call me 'Sir', I will call you 'Sir', the difference is you mean it!" He finished his intro by saying,

"You will spend an awful lot of your time here on your feet and that means your boots must fit you properly or you will be hobbling behind everyone else and 'THAT WILL NOT DO'." Emphasis made, he carried on, "Consequently, you will fall in again after dinner, at 1300 hours, (they weren't officers yet so it was still dinner and not lunch) wearing your DMS boots and we will make sure they fit you properly. Dismissed."

Jack was with Charles Telford, an ex-Guards Lance Sergeant in reality a Corporal but the Guards regarded themselves as so superior that NCOs wore the rank badges of the rank above their own but by placing Lance in front of it made it clear that they were actually a rank junior to the one they displayed but making them senior to any soldier of the same rank in any other regiment, thus giving themselves the seniority if such became an issue. In reality only the Guards regarded that as a proper way to display rank, everyone else just thought they were show off posh prats and refused to accept that one of their Lance Sergeants was superior to a line regiment Corporal! They were making their way in a smart and soldierly manner, mug and cutlery clasped in their left hands behind their backs, right hand swinging smartly to their shoulders when they were joined by Timothy Speaker a Royal Corps of Signals Corporal – the three of them were to form a tight trio to help one another through the course – who said,

"What do you make of this ensuring your boots fit malarkey; I never expected that they seem almost nice and that cannot be right?"

Charlie, no insistence on Charles here, said,

"Aye, it's wrong; it'll reveal itself soon enough." And it did. Having fallen in just before 1300 hours, the CSM appeared bang on time. He announced,

"The Cup Final starts at 1500 hours and I intend to watch all of it. So you only have two hours to break your feet in. Normally, we allow three hours for this but because of the Cup you only have two; I'm sure you'll manage. You notice I said to break your feet in; no, it was not a mistake, I did not mean your boots I meant your feet – your feet are softer than your boots so they will break in first. So that is what we'll do. ATTENTION. LEFT TURN. BY THE RIGHT QUICK MARCH." And off they went. Within 30–40 yards the CSM ordered "DOUBLE MARCH" and at that, they started trotting. At first, they were on the road but once they had left the Camp, they changed to two files, with a man of roughly the same size alongside and then into a cart track lane. They had gone about 300 yards when they were ordered to pick up the right-hand file man in a fireman's lift and to continue doubling down the lane. Jack was the right-file man and was consequently carried first and he was ever so glad to be dropped off and have to pick up the left-file man in turn. The lane was in a pretty poor state, rutted and holed, and it was therefore no surprise that Jack went over on his ankle, dropping his burden onto the lane. This happened, as luck would have it, just as the CSM was passing. Trevor Harrison had landed on his shoulder and face and had suffered a few minor grazes as a consequence and Jack who was hobbling around on his right ankle which had twisted and given way on a particularly deep hole. Having ensured that no apparently serious injury had occurred, the CSM was instantly back to hazing them onwards although this time without someone on their backs. It was unusually hot for May and, as the miles dropped off, so did the Cadets. A Landrover was following them and picking up the dropouts as the miles passed. By the time the 10 miles were up and they had doubled back into the camp, 15 of the 59 Cadets had had to be picked up. The CSM was not happy, although it was 14.45 hours and thus in time for the start of the Cup Final; in his view, there were far too many nancies amongst them, they were unfit to be soldiers of Her Majesty and that would have to be remedied, starting now. The 15 dropouts, of whom Mo was one, were ordered to the Gym and put through an hour's PT. The remainder were dismissed for the rest of the day – they had a church parade the next day and kit had to be cleaned for that, even though it was their civilian suites and hats – they are being deemed unsuitable to parade in any uniform just yet. It was during this time that Mo disappeared. Nothing was said or appeared on Orders; he just was there one minute and gone the next. However, he hadn't disappeared totally out of Jack's life and he was to reappear twice in the future. Tiredness also had not disappeared out of Jack's life.

Following the trip up, Jack's ankle had given him hell. He made it to the end of the ten miles in the main body of troops but he was limping badly. By the following morning, he could not get a shoe onto the foot, so badly swollen was it. He had to take the laces out of his right gym shoe and wear that, no sock. On parade Sgt Dewey went a bit purple when he saw it but before he could build up a good head of steam, the CSM, who was with him said,

"Is that from the fall yesterday?"

"Yes, Sir," said Jack. At that, the CSM passed on and had a go at the Cadet next to him who happened to be Horsey Fawaz. He was simply smiling at the CSM who was in first class bollocking mode, for the lightweight lime green suit Horsey was wearing was not a suitable, pun intended, defence mechanism so Horsey spent Sunday afternoon in the Guardhouse on fatigues. And Sgt Dewey passed on by.

By the following morning, Jack could not even get the plimsoll on and he therefore paraded for sick parade without a shoe on that foot at all at 0600 hrs – an inducement in itself to dissuade those only mildly unwell to parade sick. Cadets were required to parade at the Guardroom and who should be there but the CSM. He came along the line questioning Cadets as to what was wrong with them. When he reached Jack, he just looked at the bare swollen ankle and passed by. By the time the CSM had finished, half of those reporting sick had decided not to go sick of those six remaining, five were seen in the Medical Centre in the school but Jack was sent in a Landrover to the Military Hospital in Aldershot where his ankle was x-rayed and then strapped up. The Corporal Medic who strapped it up said to Jack,

"You've got a small fracture but it will be put down as a sprain lest you sue them for the carelessly incompetent way it was caused. You'll be put on light duties, no drill, PT or similarly energetic type activities for two or three weeks depending on how it heals. Report back to your Medical Centre in a week's time." Jack was to come up against the falsification of his records some 50 years later when he made a claim against the Army for the arthritis he was suffering caused by the fracture but the Judge accepted the written record of a sprain as being unlikely to have been the cause of the arthritis.

Jack remained on light duties for the next three weeks. Since he could not afford to fall behind the platoon, he had to keep up as best he could. When they did drill, he, standing at the edge of the square, mimicked most of the movements and was not too concerned since they were covering something which he was very familiar with. Since he was an experienced soldier, most of it was familiar to him but he had never been taught bayonet drill before so he paid close attention to it. Exercises in the field were awkward since he could not keep up with the platoon on some of them but as this was still basic soldiering, with which he was very familiar that did not matter too much either. The fact that he was putting in this effort did not go unnoticed although Jack felt the CSM's view would be that he would expect soldiers to walk on their stumps if their feet had been blown off on mines!

Chapter 4

It took three weeks for Jack to be signed back to full duties. They had covered in the three weeks the amount of work that recruits to a Corps would take six weeks to cover. They now started on more advanced infantry training with more time spent in the training areas around Mons. They would start out with one set of commanders, Platoon Commander, Platoon Sergeant, three Corporal Section Commanders, three Lance Corporals, Cadets assigned to the radio, 2" mortar, the GPMG – three of them with the Lance Corporals commanding the gun, a runner and any other odds and sods the Staff thought appropriate. After anything between five and 20 minutes, the Staff would blow the whistle and everyone changed around. Most Cadets yearned just to be a rifleman and do what others ordered; thus, they would avoid being criticised loudly in front of everyone else and left to feel much degraded. One would have imagined that the criticism would have been constructive leaving the Cadet knowing better what to do next time. Not so. Negativity spread throughout the Platoon.

At the end of six weeks, they faced a written exam. At the end of each day, they were required to fall in in full combat kit and rifle and undertake a route march which took them away from Mons. The lorry to bring them back would leave at a particular time and if they hadn't made it to the lorry by that time, it would leave without them ensuring that they would then have to march the ten or so miles back again. The incentive to get there on or before time was therefore considerable; the drill tests, written map reading tests and questions regarding radio operation and procedures along with the alphabet suitable for use on the radio and simple coding/decoding made up the exams at the end of the six weeks. Failure in any of the tests meant back-squadding or returning to unit although serving soldiers very rarely received the RTUing since they were already trained soldiers.

Every night when the training day finished, nominally 1800 hrs, they discovered that the training staff had thought up some little task to occupy them – most nights it was a ten-mile march along a compass bearing with the lorry somewhere along it to bring them back at a specific time. Sometimes they were scheduled to load rounds into belt clips for the machine guns – they got through belts at an astonishing rate and the task was hated because it tore fingers to shreds. One that Jack recognised offered benefits to the Cadets was the cleaning tasks in the offices. Rather than pay cleaners to clean the offices, empty the bins, clean the toilets, polish the floors and any other demeaning task needing doing, a number of Cadets were rostered to the cleaning duties each night. The benefit referred to was the exam papers and Jack's experience as a clerk. The papers were run off on Gestetner printers. The typed wax sheets were smoothed onto the rollers and the handle rotated several times for the ink to be squeezed through the print holes to get clear copies for the Cadets. It meant that, although faint, there were initially barely legible copies to be thrown away; they were too faint to be used so no clerk would pick up those first few copies, but if you wanted to know what the exam was to be the day (or two) before the exam, the waste bin was the answer and Jack knew it! Not perhaps the 'officer and gentleman' behaviour but they were being taught that winning was what mattered so win they did – but carefully; it would not do for everyone to get every answer correct. And they were still shattered at the end of every day.

The seventh week was spent on Dartmoor, an area notorious for bad weather. Although they didn't know it at the time, the Company that would follow on eight weeks behind them would lose two overseas Cadets to hypothermia on the Moor. There was to be very little in the way of playing soldiers; the military exercise was to be marching over the Moor in groups of three or so; to make sure they were really stretched before making their way to map reference points and signing in. The vast majority of which were at the top of the most exposed tors and they then had to camp at night using only the kit they could carry with them. It meant they were exhausted night after night with the effort of climbing thousands of feet carrying almost 100lbs of kit. Occasionally, they met other groups but there was little time for chat as their signing in at a point had to be done in a very narrow time band. Most days involved the better part of 30 miles carrying personal kit plus, changed daily, an assortment of additional weapons and kit. The most useless kit they carried were the radios which supposedly had a range of 2–3 miles but which in reality could not reach much more than a mile to a mile and a quarter. Indeed in some areas, the range was down to no more than a few hundred yards – something which was to contribute to the deaths of the two in the following Company, as they were unable to call for assistance. They even were kept short of rations as was the situation sometimes during real wars. In Jack's group of three, they sheltered in a small cave-like indent on the top of a tor in pouring rain. Cold and hungry, they filled a mess tin with the remains of anything they had, onion soup flakes, apple flakes, broken biscuits, Oxo cubes, curry powder, some jam from a tube, some processed cheese and some dried powder, which because it was in a brown paper bag, could not be identified. All mixed up with a little water, it provided almost a full mess tin full to be shared between the three of them and was, in Jack's opinion, one of the best meals he ever had. It also taught them always to have a reserve of food to fall back on!

The week tested map-reading skills, self-support skills such as cooking hot meals but mainly was a severe test of physicality; they had been forced to travel many miles per day over rough and testing terrain and it was no surprise that they lost three Cadets but one of them, the American Marine was a surprise, he didn't appear to be struggling with the physical side of things and since they were never told the reason a Cadet disappeared, it remained forever a mystery.

Chapter 5

The training intensified building up to the next exercise which was due to take place at Week 15 in the Thetford training area in Norfolk – years later to be used for the filming of outside shots for *Dad's Army*. When the programme was pinned up a couple of days before they travelled on the Monday, it listed all sorts of exercises advance to contact, defence, retreats, house/building clearing, ambushes, recce patrols and other types of patrols, the use of explosives to destroy dud rounds, lots of live firing where real bullets were used in exercises – paper targets of course! Besides the personal weapons, SLRs, SMGs and pistols, they moved on to platoon weapons like the 84mm Carl Gustav anti-tank recoilless rifle; they were the first to be trained on it in the British Army; previous courses had been trained in the 3.5-inch Rocket Launcher, commonly called a bazooka. The bazooka fired a rocket which was awkward to load, accelerated up the tube and then the rocket free floated in an arc to the target. Judging range was difficult but essential if the rocket was to hit its target and in strong crosswinds, learning to aim off to allow for drift was extremely difficult. The Carl Gustav was miles ahead. It fired a shell at something over 1,000 feet per second, so it had a flat trajectory and thus caused less difficulty estimating range; it was a hard-hitting round with varieties of ammunition. Being a recoilless rifle, half the force drove the round out the front and half the blast went out the back, meaning that both the bazooka and the Carl Gustav had a danger area behind them. They also left a huge cloud of dust and smoke behind them which meant that their position was easily identifiable by an enemy so shoot and scoot was the order of the day for both weapons!

They were also to be trained to fire the 2-inch mortar using smoke and parachute illuminating rounds. Generally regarded with disfavour by senior officers, the troops who used them loved them because although they were difficult to range accurately, they were light to carry, as was their ammunition, and they provided a facility of explosive power, smoke generation or light at night, one which was often needed but unavailable in any other way.

The one thing not showing on the programme was any time for sleep. Every night had some form of exercise going on but no down time for sleep. When questioned about this, Staff Dewey's response was only,

"What times were allocated for sleep during the Second World War, the Korean War or the invasion of Suez?"

They did not look forward to Thetford.

Initially, they were based in a hutted camp but since they were carrying out exercises every night, they had little chance to sleep there. At first, they carried out the exercises they had been carrying out since the start of their training but the heavier weapons training was gradually introduced. The first weapon was the Carl Gustav. Even the permanent staff were excited about this one, as all previous courses had been taught the bazooka. The bazooka fired a 3.5-inch diameter rocket. The Carl Gustave fired an 84mm shell, very slightly smaller in diameter but a world away in pyrotechnics. Handled by a two-man team, one loaded the shell into the back of the tube, rifled and just over a yard long, and the other fired it.

They were taken to a range where a tank-sized and shaped target, timber framed and covered in a hessian/canvas material, had been set up two hundred yards away from the firing point. The first pair were called forward – the rest of the platoon was off to the side so that they would not be caught by the back blast – and immediately ran into trouble. The shell looked exactly like a shell should look like but as it was slid into the tube there was no breech mechanism to lock it or secure it against. The CG relied on the loader placing the round fully into the tube with the detonation point, hit by the firing pin, lined up exactly under where the pin would strike when the trigger was squeezed. Unfortunately, the two did not line up and the shell could not be gripped to pull it out as it was a tight fit in the barrel. Although the round was inert in the sense, it did not have a live head on it – too expensive just for training – it did have a fully loaded base to drive the shell forward. Consequently, it was being treated very, very carefully indeed. Eventually, the shell was pushed through the barrel using the CSM's pace stick (Used for measuring paces during drill) with a ground sheet held under the barrel to catch the round and stop it dropping onto the ground.

It was then reloaded into the barrel; careful note having been taken of where the firing pin shot out of the hole and where the detonator of the shell had to meet it. This was probably against all the weapon-handling rules, but no one had yet seen them! The first round was fired and scored a direct hit at the base of the 'turret' of the target tank. The pair then changed over with the loader becoming the firer and the firer the loader. The second round was again badly loaded and wouldn't fire. The first pair were overseas Cadets; looking around, Sgt Dewey's eyes lighted on Jack. Dewey and Jack unloaded the round and Dewey had Jack load it, having shown him carefully how to do it. Dewey fired and the round went almost through the same hole; it was phenomenally accurate. To Jack it seemed like the world had ended. The firer and loader were at the exact centre of the bang with the noise swirling away from them through 360 degrees. It was a bloody big bang and a bloody big shock, almost impossible to describe. Being recoilless the firer only received a strong shove through the shoulder but the explosion was something to write home about. Years later, Jack was to compare it to the Navy; they fired 4.5-inch guns on their ships at targets on the Falklands from more than 10 miles away, here were poor bloody squaddies firing shells only an inch smaller from the shoulder!

The overseas Cadets, for some reason, were having trouble loading the shells accurately and tipping them out to start again; this was not only risky but time consuming. Jack and Charlie Telford were up next and neither of them had a problem loading or firing and both hit the target at the base of the turret. As they went to leave, Dewey called out for Jack to stay and he ended up loading all the rest of the rounds. On the one hand, he became an expert loader but he also suffered the proximity to more than 20 rounds being fired and that left him deafened and shaken up for several hours afterwards. And he was shattered at the end of the day.

As time passed and they carried out all the exercises set out in the programme, Jack noticed that the Cadets destined for the Army's technical/specialist Corps were only given the acting Platoon Commander's position for simple tasks like moving the Platoon from one position on the training area to another. They were never given command tasks for the important exercises like advance to contact where real command had to be exercised. At first, he said nothing to anyone else but after the fourth day with, effectively, only two days remaining, he spoke to Tim Speaker, the ex-Signals Corporal who immediately said,

"Yes, I've noticed that too. What do you think we should do about it?"

"Well, it looks to me that because we are aimed at Corps, where command of units in the field are somewhat unlikely, in my case for example, I am likely to be posted to a vehicle depot if I get my choice and there will be lots of more senior officers around and my ability to command or not is likely to be unimportant; they are probably wanting to have a closer look at infanteers, as they will more quickly be exposed to commanding troops. Should we speak to Dewey when we get the chance, do you think?"

"Yes," said Tim. They had a short break from soldiering when they were transported in the back of a three-tonner to the ranges. Jack, who was sitting next to Dewey, asked him if he might ask a question and, given the go ahead, put the observations to him. All they got in reply was a "you'll get plenty of command tasks before this course is over, Mr Hughes" and that was it. In the event the situation did not change to any great degree and since the report received at the halfway mark through the course was satisfactory, as far as Jack was concerned, he was happy enough to let the subject go, especially as it meant fewer command tasks and fewer bollockings – praise was always lacking. And he was still tired at the end of the day.

The training for setting destruction charges was particularly interesting for Jack as he had experienced the realities of disposing of faulty ordnance in Aden when the troops had been throwing the dud shells into the toilet trench as a way of disposing of them. (See 'It must have been the compo' for the full story.) At Thetford, they set varying lengths of fuse cord for different lengths of time and inserted them into blocks of about 4 oz. of nitrocellulose (gun cotton to the Cadets). The two most common detonators were detonated either by a burning fuse reaching a detonator or by an electrical detonator detonated by an electric charge from a battery. Setting the detonators into the gun cotton and carrying it out to an open space was a bit hairy as was, especially, pushing the detonator into the gun cotton, something the Armourer Sergeant demonstrating the procedure described as frequently leading to the end of the Cadet doing it. Jack was never quite sure how true these stories were but as the Sgt didn't take cover whilst this was being done, even by absolute novices, Jack was pretty sure it was all bullshit just to scare the Cadets into treating the gun cotton with respect. What he did know from Aden was that walking out into the open, when the enemy had you in their sights, carrying a dud a round that conceivably could detonate of its own accord, or if hit by a bullet, setting it down on the ground and then setting the fuse and detonator and then walking, walking not running away, was decidedly dodgy and dropping it into the shit pit was infinitely preferable – apart, of course, from when the CSM pours petrol down there and ignites it!

As far as setting the charges and detonating them, that exercise went without incident. However, with a substantial amount of guncotton left over – enough for a full platoon had been drawn from the Armoury but the platoon had lost five Cadets already and Jack noticed that when the foreign Cadets did their practices, the amount of guncotton used was much less than that for the UK Cadets so perhaps there was something to the dangers of it after all – the Sergeant didn't want to take it back to Mons – transporting explosives being bound about with loads of regulations and requirements, so he told one of the Cadets to burn it on the site where the detonations had taken place. So far so good. Having explained that the explosive could safely be burned, he neglected to mention that it should be in small quantities at a time. When he turned around and looked, there was a substantial bonfire with flame leaping six feet or so in the air. The only one near the bonfire was the Cadet ordered to burn it and the Sgt, taking in what was happening, screamed out,

"Get out of there, Sir, run for it." The Cadet ran. As he reached the Sgt, the temperature in the bonfire reached detonation point and exploded. It was a lovely bang, heard miles away; being in the open, the explosion took the line of least resistance and exploded upwards into the air doing no damage apart from to the Cadet's rifle which he had left by the burning gun cotton. The SLR was seen to soar high up into the air and then fall back down again. When the Cadet picked it up, it was to discover that the barrel had been bent through a 90-degree curve and was now ideal for shooting around corners!

The Armourer Sergeant threatened the Cadet with an enormous bill for the damage to Her Majesty's property but in the event, the Cadet's rifle was replaced with nothing said – probably due to the fact that the Sgt gave him the order to burn the gun cotton without proper instructions as to how that should be done!

As the week progressed, so their tiredness increased as did their irritability. Sleep was snatched whenever possible and Jack discovered that it was possible to enter into a sleep state whilst walking along. He had read about it and heard other soldiers talking about it but had never believed it – now he did.

Chapter 6

The platoon gradually developed an intense hatred of the demonstration platoon from one of the Guard's Regiments. Part of their role was to demonstrate actions for the Cadets which would then be practiced by the Cadets. That was fair enough. But they also played the part of a live enemy so that they would send a small patrol at night to attack the Cadets' positions. That small patrol would then return to their camp at which another patrol of three or four would come out and carry on disturbing the Cadets' night so that sleep was impossible. Tiredness brings hatred on the causer and thus the Guards were hated. With these rotations carrying on every night, the Cadets could not sleep but the Guards did. In addition, the Cadets had to do everything, carrying full belt kit and small pack on their backs – about 60lbs in weight plus whatever the extra weapon was for the role the Cadet was acting at the time; a GPMG weighing dam nearly 30lbs with a 500-round belt attached, or a 2inch mortar and half a dozen mortar rounds or a radio weighing 15 to 20lbs plus spare batteries or the Carl Gustav weighing 36lbs (later versions were reduced to 22lbs) – much welcomed for the troops who had to carry it but that was for the future as far as the Cadets were concerned, their weight was 36lbs; the equivalent of 18 2lb bags of sugar! The most popular weapon was the Very Signal Pistol firing a 1inch flare (in a variety of colours); it only weighed a couple of pounds and was a doddle to carry. Trying to chase and catch the Guards, or escape from them, was simply impossible as all they were carrying was a personal weapon and a few magazines as opposed to the Cadets' almost 100lbs – and this up or down steep hill sides, even flat Norfolk has steep hills if you look hard enough! They thought Thetford was bad, but once they got to Wales, they developed a love for Thetford and hatred for the Welsh training areas as they were all mountains! So the Cadets hate got stronger which finally was to come to a head during the final night of Battle Camp in Wales some weeks ahead.

During that week, they carried out all the normal procedures they had been taught; platoon in advance to contact, breaking contact, night and day recces and fighting patrols, attempts to capture prisoners, etc. Unlike previous practice of these skills, almost all of these were done with live ammunition. Consequently, they had to be shot on the ranges, live rounds flying all over the countryside was not on. They also included march and shoot competitions where they were required to cover five miles in an hour carrying full kit and then shoot at paper targets (the Cadets would have quite liked them to have been the Guards but this wasn't allowed!); their individual scores were recorded when they were all firing their rifles. Some of the firing was done at mixed, moving targets for both rifles and GPMGs and recording those scores were impossible; Jack for example managed to fire two 500-round belts in two and a half minutes absolutely shredding the target so much that the hits could not be counted.

At the start of the first march and shoot, they were told there would be a barrel of beer for the winners! Up until then, the most that happened was that the winners received a "well done" from the senior person there and the losers were told "better luck next time" and to "try harder". Jack and the other serving soldiers rapidly worked out that they needed to appear to be trying hard, to avoid punishment for slacking, but not that hard that they were exhausted; after all, a 'well done' was a pretty crappy reward. The promise of a barrel of beer was a whole new ball game and Jack's Platoon which had lost every competition to date won the barrel of beer by coming in eight minutes before No 2 Platoon. And this pattern was repeated every time there was a tangible reward. They had wondered how they would handle a barrel of beer but in the event it took the form of two crates of 48 bottles of beer – not a problem to deal with. No 2 Platoon never did suss the value of a real prize.

Chapter 7

The travel back to Mons at the end of the week passed extremely quickly even though they were in a clatty old bus, noisy, smelly and apparently with no suspension whatsoever. It passed so quickly because they were all asleep. They obeyed the old Army maxim:

Never stand when you can sit,
Never sit when you can lie down,
Never be awake when you can be asleep.

That had been practiced in full during the week, which just ended with odd scraps of sleep snatched whenever they could!

Getting back late on the Saturday afternoon, they spent all of Sunday cleaning and sorting out kit ready for Monday morning.

They were a little surprised that notices were placed on the noticeboards for four Cadets to parade at 0900 hrs for Company Commanders Orders. This had not happened when they returned from Dartmoor, when they carried out the week-long exercise there so there was intense speculation as to what it was about. When they returned to their rooms before dinner, having been drilled all morning, it was to discover all four were gone. Over the next few days, they discovered that three had been failed and discharged, one had been back-squadded to the following Company but had refused and had been returned to unit – doing another eight weeks of Mons training, well a commission was just not worth it. There was intense speculation as to how the four had been selected; as far as the Cadets were concerned, they had carried out all their tasks as well as any of the others. Mons and the Army not being exactly democratic organisations, they never did find out how the decisions were made.

With just 10 weeks left to their passing-out parade, the tempo accelerated and the working days got longer. The senior company to them was due to pass out in two weeks, eight weeks before them. They had to take part in rehearsals for that parade. The format should have been exactly the same as for theirs so that their passing out parade would normally have benefitted from the previous drills for the one eight weeks ahead of them and the one 16 weeks ahead, there being an intake every eight weeks. However, with Christmas and the other significant holidays in the year, this pattern could not be followed exactly – eight didn't divide evenly into 52 either and Jack's platoon had been affected such that there was only the company eight weeks ahead of them throughout their time whereas normally they could have expected two Companies ahead of them reducing to one and then to none as they were then the Company passing out.

Consequently, the passing-out parades were very demanding, especially of the junior Company who had had only eight weeks of training up to that time.

During the build-up parades, the NCOs became more and more pernickety and bloody minded such that on one day, Jack was picked on and ordered to get his hair cut – a sign that they couldn't actually fault him but he had somehow pissed them off – five times! The fourth time, the barber didn't actually cut his hair, there was hardly enough to cast a shadow on his bonce but gave him the chitty as proof of the hair cut but he did charge Jack the two shillings anyway. When Jack turned up for the fifth time, he gave Jack the chitty and said,

"I don't have the heart to charge you again, Sir, but would you please stop breaking the record which previously stood at three times in one day."

On the same day in PT, Jack whispered to Charlie Telford who was next to him. The PTI was, as usual, rabbiting on about a healthy body was a healthy mind when Jack whispered, "Tell that to bloody Einstein," without realising that one of the other PTIs was standing right behind him. Jack's comment was equal to running into a synagogue and shouting "Pork pie" as far as the saintliness of PT and fitness was concerned. The PTI went ballistic and clearly had a hissy fit because Jack found himself parading at the Guardroom to show various pieces of kit at 0600 hrs for the next three mornings, Friday, Saturday and Sunday. Sunday was the worst because it was the one day in the week when they could get a bit of a lie in. Jack vowed if he could ever get his hands on the narcissistic little bastard, either when he was commissioned or even whilst still at Mons on a night exercise, the little bastard would be walking around holding his testicles in a jar, looking for someone with an antiseptic needle and thread in their Housewife (a Housewife was a small bag containing needles, thread, wool, buttons etc. for repair of socks or other items of uniform with which all soldiers were issued!), to sew them back on. Jack had already developed a hatred of PTIs before he arrived, to the extent that he made the mistake of asking the Chief PTI what battle honours the Physical Training Corps had who responded with more early morning parades at the Guardroom for Jack.

The week of the senior Company passing-out parade dawned. The actual passing-out parade took place on a Friday. On the Thursday evening at 1800 hours, a short Church Service took place in the Garrison Church which was compulsory for all Cadets and optional for the families of the Cadets who were to pass out. For the senior Company, the Thursday was taken up with handing in all the rest of their kit that was to be no longer theirs whilst for Jack's Company, they spent half the day cleaning kit for the next day and half the day in drill. The Wednesday was the Commandant's Parade which was the full passing-out parade, band and all, under the eagle eye of the Commandant whose performance as Commandant would be largely measured by quality of the Cadets, their drill and turn out. The Tuesday was Adjutant's Parade where, although there was no band, the whole parade would be run through to make sure they would be good enough for the Commandant's Parade. The Monday parade was taken by the RSM who would make sure that the parade was perfect so no fault could be found during the rest of the week which could be laid at the Staff's door. As a Company would normally go through this process three times at Mons, one could say that parades were not exactly high on the Cadets' list of favourite pastimes, all except the very last one, of course, since it meant they were now finished with Mons and would become commissioned officers from midnight – not immediately following the parade so as to prevent any harassing of the staff by new officers wanting to get their own back for perceived harassment during the previous six months. As it had been announced that Field Marshall Montgomery had asked to take this parade, a godson, grandson of a former Prime Minister, son of a Minister for War and aimed at Aide Camp to a senior Royal, politics and a Minister's Portfolio by 40 years of age, was one of the Cadets passing out. The parades each lasted twice as long as normal, they had to do it twice each time, the view of the Cadets as to the panicking of the staff and the presence of Montgomery was pretty well indescribable without using heavyweight Anglo-Saxon!

For the first time they were to wear their complete best outfit. White belts and bayonet scabbards which were bastards to clean – especially as no one had a white cleaner, it never having been necessary before. The tailored Service Dress did not fit properly for many of the Cadets. They had been measured during their first week at Mons and the sheer physicality of the programme developing muscles where there had never been any, the loss of weight made up of fat all meant that the tailors attended on the Friday before the first parade on the Monday and, working over the weekend, made all the necessary alterations – something that happened before every passing-out parade. The worst discovery was that their best boots which had lovingly, well not exactly lovingly but with considerable time and effort devoted to the bulling of them, were too small! The rubbing in of water and polish over and over had caused them to shrink just enough to be difficult to get on and just enough to make them bloody uncomfortable. Jack escaped both problems having an athletic figure on arrival which had changed not at all and his best boots, hidden away in his locker with the new issue boots displayed at the foot of his bed for inspections, fitted him comfortably from his Army Cadet and other rank service.

Most Cadets did not wish to wear their best boots, not because they were too small and uncomfortable but because the very act of wearing them could potentially cause chipping and cracking to the thick layers of polish built up over many hours. There was no way known to them to repair such damage, because they would have to repair the kit ready for their own passing-out parade in eight weeks' time; it would mean scraping the damaged polish from the toe or heel cap and starting all over – hours and hours of work. In Jack's case, lurking in his locker was a bottle of Luton Hat Dye which renovated scratches within seconds. He was torn as to whether he should make it available to all the other Cadets or limit it to those he was close to. As there was only a small amount left in the bottle and with a further five days that week and the run-up days to his own passing-out parade when damage could occur again, he decided that he would keep it to himself.

The Staff got rattier and rattier the closer it got to Battle Camp which was the final formal test of the Cadets but Cadets still continued to disappear. The least infringement, being the last on parade, even though not late, earned a couple of hours in the Guardroom joining up links to bullets to form 500-round belts. Cruel on the fingers, it was amazing looking around how many Cadets had strips of bandages around their fingers. Mons and Sandhurst between them were reputed to consume 60% of the entire Army's training ammunition. Certainly it was a world apart from the Army Cadet force where five rounds of blank ammunition had to last the entire two-week camp. At Mons, they always set out with four full magazines in their pouches and a full magazine on the rifle; in addition, they would carry a couple of bandoleers, each of 50 rounds, 2–4 smoke grenades, 3 or 4 thunder flashes, 2 or 3 2" mortar bombs – a mix of smoke or parachute illuminating, a belt or two for the GPMG and if armed with a Carl Gustav, a round or two of ammunition for that. It was hardly surprising that the first time they attacked, or were attacked, it resulted in an enormous amount of ammunition being fired off or 'accidentally' dropped under a bush – they didn't mind being donkeys in real-life situations but carrying immense loads for sadistic NCOs jealous of their forthcoming commissions was another thing. Live ball ammunition was handled slightly differently because it was too dangerous to leave lying around. The amounts issued, though, were just as generous.

In one exercise, they were scheduled to carry out helicopter exercises on Salisbury Plain for two days. The intention was to practice all aspects of helicopter usage. They were to be carried to a spot and unloaded on the ground, be picked up at another point and even abseil down a helo 30 feet above the ground, simulating not being able to land in the jungle but nevertheless having to descend from a helicopter hovering over the make-believe jungle, there wasn't much jungle on Salisbury Plain so fir and pine trees had to stand in. For whatever reason, the powers that be decided the abseiling down a rope would be practiced first i.e., the hardest and most dangerous first. The first drop of eight Cadets went off without a hitch. Jack was in the second drop. Acting the role of a Rifleman, he was scheduled to follow the GPMG gunner who, landing first, would be able to pour out a stream of fire if the landing was opposed. The rope, at 30 feet, or so, was long enough for three Cadets to descend at once, speed being of the essence. Longer ropes were used in real jungle drops since the trees could be a 100ft or more in height – it was no good being dropped in the treetops! Jack had just gripped the rope and swung out of the helicopter when the Cadet about four feet below him dropped the GPMG. Well, he didn't so much as drop it, as it fell not having been secured properly to the sling that should have securely held it to him as he used his hands to grip the rope and descend. Dropping butt first, it hammered about four inches into the ground. Worse, the cunt (no other suitable word for him!) had loaded a 50-round belt and cocked the mechanism. He swore he had applied the safety catch but when examined, it was in the off position – it was possible the jarring could have moved it but doubt remained. Even so the gun should not have fired without the trigger being pulled but the fact was that it did. Five or six rounds burst forth from the gun with two of them being tracer.

Jack forever after swore that one went past his left side and one past his right. How the rounds missed the helicopter, no one ever knew, but what they did know was that the helicopter immediately landed, disembarked the remaining Cadets and flew away never to be seen again. Apparently, the RAF didn't like being near real bullets. The Cadet who dropped the gun, an overseas Cadet, was taken aside and never seen again, his bed space was empty when they returned to Mons; in fact, he was the only overseas Cadet, other than Mohammad Mohammad, to be thrown out. They completed the rest of their helicopter training with a Landrover acting the part of the chopper and Cadets' imagination providing the rest! It was a pity particularly for Jack as he was to carry out helicopter duties in the future in a real war environment.

Chapter 8

It was at this stage the nominations of Cadets who were to be promoted to authoritarian positions were announced. The most senior one was the role of Senior Under Officer awarded to J Jowett. He had shown a most incredible radar to detect the imminent arrival of a member of the Permanent Staff to enable him to appear to be lecturing the Cadets around him whenever a Staffy appeared. They, of course, only ever saw an extremely conscientious Cadet. The true situation was that he was a universally detested little shit who failed to carry his weight in the duties cleaning and maintaining the common areas of the spider and ablutions. His ability to command the other Cadets was non-existent when the staff were not around. Consequently, he only gave orders in front of Staff Dewey when he knew the Cadets could not refuse. The other appointments of Under Officer, Junior Under Officer (2), were made up of quite decent blokes – Charlie Telford being one. The two foreign Cadets were, obviously, positive discrimination, long before the term had come into general parlance and were made to keep foreign governments happy. Jack read, shortly after leaving Mons a short article in Soldier Magazine which had analysed the subsequent success of the Sword of Honour (Sandhurst) and the Mons equivalents and the truth appeared to be that once into their units they had disappeared without trace or achieving any fame whatsoever. Jack had no idea about the Sandhurst ones but that confirmed exactly what he and the other Cadets expected of Jowett.

Helicopter working reappeared a few days after the dropped gun incident but this time with an Army Air Corps Scout rather than the RAF Wessex. The task they were briefed on was to release from capture a General who was to be transported by road to an insurgent interrogation centre where all his extremely valuable intelligence knowledge would be tortured out of him. Their own intelligence had found out when and how many guards, two, would be with him, the route he was to be taken and the timings. The route ran from a base, in fact an Officers' Mess just off the A30, along the A30 for three miles and then down a side road which led across a training area. The A30 had been marked in red on their maps as out of bounds; stopping traffic on a Saturday on the A30 in summer with heavy summer traffic even for just the few minutes ambushing the lorry and loading the General onto the Scout would take too much time, be likely to cause havoc on a this very busy road and thus was unacceptable. They were also told that the demonstration platoon of the Guards would be sent after them so they had to move fast and leave no evidence of where they had gone. Since the length of road where an ambush could be successfully carried out on was only about a mile long and they would be carrying full kit – dam nearly a 100lbs and the Guards would only be carrying belt kit for spare magazines, the likelihood of them being found and caught was extremely high. They were given the details of the exercise just after dinner and were given the afternoon to come up with their own individual plan which was to be handed in at 1600 hrs. At 1800 hrs, they would be told whose plan had been accepted and who would be carrying out the various command positions – the ranks of the official SUO, UOs and JUOs were ignored for training purposes.

It was pretty obvious to Jack that they were on a loser; the area that they had to operate within made sure of that, so he had to come up with a plan where the ground rules were made to work for them rather than against them.

As it happened, Jack knew the barracks where the General was being 'held'; it had an indoor rifle range where he had shot in competitions three or four times a year. Use of that insider knowledge would be held against him if it came out so he had to get around that. He knew that the gates to the barracks stood about 30–40 yds down the side road. A very carefully examination of the maps they had been given showed that the clerk who had marked up all the maps had done so fairly lackadaisically and whilst the A30 had been marked red the little side turning had not and it stopped some yards short of the side turning to the training area. The written instructions about not landing on the A30 were very clear but nothing was said about the side turning into the barracks. The instructions also said that the General was likely to be guarded by two guards.

Jack's plan was therefore to send a recce patrol to the barracks to measure the road width and length to ensure there was enough room for the Scout to land and hide the fact that Jack knew the area; Jack was sure that it was but he had to be sure for the powers that be. Assuming there was a snatch squad of three plus the commander, they would invade the barracks 10 minutes before the time they had been told the lorry would be leaving. At the same time, the Scout would be called in giving the patrol about 10 minutes to grab the General. There were no sentries at the barracks but they would need to leave two Cadets at the entrance to the street to stop someone trying to access it as the Scout was landing. They should be away with the General in 5–10 minutes. In the meantime, the rest of the platoon would be making its way from Mons, leaving at 0400 hrs, to the RV point they were to reach without the Guards platoon catching up with them; a matter of four miles in two hours, easy peasy, especially as the enemy platoon's reveille time wasn't until 0630 hrs. They were to dig in for all round defence on arrival. Jack, leading the rescue squad, was to leave at 0630 hrs with three miles to cover by 0730. The activity of Jack and the squad was to be as obvious and noisy as possible to alert the enemy platoon that they were only just leaving for the exercise; in fact, the main body should be dug in at the finish point by this time.

Jack did not expect his plan to be picked. It was a bit naughty in that it depended on the snatch squad and the remainder of the platoon operating at hours which ignored the assumed (but not ordered!) hours for the exercise and the place the snatch would be expected to take place i.e., not in the two to three miles through the training area but right at the barracks at the start. He was therefore more than a little surprised when Staff Dewey sent for him and started asking questions about his plan. Jack had to reveal he knew the barracks where the General would be starting from having shot there on the indoor range as an Army Cadet Force Cadet. He expected to be told that the access road to the A30 was out of bounds. Dewey asked to see Jack's map and accepted that the access was indeed not covered in red and was therefore a legitimate area which could be accessed. He revealed that he had examined a number of maps given to other Cadets and they all left the access road un-redded so it was not just a case of Jack's being the only one which was not red by some accident but all of them were the same. Jack was the only one to notice. It could mean that the Clerk who had done the marking up had been lazy and not bothered with the little road which only showed as a tiny stub on the one inch to the mile map or, more likely, had followed his written orders (Dewey had checked them!) which said 'colour the A30 from…' and gave two map reference points. There were no written instructions about the stub.

Dewey then revealed on point of death or worse if he, Jack, were to reveal that there was a bet between Dewey and Corporal of Horse Lamb, his counterpart in No 2 Platoon, the only other platoon in the Company, as to whose platoon could complete the exercise and rescue the General and escape to the finish point without being caught by the Guards' Demonstration Platoon. Dewey wasn't entirely sure that COH Lamb, a Guardsman himself, albeit a donkey walloper rather than a Foot Guard, wasn't passing the chosen plans for both platoons to the Guards' Platoon so that his platoon could escape and Dewey's be caught. For the three Courses that Dewy had been at Mons, the bet had been won every time by Lamb easily, too easily which was what was making Dewey suspicious. Consequently, he intended to hand in another Cadet's plan, one which placed the ambush point right at the far end of the training area from the finishing point! Jack would only be announced as the Platoon Commander after Lamb had gone home for the night and Jack would brief the platoon as soon as he was gone.

Dewey then gave Jack the rare honour of being able to choose who he wanted in the key roles. Jack chose to lead the snatch squad and for Charlie Telford to command the rest. He wanted Timothy Speaker, unlikely to be bullied by any regular officer trying to access or egress the street, to be one of the two to control the street and Dave Sprake, the biggest man in the platoon, to be part of the snatch squad with him who would intimidate the two guards by his sheer size, if they were around in the Mess where Jack expected to find the General. The other two for the snatch squad were chosen for high placings in the inter platoon cross country since the four of them would have to walk/run the eight or so miles to the finish point in about an hour and twenty minutes. The other command positions in the main body of the platoon could be anyone Dewey wanted to see in action in a particular post.

Dewey appeared as soon as Lamb had gone and the platoon was assembled and he announced the appointments leaving Jack to explain the plan. When it came to questions, Jack was inundated by questions about breaking the exercise instructions. Jack explained that there was nothing in the instructions that specifically forbad what they were about to do. He, Jack, was the planner and therefore if anyone in No 2 Platoon did complain, it would be for him to deal with; they could simply say they were following orders!

The recce patrol returned at 0130 hrs to confirm that the street was easily wide enough and long enough to land a helicopter even one bigger than a Scout. A phone call to the Duty Officer of the AAC received a somewhat grumpy confirmation – he had probably been asleep, there rarely being any flying at night – but he did confirm that they would be prepared to land there. The main body of the Platoon under the command of Charlie Telford left prompt at 0400 hrs as quietly and unobtrusively as possible. Jack saw them off and no lights came on in the 'enemy's' spider so it looked like all was going to plan – something that rarely happened. Jack's squad arrived at the barracks at 0735 hrs; he had not hurried as they would need all their energy when they had to make a run for it after the rescue. To help, Jack had all their packs taken on the small handcart with the main body. They would not need changes of clothes, mess tins and cookers etc. for the rescue but they did take four spare loaded magazines in belt pouches per man in case they had to fight along the way. Standing close to the gate they could see straight into the Officers' Mess and the General sitting at a table eating his breakfast. He was sitting with his back to them and sitting facing the General, and them, was a Lieutenant with bags of braid and cords around him – clearly his ADC.

At one minute to eight, Jack made his move, he reckoned by the time they got into the mess, it would be 0800 hrs and game on! As they entered the Ante Room it was to find two Guardsman sitting in the armchairs with their rifles propped up in the corner. Sitting away from them and unarmed was a Sergeant wearing the Royal Logistic Corps uniform, probably the General's driver. Dave Sprake immediately threatened the two Guardsmen and had them lying down on their fronts in a corner of the Ante-room with their rifles safely moved to the far corner as quick as you like. Jack told the Sergeant to stay where he was. Entering the dining room there were two officers sitting at a long table and the General and his Aide at a small table in the corner by the window. Jack said to the two officers,

"Gentlemen I have just shot you and you are to take no further part in the proceedings." He said this as he didn't want to actually fire his rifle in the Mess and certainly not as he approached the General's table. As he did so he realised that he knew the General. During their briefing they had not been told the General's name just that he would be wearing a Lieutenant General's uniform. Half of the Cadets thought it would probably be a Mons Staffer dressed as a General for the exercise and the other half didn't care a jot who it was. It was General Sir John Magrill, the Commander of 1 Br Corps (BAOR) based in Bielefeld, at least he was when Jack had been based there before passing the RCB. Jack had had an accident passing between some swing doors whilst carrying five freshly made coffees and had emptied them all over the General's trousers boiling his balls in the process! Jack had acquired some notoriety over this incident. *(For the full story read, 'It must have been the compo' the first in this trilogy.)*

Jack was wearing full combat kit and his face was covered in green and brown camouflage creams so he felt reasonably secure that the General would not recognise him. He had intended to approach the General, give him a butt salute and ask him to come out to the Scout which was just audible in the distance. Unfortunately, the Aide de Camp ruined this. He started to rise from the table whilst at the same time, in a loud voice, started going on about "you can't come in here, it's too early" and as he did so the tablecloth caught in his uniform and started to be dragged off the table as he stood. Jack pointed his rifle at the prat and shouted,

"Keep still. It has gone 0800 hrs and the exercise has started. It is perfectly within the rules for me to be here, there is nothing saying the Mess is out of bounds. Sit back down and let the General finish his coffee; he doesn't want to boil his balls again." Jack simply could not resist adding the 'again' at the end of his sentence. At that, the General stood up and came right over to Jack and started examining him closely under the camouflage. After a thorough examination, he said,

"You're quite right, young Hughes. I do not. I do need to pick up my hat and briefcase in the Ante-room and then I am all yours. Separate to the exercise rules, my Aide needs to come with me. We will be flying to the MOD in London for a meeting and then we shall be flying back to 1Br Corps in Germany. The Scout has sufficient seating and I am quite glad to be getting an early start as the later timings are a bit tight." Turning to his Aide, he said, "This young man, as a Private Soldier in 1Br Corps once emptied scalding coffee all over me and it was entirely my fault. He became known thereafter as the man who boiled the General's balls and he was quite right to shout at you to sit back down to prevent it happening again. Twice would have been far too much and the end of your career in the Army. Think on that."

A chastened Lieutenant followed Jack and the General into the Anteroom. Taking in the situation at a glance the General gestured for Jack to hand him his rifle whereupon he cocked it and shot each of the two Guardsmen lying on the ground. "They didn't half jump!" he said, "They were enjoying their role of Guards far too much bossing me about and shouting." Speaking to them he said, "Since you have been shot dead you will under no circumstances tell any of your Platoon that will undoubtedly arrive here in a while what happened. That is a direct order. You will leave them to work everything out for themselves." Turning to Jack, he asked,

"Have you had any breakfast yet?"

"No, Sir," said Jack.

"The end camp is a fair way from here, isn't it?"

"About eight miles, Sir, and we have just over an hour to do it, so we should be alright."

Turning to the Mess Manager who had been drawn to the sound of the shots, the General said,

"Knock up some bacon sandwiches or something quickly for these two chaps…"

"Four, Sir, I have two men guarding the road to make it safe for the Scout to land." The Scout was overhead by this time and gradually descending into the road.

"Four packs of sandwiches, a few apples and some cheese as soon as possible. I presume that a quick-thinking commander would realise that the vehicle that was due to transport me and the two Guards could also be used to transport the rescue squad and would escape in it?"

"I did think of that, Sir, but I don't have the authority to sign the work ticket so I planned to run."

"But I do. Sergeant McDuff, take these four gentlemen wherever they want to go but make sure that you are at the MOD this afternoon at 1600 hrs ready to take me out to Northolt." At that, he shook Jack's hand and was gone. He and his aide boarded the Scout and with a scream of the jet engine, it was gone.

The bacon and sausage sandwiches, courtesy of the Mess Manager, with cheese and apples arrived in remarkably quick time – it was amazing what a General could achieve. The ride in the General's Staff car to the exercise end point only took 15 minutes, or so, just enough time to finish the sandwiches. As they said goodbye to Sergeant McDuff, he saluted Jack, which strictly he should not have done since Jack was only an officer cadet, and said,

"Good luck, Sir, you've just put the General in a good mood and that counts for a lot for me."

Finding the rest of the dug in Platoon was not that easy as they were well camouflaged but find them they did. Present were Sgt Dewey and Captain Cleary, responsible for their training, the latter of whom they had seen precious little. Jack was closely questioned, very closely, on the events, but when he said that the General had ordered them bacon sarnies, cheese and apples and the Mess Manager had added sausages, Capt. Cleary said,

"Well, if the General himself thought fit to order the sarnies, it must have gone well." Jack felt it better to omit the coffee incident and that he and the General had met before at HQ BAOR. It was only just before 0900 hrs and the exercise had been scheduled to finish about midday so there was no transport available to take them back to Mons. Sgt Dewey suggested that they march back to Mons and get on with the preparations for Battle Camp which was now only a few days away. Cleary agreed, it seemed somewhat reluctantly, and the way he was dragging behind after 15 mins or so showed why; he was nowhere near as fit as the Cadets were now and he had trouble keeping up. Still he made it to Mons with them demonstrating the level of determination required of an officer.

Chapter 9

In which the CSM plays the part of a water lily.

The amount of kit that had to be got ready for the ten-day battle camp was incredible. Besides all their own individual kit, there were the platoon weapons, GPMGs, SMGs, 2" Mortars, Carl Gustavs, Signal Pistols, radios, batteries, cookers, tents – mainly two-man bivouacs, barbed wire, entrenching tools, batteries, but not surprisingly food. It was the last week in September as they prepared to leave with October passing out parade just a spit away – failure at this stage was just an unbearable thought. The weather since May when the course started had generally been good, certainly too good for the CSM who continually complained that they were having it too soft whenever it was not raining when they were out of the school on exercises. He had his wish, however, as they arrived at a track leading off the main road running up into the Brecon Beacons. They had travelled all the way from Mons in beautiful sunshine and as they were debussing so it started to rain. They were not to know that it was going to rain for the entire 10 days they were there but it would.

Their first task was to set up the camp that was to operate as their home base for the 10 days even though they would spend most of their time away from it during the next 10 days. They were each issued with a two-man bivouac tent. Supposedly large enough for two men but they were, in fact, only just big enough for one. Set low to the ground, it was actually impossible to sit upright inside one. Old, warn and thin, the absolute rule was under no circumstances should one touch the canvas inside as, if it was raining, and it was, the touch somehow allowed the water outside to drip into the inside. It didn't take many touches to ensure that there was more water inside the tent than outside! Digging water runaway trenches around the wall bases did very little to drain water away as there was only the thinnest possible layer of soil over rock to dig channels in. The key was to select, if possible any mound area so that the water would run away naturally. Fortunately, the CSM wasn't around at this time; it was rumoured that he was up in the hills at a shrine to the rain god making a sacrifice – or they would have had to line the tents up in nice straight and soldier like lines. By the time he returned, the barbed wire had been strung around the camp and there wasn't sufficient time to move the tents before the first exercise was due to start. Jack was therefore lucky that he and Charlie Telford working as a team had been able to place their two tents on the summit of the minor mound which was to be their home base and which at least kept most of the water from running under the walls and into the tents.

All the exercises started that evening – no rest for the wicked or officer cadets. They were to follow the pattern of Thetford in that no time was scheduled for sleep but because not all the exercises involved all the Cadets at the same time; for example when recce or fighting or snatch patrols were sent out, the remainder of the platoon, apart from those on sentry duty, were able to snatch some sleep – a more realistic war situation than having all the Cadets doing all the exercises all the time. Initially, Jack had no responsible positions to fill and just took the part he was ordered to be. On the third night, he was listed as a Rifleman in a recce patrol. Led by Terry Harris, a superb athlete who had raced in and won the Devizes to London canoe race on more than one occasion, Jack and an overseas Cadet, Mwanza NGumi, made up the rest of the patrol. Jack was concerned since the briefing made it clear that they were to find the Guards' platoon position and determine the layout and extent of the camp with almost nothing in the way of kit to assist them; what they did have was almost useless as the prismatic compass which they had been issued was so faded as to be almost illegible. They were to determine the best avenue to attack the place the following morning by the full Platoon. The Guards were no fools and having carried out this role with previous Companies passing through Mons knew that a patrol would be programmed to be out looking for them. It was even thought by the Cadets that the 'enemy' always knew their plans because the permanent staff told them. There had been previous encounters where snatch squads and fighting patrols had come into contact with the Guards very easily and some of the subsequent roughing up had been quite extensive.

Jack's concern was that NGumi was notorious as an idle, useless specimen, who, if he had been English, would have been thrown out, but, as an overseas Cadet whose country was paying good money for him to go through Mons, he, like many of the other overseas Cadets was just allowed to carry on. Indeed realised Jack when thinking about this, the only overseas Cadets to compulsory disappear were Mohammed and one whose name he had forgotten who almost shot down their helicopter. Not one of the others had been dropped or even back squadded. Jack, following a previous policy he had adopted i.e., to get rid of weak links whenever possible, wanted to get rid of NGumi – he was almost certainly likely to make a noise, blunder into an enemy trip wire or in some way get them caught or found out. It was a relatively easy matter when he and NGumi were carrying a box of Carl Gustav ammunition for Jack to stumble forward so that the box dropped on NGumi's outstretched ankle. Jack made the leading expressions of concern including you ought to report that in case you've broken something and to prevent it getting any worse knowing the NGumi, being the skiver he was, would use it to get out of the exercise. And sure enough within a few minutes the ankle had swollen a bit and, shown to Staff Dewey, quickly resulted in him being carted off to the medical room in Sennybridge Camp; British Cadets would have been expected to carry on as they would have been the situation in a real war, but overseas Cadets were precious and not to be driven too hard – cotton wool and mollycoddling was the order of the day for them – and after all, if they didn't reach the same standards as the Brits that would not be too serious because if we ever got around to fighting them (as Jack had with Mohammed!), they would be a second class enemy and relatively easy meat. So NGumi disappeared and another Cadet, Tim Barton, an African Cadet despite his very English sounding name, very fit and powerful – useful if they did get into a bundle with the Guards – replaced him and Jack had achieved his mantra to get rid of bad ones, don't let them drag the team down.

The bombshell dropped on them as they were about to leave. The CSM was to accompany them to monitor and mark their performance. This was seriously bad news. As time had progressed, they had come to detest him almost as much as the Demonstration Platoon. He really was like one of those war comics where the hero is massive – at least 6ft 8ins tall, built like the proverbial and square shithouse, square shoulders, square head, square ears, square hands, square nose and even square eye balls, always immaculately turned out, brilliant at spotting mistakes and heavy to jump on them; his job of course, but all the Brit Cadets felt that he carried a chip on his shoulder, a massive one to match his size that he was not an officer and therefore hated the English who he blamed for this situation. He wasn't going to be one, an officer, but this bunch of useless Cadets would be and in due course, if he was unlucky, he would have to salute them and call them "Sir" and mean it. His only redeeming feature was that as a member of a highland regiment, he wore a kilt and this provided endless amusement as to whether anything was worn under it and to the Arab and African Cadets, they could not believe that a fighting British soldier could wear a skirt; even though the Arabs wore a very similar but lightweight cotton role of cloth called a *longi* which also looked like a skirt. That had provided endless amusement in Aden when an Arab walking past a pack of pi-dogs, would be chased by them. The funny bit was to see the Arab lift his skirt up to be able to run faster. Jack thus knew whether they wore anything under their skirts too!

Their camp was perched on the top of an exposed and barren mountaintop. It had been raining, sometimes heavily sometimes lightly since they had arrived three days before. Consequently, they were soaked to the skin. In those three days, their spare socks, shirts and underdungers had been put on in the hope that the wet ones taken off would dry in their bivouacs before these new dry ones got wet through in turn but they hadn't. Now everything was wet. The trenches, such as they were, were full of water with a thin layer of ice on them in the mornings. When the Guards attacked them, which was pretty well continually, they were supposed to jump into the trenches. They should have been at least four/five feet deep, two feet wide and six feet long. Half the trench should have been covered by canvas with a foot or two of soil on top so that in the event of a nuclear threat, they could shelter in the covered part, both of them, and the theory was that they would thus survive a one-kiloton nuclear detonation only 800 yards away. The fact that the residual radiation would kill them if the explosion didn't was quietly forgotten. Since the trenches, ranging from one to two feet deep at best, were full of water meant that there was no way the Cadets would jump into them; they were wet enough as it was without jumping into the ice-cold water. The ground by the trenches would just have to be laid on – in the dark if the permanent staff couldn't see you the Cadets stood up to return fire.

This night it wasn't just raining it was pouring. Not only was it dark, dark as pitch and freezing cold, the wind was blowing a bloody gale and the wind was blowing up the valley so hard that the rain wasn't falling it was being blown up into the air. Jack, and he was sure the other Cadets, was utterly and completely miserable, wet through, scheduled for a rotten task and now the bloody CSM was coming with them. Mind you he was supposed to be happier the worse the weather was so maybe he would be in a good mood!

All they were given was a compass direction and a map square reference where the enemy were supposed to be. It was so dark that visibility wasn't much more than a yard or two. The fluorescent paint on the prismatic compass had long faded into invisibility – the date on it was 1941 and it did point north; however, that wasn't a lot of help if you couldn't see the bloody needle. The patrol, three Officer Cadets and the CSM, left through their wire at 0100 hrs. Being careful not to fall over any of their own trip wires, they were led off by Terry who had so far sailed through the physical aspects of the course having, in a previous life, been a sports teacher and very considerable athlete in his own right – something that was to be the downfall of the CSM. Following the predetermined compass course down the exposed side of the mountain was hard enough, the rain was blowing into their faces and keeping their eyes open was almost impossible. Consequently, they kept their heads down and followed the one in front by looking at their heels. The bearing they should have followed did not involve a tarn (lake); the one they actually followed did. They had been struggling to move through a piece of Forestry Commission land which contained closely placed pine trees, fallen branches, nil visibility and a thousand and one branches, twigs and bushes to trip over, into and receive full in the face having swung back from the person in front. For the Cadets it was bad enough but for the CSM it must have been purgatory with his lower bare legs largely unprotected by his kilt.

Terry became aware of the tarn at the very last nanosecond. The rain had been driving into their faces so they all had their heads down to avoid it. Terry, about to put his right foot down, suddenly somehow sensed that there was not going to be any ground under it – afterwards, as hero of the hour, he could only explain it as "I suddenly knew there was nothing there" and reacting so fast, he didn't even appear to think about it, he spun on his left foot, which was still on the ground, and headed off at right angles to his left. The CSM, victim of the rain for which he had prayed and left offerings to the Rain God for, head down and not paying close enough attention, proceeded to step straight into the tarn! For such a square man, the ripples spreading out across the tarn were so circular, but in keeping with his reputation, were considerable and loud.

As the three Cadets gathered at the bank, the clouds opened and a huge moon shone a searchlight brilliance on the scene. They were greeted with the sight of the CSM standing there, up to his waist in water, his kilt floating out around him like a giant lily pad, with perched in the middle of it this square 'frog' who proceeded to speak!

"I s'ppose you think that's bluidy funny?"

"YES SIR!"

"And I s'ppose y're goin' to tell everyone aboot this when we get back?"

"YESS SIR!" from all three – and they did. The task could not be abandoned just because the CSM had got his kilt wet so they carried on. The CSM changed his position to last in the patrol, immediately behind Jack. The moon was now giving them a window of opportunity to see where they were and replot a route to where they were supposed to go. Jack could here funny noises from behind him and so he turned and looked to see what was going on. What was going on was the CSM had taken his kilt off and was ringing the water out of it.

"Face front," came the command from the CSM but not before Jack had the opportunity to determine the answer to the age-old question, 'did a Scotsman wear anything under his kilt?' and he did indeed discover the answer.

They could not find the enemy position. Thanks to the moon, they were able to accurately determine where they were and that that was the middle of the square designated on the map as being the believed enemy position. They carried out two circular sweeps each further out from the centre and there was still no sigh of an encampment. Terry, as the patrol commander, consulted with the other two members and asked their opinion as to what they should do. Tim simply said,

"You're the Patrol Commander, you decide."

"Jack?"

"We have the CSM with us to provide evidence that we did find the designated area and that we found nothing there or on the two sweeps around it. Also, although we three are wet, we are at least wearing full combat uniform. The CSM's legs are exposed covered only partly by a wet kilt and there is potential danger to him if he gets hypothermia. He's been muttering and mumbling to himself for a while, I can't work out what he's saying but it sounds like he isn't quite with it. I think we should return to camp and let another member of the Staff know what's happened."

"That's decided then. We're going back." No sooner had he said that than the clouds started covering over the moon and the rain started again – it was nice it had stopped for the ten minutes it had, even though they had not dried out at all. The rain had been in their face on the way out from the base and therefore should have been on their backs on their return, but no, the Rain God had his mojo working full bore in response to the CSM's prayers and it was in their face returning. Fortunately, the return was incident free – no fighting patrols from the Guards found them – and they returned to camp at 0500 hrs. By the time they got back, the CSM had been silent for the last ten minutes or so, stumbling along and occasionally falling, he must have been driven by sheer willpower alone. Tim spoke quietly to Sgt Dewey and he and the CSM disappeared. The story of the lily pad frog and the CSM spread rapidly around the base and guffaws of laughter could be heard all over.

Jack managed to grab just over an hour's sleep before they were once more assembled for the next exercise. A Landrover with three staff, the CSM, Sgt Dewey and the 2nd Lt commanding the Guards platoon got out. Jack, Tim and Trevor were called over. The 2nd Lt, without explaining why his Platoon was not where it was supposed to have been apologised to the three of them that his men had not been where they should have been. He confirmed that they, the patrol, had indeed found the right area and he gave them a brief description of the camp, the sort of information they would have been able to determine if the Guards had been where they should have been. They were then dismissed to carry on. As he turned away, Jack looked at the CSM who gave him the slightest of nods. *About all that I could expect*, supposed Jack; still the man was on his feet and functioning, so that said something about him.

Chapter 10

The days passed slowly. They were packed with military exercises although, as at Thetford, those intended for the infantry and armoured regiments were most often put into the command roles; not that Jack minded. The obscurity of a rifleman suited him very well. Life continued to be hell with the Guards enemy disturbing them intermittently all night every night; they could never escape from them, or catch them, whichever was the exercise because, laden down with full kit, occasionally up to 100lbs, as they were the odds were always against them. The only time they got even was when they actually clashed in fighting patrols; sentry snatches and when they managed to catch any of the Guards who were sneaking up on them. The clashes were quite physical and more physicality was applied, the more tired the Cadets became. Indeed as the 10 days progressed and the better the Cadets became, the more the clashes occurred and the violence escalated, indeed it became so bad that the Company Commander, Major Happie, the only man in the Company taller than the CSM, had to address them to tone it down. The Cadets did, however, detect a degree of smug satisfaction in his face that the Guards, who overbearingly regarded themselves as superior to everyone else, had to come to him to ask for some protection.

Nearer the end of the 10 days came the more the pressure was applied. Two Cadets disappeared back to Civvy Street and tempers became shorter still especially against the Cadets who were not carrying their weight, mainly overseas Cadets the Brits started giving them the unpleasant tasks, filling in the full lavatory holes and digging new ones being the worst. When they complained to the Brits that this was happening, it was made clear to them that only some of the overseas Cadets were given this task, those who pulled their weight were not. Complaints to the Permanent Staff were dealt with by them pointing out that it was not overseas Cadets who were being picked on because of their race but anyone idle because of their idleness – the CSM did not like idleness, he had a passion against it; it was one of the duties of a CSM to root it out and any Cadet complaining to him soon had it rooted out very thoroughly and finally. He was much better at rooting than any dentist!

They were building up to the final exercise. They did not know what form it would take but that it would be hard, unpleasant and extremely demanding was a given. They were made aware that senior officers would be visiting and watching and this meant that they had to show a high degree of skill at every task.

Their very last evening was still wet, still cold and still bloody unpleasant. It had been getting dark early because of the heavy clouds and rain. They were dismissed from patrol duties for that evening, although it was made clear that the Guards' platoon had not been stood down so were likely to do their damnedest to make this last evening as unpleasant as possible. Jack was able to cook up a meal on his hexamine cooker – it was a small metal square which held hexamine blocks, a bit like firelighters, and which were just about adequate, with one block, to heat a mess tin of water to the boil for a mug of tea. Two blocks were better but the Army carefully watched the issue of blocks and building up a few extras was quite difficult but not impossible – Cadets whisked away made sure that extra gash kit, hexamine blocks, tea bags, sugar and milk in particular which had been hoarded were passed on before they disappeared. Knowing that they were leaving the next day and only breakfast and a possible brew mid-morning was likely to be needed, Jack had a belting blow out. Everything he had, including his emergency rations in case they played the Thetford trick again of not bringing out rations because of 'enemy activity' went into filling up two mess tins and providing the best 'home' cooked meal of the camp even if some of the mixture, apple flakes and curry for one, was a bit odd! Jack shared with Charlie as he had not been able to build up such a stash. They had just about finished their evening cuppa, about 2000 hrs, when the sentries called out the alarm. Most of the rest of the Cadets had not finished their meals and, soaking wet and enjoying their own mega meals were not in a mood to be disturbed by any bastard enemy, Guardsman or not. The permanent staff had made a mistake – there were none of them there. They had gone to an 'O' Group, regarding the final day's exercise, in Sennybridge Camp and had left the Cadets alone.

"Fuck this for a game of soldiers," called one of the Cadets and instead of firing the parachute illumination two-inch mortar bomb straight up into the air, he fired it along the ground towards the trees where the enemy were thought to be located – about 40 yds away. Example set, it was only seconds before flares from the Very pistol one-inch in diameter and flaring beautifully were flying in the same direction. They only had three flares for the two-inch mortar but they did have a plentiful supply of smoke bombs so they were fired as well. With the air quite misted from the fine rain, the pyrotechnics produced a picture from Hell – Dante would have been quite proud! With cries like "bastards", "you mad cunts", "you fucking mad bastards", the attack broke up and the enemy hastened away. The Cadets expected trouble both from the staff for their outrageous use of the two-inch mortar and the Very pistol flares and from the Guards later in the evening during their next attack. The Cadets didn't care, so pissed off were they, they even prepared for the next attack by removing the blank firing attachments from their rifles. Yellow in colour and thus easily identifiable as being fitted to weapons when such was needed, they enabled the SLR, or any other automatic weapon to which it had been fitted to be fired without the weapon having to be cocked every time – normally done by a real bullet flying down the barrel. Without a blank firing attachment fitted, the semi-automatics would not reload. Having removed them, the Cadets were able to drop handfuls of grit down the barrel and thus fire it a bit like a shotgun. Very dangerous at very close range but mildly unpleasant if fired at say 20 or 30 yds – not likely to kill or even injure very much, but it was enough, in the dark to make anyone approaching the Cadets' camp think again. With the three mortars loaded with smoke bombs dangerous both as a flying projectile and emitting copious amounts of smoke to cause confusion and loss of direction and the three Very pistols well supplied with a variety of coloured flares, they awaited the next attack. It never came! So they had their one and only uninterrupted night. Nor was anything said to them by the staff. If the Guards had had a plan to get their own back the success of the Cadets' actions in the mini battle to come destroyed it – they did not want to face the danger of two-inch mortar bombs flying their way!

Reveille was at 0630 hrs, about an hour before first light. They each made their own breakfasts and then started to break camp; the first activity of the whole 10 days that they did joyfully. Jack had just about collapsed his tent and folded it up when he was approached by Sgt Dewey with the glad tidings that he was now the Platoon Commander and was to attend an 'O' group with the Company Commander Major Happie. It was, in fact, the first time that Jack had spoken to, or been spoken to, by him in nearly six months! The briefing was quite short and followed the same pattern as had happened throughout the 10 days. They were to advance to contact the enemy along a minor road/track starting at the base of their mountain and once contact had been achieved, they were to attack and capture that position. Jack had no questions so he was ordered back to his platoon with the move out time being 0830 hrs – time enough for it to get light for the visiting VIPs to see and not too early as to disturb their morning lie-in.

Jack was perturbed. This was the major exercise at the culmination of the camp and he had been chosen to lead. Why? Why was a non-infanteer in charge? He had no answer to that so get on with it he did. However, he was not happy at the task. All the attacks throughout the 10 days had followed the same format, indeed the same format that was followed throughout the entire British Army. When faced with an enemy in front of you, you only had three choices, to attack from the front, to attack from the left flank or to attack from the right flank. Continuous trench lines, as in the First World War gave only one attacking position – from the front. This was normally unacceptable – too many casualties so right or left flanking it had to be. Looking at the enemy's position and the ground around and leading up to it normally revealed the best direction from which to attack. However, that information was also available to the enemy, simply by looking at the ground themselves and it was therefore quite easy to prepare defences for an attack from that direction. How, therefore, to do it differently and attack in a manner the enemy would not expect?

Jack spoke to Charlie Telford who had just packed up his tent.

"Charlie, collect Terry Harris and another fit Cadet and" – showing him the map – "get yourself along this road as far as you can but make sure you are back here by 0820 hrs – that gives you about an hour. Leave your packs, I'll have them watched, I want you to look for the Guards' positions. There are bound to be at least two, possibly three, to fill in the time for the whole morning. Every contact with them results in the same old actions; fire, drop down, observe, fire and move and then the Platoon Commander assesses the position, decides to go left or right flanking, gives orders to the gun group(s) and assaulting groups and then gets going. It always takes about 30 minutes and the enemy is pretty sure where we're coming from and when. I want to do it differently. If you can find where the first enemy position is and a way past it, we may be able to get behind them and attack them from there. Look for ways through the woods, up the fields behind the stone walls whatever but, whatever you do, don't be seen. Questions?"

"None."

"Get going and see if you can leave the camp without any of the permanent staff seeing you go. Good luck."

Charlie left and Jack started getting the platoon site cleaned up. The lazy bastards were given the shit pits to fill in, and, chasing the others, had the Platoon getting ready to move off at 0830 hrs. Tim Speaker was given the task of guarding the recce patrol's heavy kit. At 0810 hrs, Jack was approached by Sgt Dewey, again, who asked,

"Can you explain to me why Mr Telford and two other Cadets are making their way up the backside of this mountain in an apparent attempt not to be seen?" Jack had come to respect Dewey during his time at Mons and, making his mind up immediately, told him the orders he had given Charlie and why he had done so. Dewey looked at him for what seemed like an eternity and then said,

"I suppose that as the Platoon Commander, you believed you had the authority to order such a patrol?"

"Yes, Staff."

"Well, let's see what Mr Telford has found out."

Jack could tell by the smile on Charlie's face that he had good news to impart. And he did. He explained that they had found the enemy's first position only 3 or 400 yds from the start point. The Guards weren't expecting any activity by the Cadets until after 0830 hrs and so were walking around openly preparing their position. It was an old gatehouse much tumbled down. It occupied the right-hand side of the track and a dry stonewall in poor condition stretched off to the right disappearing in the bushes and trees which had grown up since it was built. To the left side of the road, the wall was in good condition for about 25 yards but after that, it deteriorated and there were ample holes for a body of men to pass through it. Charlie and the patrol had done just that without the three Guardsman at the gatehouse seeing them. About 150 yds further on was what looked like a fallen down cottage where a largish number of Guardsmen were milling around, smoking and chatting; the preparation of their position was progressing in a fairly desultory fashion, the ruins, which had almost certainly been used by them before, provided an ideal position for defence. The trees and bushes started thinning out about 35 yds past that position such that it was completely surrounded by open space, again ideal for defence. Charlie thought that there were about 20 Guards at that, probably, therefore, their main position. With the three at the first position that left about seven Guardsmen unaccounted for. As Jack started to ask,

"Was there—" Charlie interrupted and said,

"Any sign of the rest? I think I got a glimpse of a third position about 50–70 yds further on but the rain was limiting visibility so I couldn't be totally sure but it would make sense for them to have defence in depth because they've done that during every exercise." It pained Charlie, that as a Guardsman, they were so predictable and a mere Headquarters Clerk had sussed out their plan but he was honest enough to say that he thought Jack was right.

"Right," said Jack, "O group." Time was getting a bit tight but he had time to set out the duties of each of the Sections.

"No 1 Section," commanded by Charlie Telford, who had recce'd the position and was extremely competent in Jack's opinion, "You are to take the lead and creep around the first enemy position and attack them from the rear on my signal. The gatehouse is in poor condition but the rear wall and most of the roof is still standing and it is a good bet that they'll shelter from the rain under it for as long as possible. That rear wall should give you cover to get right up to the Guards before they even see you or are aware of your presence. Do whatever is necessary to make sure that they have no opportunity to fire a shot or give a vocal warning." Jack was sure that they would do just that. "Leave two O/Cadets to guard the captured enemy and those two should be two biggest buggers well able and reliable to flatten any escape attempt or any attempt to warn the others." Violence had been used by the Guards when they formed snatch squads etc. and that, as far as Jack was concerned was to be practiced on them in return if necessary. "The remaining six Cadets are to join No 3 Section once that has been done."

No 2 Section was to be the firefight group. Their task was to pass around No 1 Section and make their way to the edge of the woods before the second, main enemy position. Until the signal was given, they were to remain hidden in the trees. One man was to lead by about 10 yds to limit the chance of the enemy seeing how many of the Platoon were making their approach. Jack didn't want numbers wandering around and giving their presence away so one man, taking care, could identify the limit to which they could advance. No 2 Section was to be beefed up with the 2 GPMGs from the other sections and was to be provided with all bar three of the remaining smoke grenades and thunder flashes. When the signal was given, they were to emerge into the open as though they didn't have a care in the world. Jack hoped the Guards, seeing them coming, would open fire on them as standard practice. At which No 2 Section should retreat into the woods as standard practice. The Guards would then be expecting that the O/Cdt Platoon Commander would hold an 'O' Group, as standard practice, and that 30 mins, or so, later they could expect fire to be rained down on them in an attempt to keep their heads down whilst the rest of the Platoon went left or right flanking as standard practice. The problem for the Guards, although they did not know it, was that there would be no 'O' Group and 30 mins, or so, to rest. Jack was carrying out the 'O' Group now and the wandering into the open would only happen on Jack's signal. Only then would the six men of No 2 Section, three GPMG gunners and three riflemen, which Jack deemed sufficient to appear to be the head of the Cadet platoon wandering into the open, would do so. On command, they would pour fire, smoke grenades, mortar bombs and thunder flashes into the Guards' position.

Before this happened, No 3 Section was to crawl up the mountain, by the side of a dry stonewall, that Charlie had identified, as going up the hill for about 40 yds and then turning along the side of the mountain to run parallel to the road – ideal to let them get close to the enemy without being seen. Section 3, nine men, plus the remainder of Section 2, two men, was to lead off so that it would be to the right of the line when they formed line to advance down the hill against the main, 2nd, enemy position. The remainder of No 1 Section, six men, was to follow the others up the hill and then along the wall so that they would form the left of the line making a line of 17 men for the assault. No 3 Section was to be formed so that the biggest and fittest men formed the right of the line, seven of them, as they were to swing right having passed through the enemy position 'killing' everyone they encountered and dash for the third position. Jack wanted as many smoke mortar rounds and smoke grenades as possible to be fired into the area between the No 2 Fire Section fire point and beyond the second enemy position to reduce visibility as much as possible. The remaining three smoke grenades were to be thrown by No 3 Sections strongest throwers into the area between the second enemy position and the 3rd fall-back position. He hoped that the remaining Guardsmen, probably about seven allowing for three at the first position, 20 at the second leaving seven from a platoon of 30, would not suspect that their position had been discovered. The smoke and the rain mist together would limit their visibility of the main site and the smoke, thrown by No 3 Section between their main position and the Guards' third position, would simply be thought to be smoke drift from the main battle and No 3 Section, nine men in all, would be able to run on them out of the smoke in a frontal assault, this within only two or three minutes of the start of the assault on the main position. They would be expecting, Jack hoped, that there would be at least 30 mins or more spent by the Cadets clearing the main site, during which they could shelter from the rain in the rear ruined gatehouse and only emerge from it to be ready when the Cadet Platoon started off towards them having cleared the Guards' second position. As usual, the Guards would fire at the Cadets as soon as they appeared and there would be, as usual, about 30 mins of O Group before they attacked the third position. What they would not expect, he hoped, was that they would be prepared for a section charging in on them from the smoke almost as soon as the second battle started. That was the plan outlined. Jack dealt with a number of questions and, by the skin of his teeth, was ready when Staff Dewey called out.

"Mr Hughes, Mr Fawaz, here please." Once they had assembled he said, "Mr Fawaz, you are now the Platoon Commander, you, Mr Hughes are a Rifleman replacing Mr Fawaz in No 3 Section." Jack was staggered. Whilst it was quite common for Cadets to change roles during an exercise, for it to happen now, just as the action was due to start was an absolute bummer; in fact, Jack became more and more angry at the thought of Horsey, so named because he abandoned the Mustang sports car in the drill shed blocking all entry on the day they reported to Mons, getting the credit if the plan succeeded and he was just about to complain to Sgt Dewey when he spoke to Fawaz,

"You do not have much time, Mr Fawaz, to formulate a new plan, which you are, of course, entitled to do. On the other hand, you could consider that Mr Hughes's plan is an excellent one, different to anything that has been seen before and, for that reason, very likely to succeed, also the platoon know what it is. You could thus decide to adopt it. You have five seconds to make up your mind and consider that you have no time at all to brief the platoon on your plan, whatever it might be. By the way, Mr Fawaz, you might like to know that there is a Brigadier from your Army, in charge of training, up on that mountain over there with a British Army Major General, who have both come to watch the exercise. So have you decided to follow Mr Hughes's plan; you have. Good choice, Sir. Let's get going, shall we?" And at that, he was off. Horsey said not a word throughout.

This exercise was somewhat different to any of the previous ones they had taken part in that, this time, they had Umpires who would decide who was killed or wounded. There was one Umpire at each enemy site and one with each section of the Cadets' platoon.

Charlie led away with No 1 Section and 2 and 3 followed about 10 mins behind. No 2 Section, for the exercise, the three GPMG gunners and the three riflemen, carried straight on past the turn off No 1 had taken and then stopped after about 25 yards whilst still in the woods and out of sight of the main enemy position. No 3 Section, augmented by the two men from No 2 Section, followed them but stopped short at the wall going off to the right. They had only been in position for five mins or so when No 1 Section arrived, all of them with huge smiles on their faces. Charlie whispered to Horsey Fawaz that not only had they captured the three Guards in the first position, but they had also captured the Platoon Commander who was making a final inspection of it. The whisper came down the line that Charlie, no love lost between his Guards Regiment, and the other Guards forming the enemy, had been unable to resist saying to their 2nd Lt,

"For you, Sir, the war is over." It came out later that the Lt had not been too pleased at his capture and had had to be restrained from pulling rank on the two O/Cadets left as guards, attempting to order them to release him but he was restrained by the Umpire a Captain in a Shire regiment who had no love for, in his view, the stuck up and rather supercilious Guards' regiments claiming superiority and seniority over everyone else.

No 3 Section, the remnants of Nos 1 and 2 Sections, started making their way alongside the wall up the side of the mountain. They were only able to progress about 20 yds before the trees petered out and they had to start crawling along the side of the wall. Not only was it physically exhausting crawling lugging all their kit but the sheep had obviously formed a track alongside the wall which was consequently very muddy and covered in sheep shit. Such are the pleasures of soldiering! They reached the turning point without having been spotted and crawled along, still hidden by the wall and slithering in sheep shit until they were opposite the enemy position some 30 yds or so down the hill. Careful observations by Horsey had taken in Guardsmen lying around, smoking, berets off, most of them squeezed under the buildings dilapidated roof, and clearly unaware of the Cadets' proximity. The Cadets were keen to get at them; they had been on the receiving end of the agro for 10 days; they were tired, wet and thoroughly pissed off at the Guards. So when the order came whispered down the line, "Prepare to advance," they were ready for it. They were not ready for the "fix bayonets" which followed it. Bayonets were fixed automatically when "prepare to advance" was given when they were using ball ammunition and paper target enemies. Bayonets were not fixed when the enemy was a live one because of the obvious dangers. With shared grins, the Cadets fixed bayonets. They were delighted to do so. They hated the Guards with a passion that had grown through six months and escalated enormously during the ten days of battle camp. The order was given by Horsey who was unlikely to get into much trouble for it so they obeyed!

Horsey passed the order to No 2; fire party to advance. The first of them was immediately spotted by a Guardsman as he exited the wood and the alarm was sounded – they were at least that well prepared. The No 2 Section soldier ran back to the gun line at the wood edge as they started pouring fire into the Guards' position. Some of the Guards spilling out of the ruin were exposed in the open and it was these who suffered. The Umpire called out "killed" and "wounded" as he walked across the front of the Guards' position. It is a common maxim that no plan ever survives first contact with the enemy and this time was no exception except it was the Guards' defence plan that did not survive, not the Cadets' that fell apart. One of those killed in the initial burst was the Platoon Sergeant leaving no obvious leader at their moment of greatest need, the Platoon Commander having been captured a few minutes before. This activity kept all of the Guards concentrated on their front with the Sgt trying to argue, unsuccessfully, with the Umpire that he was not dead.

Meanwhile, "Advance" came down the main line of Cadets at which they all stood up and stepped/climbed over the wall – only about three feet high and less than that where it had fallen into disrepair. Jack, right hand man, immediately fixed his eyes on a Guardsman who was lying on his back, beret off and fag on, firing blanks into the sky in a desultory manner with no attempt at taking aim. The Cadets' assault line, 17 Cadets strong, armed to the teeth and covered in camouflage paint walked steadily down towards the Guards with their rifles, bayonets fixed, held out in front of them ready to stab the Guards. It was this last that clinched it for the Cadets. They had already established the Cadets' mad badness the night before by firing two-inch mortar bombs and flares from the Very pistol directly at the Guards attacking the camp. The word for this had clearly spread amongst the Guards so the sight of gleaming bayonets pointing directly at them by these madmen was the final straw. By the time they were spotted, they were only between 10 and 15 yds from the Guards. As soon as they were spotted, Horsey screamed "charge" and the assault was on. Screaming like the lunatics they clearly were, the Cadets broke into a charge which given the amount of kit they were carrying was not very fast, fortunately for the Guards.

Jack's target was up and off at a rate that would have made a 100-yd sprinter envious. Jack had some momentum from coming down the slope but the Guardsman, unencumbered by any kit and leaving his beret behind, was off like a rocket. Jack got to about 5yds from him but by this time the Guard was still accelerating, by now, up the other slope of the valley and Jack was being dragged back by his kit and the upward slope. Jack was screaming his curses.

"Come here, you little bastard; I'm going to pay you back; I'm going to introduce you to some fine English steel." These were just some of the sweet-talk words he aimed at the Guardsman. He didn't really want to hurt him very much – just stab the bayonet an inch or less into his arse, but the Guardsman was, unreasonably, having none of it. Jack considered throwing his rifle at him, like a javelin, but he couldn't be sure of his accuracy and anyway he needed the rifle for his next task.

So with considerable frustration, Jack slowed to a stop and looked around him. The three designated Cadets had just thrown the last three smoke grenades to thicken up the smoke which fortunately had been gently blowing up the valley. Picking up the abandoned beret, Jack joined the left of the assault line – only seven strong now, two of them adjudged to have been killed in the assault by the Umpire. Moving off at a steady trot, they disappeared quickly from view of the main assault, so thick was the smoke. Indeed, it was only the track that showed them the route to follow. They were only 10 or 15 yds from the final position before they were spotted by the defenders. Again the command to charge was given, this time by the Section Commander, O/C Tim Barton, and charge they did. Although the Guards were more or less alert at this position, they stood no chance; not expecting a frontal charge, they were disbursed to both sides of the gatehouse so that only the end Guard from each line was able to turn and face the charge. They too were horrified when they saw the fixed bayonets and their reaction was mainly to surrender such was the reputation the Cadets had established the night before but 10 days of no sleep had earned them a good going over and that is what they got. Jack often wondered for years later why it was the Umpires had not stepped in and ordered the unfixing as soon as they were fixed. Maybe they didn't like the Guards very much either Maybe they thought it exceeded their authority or maybe it just happened too quickly and it all happened before they could give the order. Anyway they didn't. Jack and the Cadets just secured the position and the prisoners and waited for orders.

They weren't long in coming with a whistle blowing and a runner appearing to order them to assemble at the main position. It was only a few minutes to walk back. The artificial smoke had largely cleared by this time and the rain had slackened to a light drizzle. Forming three sides of a square, they waited for the explosion. It was obvious one was coming. They knew they had been somewhat naughty and judging by Major Happie, who was stalking about looking like a bulldog who had just swallowed a wasp, unhappiness was about to descend on them. Happie did not look happy either. The first thing he said when they were all reported as being present was to,

"Unfix those bloody bayonets and—" Before he could say anymore, two Landrovers drove up the track, the first one with the Star Plate of a Major General uncovered and on show. The CSM called them all to attention as the General got out and walked over to the Cadets. Major Happie saluted. The General returned the salute and then shook hands with Happie. Following him were two Generals in somewhat exotic, foreign, uniforms and a couple of Brigadiers. Hovering in the background were a couple of Subalterns, the normal 'gophers' to be found around any General Officer.

The Major General introduced himself as being in charge of Army Training and the other Senior Officers as being his counterpart in their Armies. He immediately asked who the Platoon Commander for the exercise was. Horsey trying to reduce himself in size and hide behind a couple of other Cadets called out quietly,

"I was, Sir."

"Step forward. You are?"

"Officer Cadet Fawaz of the United Arab States Army, Sir."

"How did you come up with that plan?" This was delivered rather sternly and Fawaz, knowing that fixing bayonets was quite a serious crime, was only too delighted to throw the blame elsewhere said,

"It was O/Cadet Hughes's plan, Sir. He sent out the recce patrol without orders and then carried out the 'O' Group. Just as we were about to move off Staff Dewey changed the command roles around and, as there was no time to come up with another plan, I carried on with his plan, Sir."

Gee thanks, thought Jack. *I hated them in Aden and I hate them again now.* He didn't need to put that "without orders" in or even mention the recce patrol. *The little shit is trying to slide out from under his 'fix bayonets' order by diverting blame to me.*

"I see," said the General, "the credit for the success of this attack therefore belongs to O/Cdt Hughes?"

"Oh yes, Sir."

"It does you credit not to claim credit that belongs to someone else, Mr Fawaz." Calling for Jack to step forward, he said,

"We were able to watch the whole attack developing from up on the ridge. Although there was a lot of smoke and rain, we were above most of it and able to look down on the fight. The plan for this morning shows a sequence of three attacks taking up virtually all the morning it not being possible to be too precise in these matters. However, by your silent attack on the first position without the normal firefight and delays for 'O' groups the position had been overrun in just five minutes. Moving your assault force up the mountain by the side of the wall was masterly. You held back your fire group until you were in position to assault the main position and only then did you give the word for the fire group, and even then only one of them, to reveal himself to start the fight. The Guards were clearly expecting a half hour 'O' group or something like that because they were just lying around not ready as your assault force came down the hill at them. You must have been only 10 yds or little more before they saw you and then, very sensibly, they decided their position could not be held and they scarpered. We saw the extra smoke grenades detonated to give you cover for the frontal assault on the third position which again took place without an 'O' group. By the way, how did you know the position was there?"

"I sent out the recce patrol first thing and they found all three positions, Sir."

"Anyway, once more, the Guards at the third position were also taken by surprise and they too, very sensibly, decided to scarper or surrender. The whole exercise took less than half an hour and that was nothing short of brilliant. You are to be congratulated O/Cadet Hughes for such a masterful plan. The key factor was surprise. You are Kohima Company and named after the Kohima battle that turned out to be a major surprise for the Japanese and the turning point of the war in Burma. It was the first occasion that the British Army, which had been surrounded at Kohima, did not try to break out but decided to stay put and fight. The Japs had anticipated that the British would behave in the manner they had exhibited throughout the war to that date i.e., split up and try to break out when surrounded. We did not do that. Developed by Field Marshal Slim and made possible by the immense build-up of air support, they had an enormous air fleet capable of huge air drops to surrounded forces to enable them to fight and defeat the Japanese at that site. The Japanese had anticipated the actions of the British running as normal and they could then live of the supplies left behind. When this didn't happen, the Japanese kept attacking and kept being beaten off so that they were eventually forced to retreat starving and having lost a huge number of their attacking soldiers. Those that did survive were malnourished and disease ridden and were relatively easy meat for the relieving forces. I know this because I was a very junior Subaltern in the main regiment defending Kohima. Now this little battle this morning wasn't quite in the same category as Kohima of course but it does illustrate comprehensively the value of surprise against an enemy who assumed you would behave as before. Well done, O/Cadet Hughes."

"Thank you, Sir," said Jack, "but a lot of the credit should go to O/Cdt Telford who led the recce patrol and found the three positions. Without that we would have struggled."

"Quite so," said the General, "Who is O/Cadet Telford? Stand forward." Charlie stood forward and the General shook his hand and then Jack's.

"Now," he said turning to Major Happie, "I understand I have some presentations to make." Happie was not happy. He had wanted to give the platoon a good going over for the fixed bayonets and to rearrange the programme for the rest of the morning. He was unhappy that the General, by his words about presentations, had written off the rest of the morning and had moved to the presentations. The plan had indeed envisaged that the battles at the three sites would take all morning so that finishing at lunchtime would finish the battle camp quite nicely. Now they were finished by 0930 hrs. But if a general says that's it, that's it.

"Yes, Sir, if you please, was all he could say. CQMS Little, the first time any of the Company had seen him, stepped forward. The CQMS, (Company Quartermaster Sergeant – the man responsible for all their supplies,) handed the

General a piece of paper and a wrapped object about three feet long. It was the Sword of Honour and was handed to J. Jowett, the SUO (Senior Under Officer) along with suitable words. Other Certificates were handed out to the other Cadets who had earned more junior positions, again with suitable words being said, and then the CQMS handed a blue box, about 10 inches square, and a note to the General. The General said,

"We now come to the final award and I am instructed to say that the scores total achieved by this Officer Cadet as Champion at Arms beats the previous record by two points and is awarded to Officer Cadet Hughes. Jack marched forward and remembered to salute the General, something he had forgotten when he won the Surrey Lord Lieutenant's Cadet Badge as the best Army Cadet of that year. The General said a few private words and then to the platoon said,

"If O/Cadet Hughes can catch the enemy off guard in the future and shoot them as well as these scores indicate, then he won't need a platoon, he can shoot them all himself." The Cadets dutifully laughed and Jack thanked him, saluted and marched away. There was to be another presentation in a somewhat different format at the passing-out parade but the end of battle camp had traditionally seen all the presentations announced then. Jack was surprised to be accosted by CQMS Little who demanded the tankard, for that is what the box contained, back. It turned out that it was to be engraved with Jack's name etc., which could not be done before the Camp because the winner would not be known until the end of battle camp. He quite happily returned it to him, satisfied that it wasn't one of these prizes handed to the winner and then stuck back in a display cabinet only to reappear at the next presentation.

They were bussed to Sennybridge camp and allocated bed spaces by platoon, as at Mons. It was nothing short of heaven. The rooms, only wooden spiders as at Mons, were warm! They even had drying rooms and for the first time for 10 days, they were able to clean the worst of the mud off their kit and get it dry. Because the dinnertime was a bit of an unknown as the finish time could not be foreseen, a simple meal had been arranged with a slap-up meal arranged for teatime. At teatime, there were four choices of starters, four choices of main meal, steak, chicken, pork and lamb – and you could have some of each if you wished – and three choices of puddings. The Cadets were habitually used to eating about 6,000 calories per day – hard living allowance – but they comfortably exceeded that at this meal! Most of the Cadets were asleep by 2000 hrs and ready and queuing for the transport back to Mons at 0800 hrs Even after that good night, most of them slept most of the way back in a slow, noisy, grubby old coach, some on the floor, the rest draped across anything any which way they could.

They were surprised to find a set of Part One Orders on the notice board when they got back; there had never been Orders before on a Sunday night – the Orders customarily being posted on a Friday night. They were quite short. They listed the RSM's rehearsal drill parade for the following morning at 1000 hrs and the names of four Cadets to parade at the Company Office at 0945 hrs. The word went around quickly. The four were to parade at that time so that they could be fired and got rid of from the Camp by the time the parade rehearsal was over. The despondency at reading this was slowly dispersed by the realisation that the Cadets not named on the Orders had passed the course, the only actual notification they received, and would pass out on the Friday. Jack, although sorry for the four named Cadets, none of whom had he been particularly friendly with, gradually developed a huge grin on his face and shot across to the telephone box. He had been too slow and the queue was long. It was an hour before he could ring Janet and tell her the probable good news – there was still almost a week for things to go wrong!

The one major problem looming for Jack was that he was not a good swimmer. If he just floated in the water, his natural buoyancy was about 4–6 inches under water! He had swum a lot in Aden in the afternoons with Janet and had introduced her to the benefits of a mask and flippers. The first time Janet borrowed his mask, she didn't want use of the flippers, she was staggered at the amount of life in the sea – there were huge quantities of fish some of them quite large and fierce looking. Although she had been swimming off that beach for about a year, she had never been able to see underwater before. Indeed, so much life was there that she was a little frightened by it and almost swam up the beach to get away from it! She was a superb swimmer and had swum for the Army in inter-service competitions in the UK and Aden before meeting Jack and had one many medals and cups. So intense was the training she underwent that her ears were affected by it and she had ceased competition swimming just before meeting Jack. Jack was able to keep up with her whilst wearing flippers but not without.

Early on in his time at Mons all the Cadets had had to pass a swimming test. Jack couldn't pass it and had had extra training as a result. Now he had to pass the test in the last few days at Mons, before the passing-out parade or he would be failed. In the event, Jack just passed the test but he was never happy in the water and if he did swim, it was always with a mask to protect his eyes – he had caught German Measles (Rubella) at three years old which had shown up mainly in his eyes making them very vulnerable to chlorine in swimming bath water and to cold weather when his eyes would water as though he had lost a pound and found a penny.

Chapter 11

The final five days were a mixture of pleasantry and purgatory. The purgatory was the endless rehearsals for the passing-out parade on the Friday, pleasant though that parade would be. The pleasantries included handing in all their kit bar their best SD uniforms and boots, and the issuing to them of the white belt, bayonet scabbard and rifle sling for the parade use only; also good was the receipt and trying on of their officer uniforms, mess kit, shoes, mess wellingtons, gloves, hats – 3 types – and overcoat, great coat and raincoat. All paid for by a grant, which was not enough despite tricks like buying a second-hand SD as the second everyday wear uniform, Sam Brown belt, ties etc. which meant a bill to Jack of nearly £200 extra when his pay was only £20 per week! He was to discover that the bills didn't end there – there were mess bills to come and the purchase of a black-tie outfit which he wore on the Tuesday night when a 'dining in mess night' was arranged – something he was to wear only once in his entire Army service!

Monday, as ordered in the Part One Orders, was the rehearsal conducted by the RSM who had appeared before them to welcome them at the start of the course and whom they hadn't seen since the previous passing-out parade when they were the junior Company. The passing-out Company was only 44 strong, 16 had either fallen, or been pushed, by the wayside. All of them were either serving soldiers or those straight from civilian life, none of the foreign Cadets, apart from Mohammed Mohammed, had been dismissed or allowed to resign. The RSM was not happy the first time they marched the parade so they had to parade again and he didn't like that one either so they did it a third time. Jack felt the first one was the best one and that the repetitions got worse as they got more tired but the RSM obviously did not feel that way. Had he had his way they would have paraded again after dinner but appointments had been set up for the Cadets with the Regiments or Corps to which they were being posted for them to discover what they were being offered in the way of commissions, and they took precedence. But they still had to do their ten-mile hike before tea. And they were tired.

In Jack's case, the interviewer was a major, who, after the initial pleasantries said,

"Well, I have good news for you, Jack, we have found you a place at the unit you asked for, you are being posted to the RAOC Junior Leaders' Regiment at Deepcut, not so very far from here on a two-year Short Service Commission."

Jack was stunned and it evidently showed on his face. "You don't look too pleased, why is that?" Jack said,

"I wrote as my first option on the forms we filled in at the start of the course that I would like to be posted to CVD Ludgershall, which deals with 'A' vehicles (vehicles which normally operate in the front line) and failing that any 'B' vehicle depot (those that are not normally used in the front line). I did write, as the first unit, I would not like to be posted to as the Junior Leaders and my second choice not to go to would be the Recruit Depot. I am therefore very disappointed and somewhat concerned at what you have just said." Opening a file on the desk, the Major scanned through it. Jack recognised when he reached his expression of wish form by the black ink and the handwriting. Reading through it the Major said,

"Goodness so you did. I wonder how that happened." Jack knew, some idle bastard, maybe the one in front of him, had not bothered to read it at all and had selected Jack for the Junior Leaders because it was the next one on the list that needed an officer and Jack was the next one on the officer list – job done; no work or effort involved. "But what is your objection to the Junior Leaders, you would be the first subaltern on his first commissioning to be sent there, a real recognition of your qualities. Normally it is a second posting at least for Lieutenants or even Captains but by virtue of your other rank service, it's felt that you would have exactly the right experience to command a platoon of boy soldiers. As you know, they are intended to be the future leaders of the Army and someone from the ranks such as yourself having achieved a commission would be an excellent example to them as to what can be achieved?" That comment told Jack that they had decided to send him there irrespective of his wishes.

"Sir, I joined, originally the RASC, as a technical arm which would enable me to learn a trade or profession. I had served almost six years in the East Surrey Regt, an infantry one in the Army Cadet Force; I underwent two basic training courses on joining the Regular Army and have endured the last, hardest, six months of my life running up and down mountains carrying enormous loads and I have no intention of doing it anymore. That is why I said I wanted Vehicle Org and did not want Junior Leaders or the Depot. I feel very strongly about this. As a ranker, I really had no choice in where I was posted but, as a commissioned officer, I don't have to accept a posting, do I?" The Major thought about and then, using his words very carefully, tried to say that Jack had no choice whilst at the same time saying he did – typical. Jack was more and more convinced that he was the one who had not read or at least had ignored the expression of wish form and now was desperately trying to get out of the mess without it being found out. Jack then said,

"I feel so strongly about it I would rather resign my commission now than accept that posting." Jack felt he was taking a bit of a risk that his bluff would be called but he felt, after six months of being buggered around from arseholes to breakfast time, that he was dammed if he was going to spend the next two years training boy soldiers to be infantry soldiers running around the woods playing at silly buggers and shouting bang while he did so (their ammunition allocation was piss poor). Since he was only being offered a two-year commission, it would mean leaving the Army with only infantry experience, something he already had in spades. The blood drained out of the Major's face and he almost gabbled the words out when he said,

"Well, let's not be too hasty. Would you mind waiting in the next room whilst I make a few telephone calls – I'm sure we can sort this all out?" Jack said,

"Not at all, Sir." He stood up and walked out. He spent at least 15 minutes hovering outside thinking, *now I've gone and done it, he'll come back and throw the book at me.* But he didn't. He invited Jack in, invited him to sit, he hadn't been invited to sit before, and said,

"I hope I can now offer you a compromise that you will feel is acceptable to you. I cannot do anything at this late stage about your posting to the Junior Leaders next January; it is only about two months away and one of my colleagues has had a look at who is next in the pipeline and when they could become available. With Christmas also falling into that period, it is simply impossible. But, however, we can do something a bit later along. I can promise you a posting to Ludgershall after one year if you are prepared to accept a one-year posting to the Junior Leaders first. Now how does that grab you? Of course there is also every possibility that you could apply for an extension to your Short Service Commission or a transfer to a Regular Commission in the future even possibly to enable you to stay at Ludgershall longer than a year." Jack thought about it for all of a nanosecond; it was clearly the only offer he was going to get and it had not only the guarantee of Ludgershall but the possibility of an extension of his Short Service Commission at the end of it at Ludgershall. He didn't know, and would not get to know for some time, that his Army career just ended at that point. Useless jobsworths like the Major were vicious little, small minded bastards and a junior rank standing up to them whilst revealing their incompetence in doing so would be the subject of vicious and unfair treatment. There was never going to be an extension or change to a Regular Commission; besides this little Gestapo turd Jack was to upset two more senior officers who would happily put the boot in.

On Tuesday, they paraded for the Adjutant, another one they had not seen until this day. He only made them go through the parade twice before dismissing them but the RSM was unhappy so they paraded again in the afternoon for him. If he had been left on anyone's Christmas card List by that time he rapidly was deleted on Tuesday afternoon. And they completed their ten-mile hike before tea and they were still tired.

On Wednesday was the big one before the biggest one. It was the Commandant's Parade when for the first time they had a band and he, the Commandant and a Brigadier to boot, having expressed himself satisfied after just one parade, went onto everyone's Christmas card list. The remainder of the time, with no parade scheduled for the Thursday was taken up in all sorts of admin, the issuing of discharge books for all the serving soldiers and medicals for them because they were being discharged – the foreign Cadets also had medicals to prove, if their governments complained, that they were in first class physical condition; in the case of Fawaz, much better condition than when he arrived. But they still had to do their ten-mile hike before tea – this time literally just a cup of tea and a piece of cake as they were to eat dinner in the Officers' Mess later.

That night they were dined into the Officers' Mess and they all wore their Dinner Jackets for the first, an in Jack's case only, time. Although the Mess could not boast the amount of silver that most infantry regiments could it was nevertheless a very impressive sight if you had not seen one before. Jack had at the RAOC Mess in Deepcut, indeed he had waited in the Mess as part of the agro the CSM had had in for him, and Charlie had seen a Guards' Mess all done up – both far superior to Mons. After the meal and the toasts the high jinks started encouraged by the officers after the Commandant had retired. Jack knew all about the mess games and the damage and mess caused because he had had to clear up after them in Deepcut and was deeply sensitive about it. If NCOs in their clubs or messes, or soldiers in the NAAFI had behaved that way, they would have been very severely punished. He could not understand why it was all right for officers to behave as hooligans whilst at the same time dishing out punishment to more junior ranks behaving in the same way. 'Relieving stresses' did not cut it. NCOs and even soldiers experienced stress, some so severe they killed themselves, so Jack took no part in it and just quietly left when it started becoming too boisterous.

However the Wednesday was not finished. Just after 0200 hrs when Jack was deeply asleep, there was an enormous bang which woke the whole camp and surrounding area. It didn't take very long for the cause of it to be discovered; the CSM's room had been blown up. Further investigations showed that a number of dustbins, probably four or five, it was difficult to tell, had been placed in the room, explosives had been placed in the middle of them and then detonated. The CSM had the end of one of the spiders which had been modified into a comfortable couple of rooms, bedroom, lounge diner with small kitchen attached and the whole lot had been blown to hell. No one knew if the CSM had been in the rooms at the time and this was only resolved when he staggered up from the Sergeants' Mess. To say that he was not a happy bunny would have been the understatement of the year. The sight of the site and the state it was in rapidly sobered him up. And then anger set in not, surprisingly, at the damage that had been done to his home but at the realisation that someone had probably retained explosives from an exercise to be able to carry out the demolition. Every time the Cadets were on the ranges or exercises where explosives or ammunition were used they had to make a declaration at the end of it, to an NCO/Staff Member that "no live rounds, empty cases or explosives in my possession, Sir". Someone had clearly lied at that declaration and that was a serious matter for someone who was about to become 'an officer and a gentleman, whose word was his bond'. It was even more serious than the damage that had been done! It also showed a clear intent to carry out this demolition.

The rest of the night was a mess. Fire brigade, police, military equivalents, were all over the place. Everyone had to give a statement setting out exactly where they were when the explosion happened. Demands were made for the guilty party or parties to come forward – none did. And then, about 0545 hrs, the bombshell struck. The CSM had them all parade in various states of dress – it was bloody cold at five o'clock in the morning of Thursday, 12 October, and announced if the guilty parties did not come forward, then there would be no passing-out parade, they would not be commissioned and the bill for repair would be shared out amongst them! This drew loud mutterings of protest to the extent that it looked like there might be some sort of riot. It was easy to understand the CSM's anger but such a punishment for the Cadets not involved was not to be born. As the noise level grew the CSM, perhaps realising he had gone too far, dismissed them to their beds whilst further investigations were carried out.

The Thursday passed as much as normal as possible. In daylight, the extent of the damage, considerable, could be seen with bits of the building spread all around. The interior, visible to anyone, could be seen to be a right mess; some of the dustbins had been brought from the kitchens and the spread of leftover food was quite spectacular in its colours and spread, quite modern in its style really.

Considerable efforts continued to try and get the guilty ones to come forward. The Commandant had them fell in on the parade ground and did his best to bribe, coerce, jolly them into naming the guilty one. One of the voices from the back of the parade called out,

"How do you know it was us and wasn't a previous company or anyone else with a grudge against the CSM?" This comment, although anonymous, was fed back to them when they paraded again at 1500 hrs. At that parade, it was announced that as there was as yet no evidence to indicate who the guilty parties were, not even as to whether it was this company, the commissioning parade, church parade and other events would go ahead. However, they would be parading at the Guardroom every hour, on the hour starting at 2000 hrs. Not good news but if that was what it cost to get the commission, so be it and they would not be hiking 10 miles again.

The first parade was at 1750 hrs, when, in civilian suits, they were marched to the Garrison Church for a commissioning church service. Families were welcome and Jack's mum and dad attended. His wife, Janet, could not get away in time from her barracks in Mill Hill although she would be there the following day for the passing-out parade. What was a surprise was the attendance of Field Marshall Montgomery who had a godson passing out.

After the service, they fell in to be marched back to Mons when Montgomery approached the CSM. This should be interesting thought Jack.

"Sergeant Major, I have made arrangements to have dinner with my godson; there's no problem with that, is there?"

"Yes, Sir, there is. He and all the other Cadets who are passing out tomorrow are on punishment and he cannot be released whilst all the others stay."

Crikey, thought Jack, *it takes some balls for a CSM to say no to a* Field Marshall, and that's what he had just heard.

"Oh," said Montgomery in a tone that indicated he was not too pleased. "But surely you can make an exception in my case; I have travelled a long way to be here?"

"No, Sir, I cannot and some of these Cadets have relatives and visitors who have flown in from thousands of miles away and no exception is being made in their cases either." Probably Montgomery would have argued if it had just been the words but the CSM had approached him, standing so tall over the shrunken Field Marshall, who had never been big to start with, the power with which the words were delivered were a clear indicator that no exception was going to be made and at that Montgomery turned and clanked away (his sword scabbard was scraping and clanking on the ground). The CSM's salute to his back was less than smart.

And that's what happened. They paraded at the Guardroom every hour on the hour, the first time they were told they were to parade in their combat kit. That kit had been handed in during the previous day when all their kit had been handed in. So they paraded in their civvy suits. They were inspected and told to parade at 2100 hrs in their PT kit, so they paraded in their suits again and this farce went on all night until at 0700 hrs they were inspected and released by the CSM. They should have been very tired but today they were being commissioned; well, to be precise the commission came into force at midnight that night but the commissioning paraded was today and the excitement was enough to carry them through, and they had got used to going without sleep during the various exercises they had undertaken.

According to the RSM who formed them up – the commands during the parade were all to be given by Cadet Under Officers, they were late on parade. In fact they were early and it was just the RSM having a last go at them. One of the phrases he used struck a chord. He went on about him pulling their strings and them responding. When they stepped off the band burst into *Puppet on a String* which had recently won the Eurovision song contest sung by Sandie Shaw. There was no singer but the Cadets marched onto the parade ground laughing out loud at the timing of that tune, whether it was intended to be the first tune or a quick thinking Bandmaster switched it in having heard the "I pull your strings" comment they would never know.

Jack, as the tallest man in the Company – he hadn't been originally but one of the taller than him ones had disappeared halfway through the course and the other one was filling the role of an Under Officer and was marching behind the Company – It was Jack's job that when the 'eyes right' was given, he would keep looking straight ahead so that he could march in a straight line and keep the parade straight. It meant he could not have a good look at the Grandstand to see his family but they had a good look at him as the closest man to them!

At one stage, they were formed up to be inspected by General Sir John Magrill. They had all been surprised at this announcement as they had been expecting Montgomery again, especially as he had attended the church parade the night before and had been spied clanking around the school earlier in the morning. He had taken the previous parade for a godson and they had thought the same thing would happen this time. However, they were wrong; Montgomery was just there, the inspecting officer was General Magrill, Jack's almost nemesis from 1Br Corps where he had boiled the General's balls by spilling coffee all over them and 'rescued' him from captivity during an exercise when he had allowed the General to finish his coffee before conducting him to the helicopter that whisked him away. Jack hoped that he would not be recognised by the General but it wasn't to be. The General was accompanied for the inspection by the Commandant, a Brigadier, who on approaching Jack at the right of the line said,

"This is Officer Cadet Hughes, Sir, Champion at Arms with a new record score which will be hard to beat in the future." He clearly expected the General to say something about that in response. Instead he said,

"Boiled any more General's balls lately, Officer Cadet Hughes, not boiled the Brigadier's I hope." Jack could only laugh and say,

"No, sir." At that, the General turned to the Brigadier and gave him a short version of the boiling incident. The Brigadier was turning quite pale at the news the General knew far more about Jack than he did. Jack even wondered how the Commandant knew who he was to pick him out as the Champion at Arms, they had never met or spoken so Jack thought it was probably that he knew to pick Jack out either because one of the NCOs had told him he was Right Marker or that, as the only Cadet wearing a medal, it must be him.

"And is it true you threatened to blow the head off the Duty Officer in Aden?" Jack was really surprised at that one. He could only answer,

"Yes, Sir, but he was RAF." At this the General burst out laughing. The Commandant was looking quite green by this time as the General simply said,

"Good man and good luck with your career," he said and moved on. He spoke to one or two more Cadets and then addressed them from the podium for only 10mins about the future and their role in it.

They marched off to applause around to the back of the gym which was being used for drinks and canapes. Behind the gym was a cart upon which they piled their belts and bayonet scabbards. Their rifles were handed to the Armoury Sergeant who took them and piled them on the floor of a Landrover – so much for the zeroing of the sights! They all made their way into the gym to meet their families. Jack had his entire family there, his wife, Janet, Mum and Dad, Uncle Bern and Aunty Pat and their four children, his sister and her husband, the baby had been left with a sitter as he was only 12 months old, and his grandmother and grandfather. The tickets cost a fortune but as it was never going to recur he managed. The conversation was all pretty much as expected but Jack didn't notice his mother disappear. She reappeared a few minutes later het up and angry.

"Common little bastard, no fucking manners at all." This stopped all the other conversations, his mother very rarely used Anglo Saxon. It took a while to get from her that she had approached Montgomery, who was clanking and parading around the room almost giving a royal wave as he did so, and said to him,

"My son has passed out today and is a great admirer of yours; could I please have your autograph for him?" At which he looked her up and down and said,

"Madam, it is not my custom to hand out autographs like some mere film star. No, I will not. Good day to you," he said and turned his back on her. She was fuming. Like many who had survived the Second World War, Montgomery had been a hero to the population and to discover how pompous, rude and 'little' he was, was very upsetting hence her use of Anglo Saxon even though she was a Celt! Jack simply said,

"Mum don't be upset; if he had given it to you, I would simply have thrown it away. All the battles of Alamein, the D-day landings etc. were planned by better men and better Generals. The only one he planned was Arnhem, a bridge too far, a disaster costing at least 15,000 lives of first-class troops. The man is a poseur and credit stealer. I hold him in no respect whatsoever. Let it go." The party was starting to break up by then. Jack did not go around saying goodbye to all the other Cadets, he felt, as he would never meet any of them again that it was a bit pointless but he did find Staff Dewey and sold him back some of the boots and other kit he had bought from him at the start of the course!

But Mons had not finished with Jack. He had loaded all his new uniforms and kit into his car early in the morning so it was just a matter of getting in and driving away. Not to be, when he pushed the starter button, there was nothing – the battery had gone flat since it had last been used for the long weekend they had been allowed halfway through the course. He was parked too close to the wall in front to be able to insert the starter handle so to push the car back he sat in the car, held the driver's door open, put his right foot on the ground and shoved. The car started to roll and then stopped because the door had hit a bolt sticking out of the wall close on the driver's side of the vehicle. Pushing the car a bit forward, he pulled the door in closer to him and pushed the car backwards again. This time it missed the bolt and when he had sufficient space to access the front he stopped pushing. The car started first swing of the handle so it was just a matter to replace it carefully in the boot making sure it didn't foul any of the uniforms and get in closing the door as he did so. Except the door would not close! The gentle nudge against the bolt had bent the door hinges. Maths and physics says a nearly two-ton weight car moving at half a mile an hour will exert a huge amount of force on two little hinges, easily enough to bend them out of true! It is only when that happens for real that you discover precisely what that physic means. He was able to close the door on the first catch and so able to drive home. His father helped him to remove the hinges and hit them with a hammer – no luck. A seven-pound lump hammer could not belt them back into shape either. Nor could a 14lb sledgehammer! Thank heaven for a father who worked in an engineering factory where a 30-ton press did put them into order. And now Jack was an officer and there was no ten-mile hike that evening.

Chapter 12

Jack had two weeks leave following his commissioning and it was funny and frustrating that he was an officer but was not wearing his uniform and taking salutes from soldiers. The Friday following his commissioning Friday was Janet's last day in the Army. They had agreed that she would extend her service by a year, a year ago, since Jack would be in Germany and then the UK for Mons training and this would take the best part of a year. Jack tossed around in his head how he could get Janet to salute him and call him, Sir, in the little time that she was left in the Army. He telephoned the Adjutant at Mill Hill barracks where Janet was stationed and under the pretence of discussing him collecting Janet on her last day, he found out her programme for that last week. He was thus able to turn up on the Thursday in full uniform and just happen to walk down the path, which led to the Cookhouse, at the time Janet was walking towards it with her best friend, a Lance Corporal. It was therefore Janet's task to salute this officer who was walking the other way with his hat pulled quite well down over his eyes and thus unrecognisable from a distance. She had already started the salute when she realised who it was she was saluting – it had always been a standing joke between them that she would never salute him or call him Sir. Consequently she blurted out,

"You bugger, Sir," she said with a big smile on her face and then to the Lance Corporals surprise Janet kissed this tall young officer. Jack excused them both from the Lance Corporal, returned her salute when she walked away and whisked Janet off for lunch at a pub down the road recommended by the Adjutant. The Adjutant had been as surprised as Jack when he entered her office to discover that she was the 2nd Lieutenant from Houndstone Camp in Yeovil, when Jack had been on his trade training course there nearly three years before, and when he had created havoc on pay days – small world. She had told Jack, on the telephone, that Janet's last day in the Army was in fact the Thursday, some cock-up in admin, which meant Jack was able to tell Janet this and after lunch wait whilst she packed and said her goodbyes and then take her home to his parents where they were going to stay until they found a flat in the Frimley Green area whilst Jack was at the Junior Leaders Regiment. Janet was never to forgive him entirely for trapping her into saluting him but it did become a 'remember the time…' at family gatherings and events over the years.

On the Monday night of the second week, Jack's dad arrived home in a brand new white 2.4-ltr Mk2 Jaguar. It turned out that the Managing Director had asked his dad to drive him to the airport in his, the MD's car, and be there to collect him on his return on the Wednesday – subsequently, Jack's dad was to take the same journey. It meant that his dad had the car on the Tuesday. This gave Jack an idea. He had been badly treated by the Headmaster and most of the staff at his school when he had announced that he was joining the Army as a private soldier and in so doing turned down the opportunity to become the School Captain. So he asked his dad if could come with him when he went to work the following morning and then take the Jaguar for an errand he wished to run. His dad reluctantly agreed but agree he did which found Jack driving up the long drive to his old school; it comprised three large mansions spread over extensive grounds, and he parked in the visitor's space by the main front door. There were only three cars parked there anyway, the Headmaster's, the Deputy Head's and Ted Hiller's car, the Captain of the School Army Cadet Force unit, exactly the same as the last day when Jack left school four years before. Stepping out in all his uniformed splendour, Jack took his time putting on his Sam Brown, picking up his swagger stick and walking up to the door where a fourth former opened it on his approach. Asking his business, Jack replied that he wished to see Mr Hiller and gave his name. Asked to take a seat in what would originally have been the foyer, Jack chose to stand and admire the pictures hanging there, the exact same ones as to when he had carried out the self-same fourth former's duty.

Ted appeared almost immediately with a delighted grin on his face.

"So you made it," he said, "you said you would obtain a commission from the ranks and you have evidently done it. Come and tell me how you did it." He led Jack to the Staff Room and got him a coffee. Two other teachers who Jack did not recognise were there doing their best to appear uninterested whilst at the same time doing their best to hear all that was said. Jack briefly described his career and added that he thought he had received the recommendation for the commission based on the fact that he had shot a terrorist in Aden who had been attempting to grenade the Officers' Mess. The two teacher's eyes were out on stalks at that. Being a Tuesday it was the day in the week when the Army Cadets wore their uniforms to school and paraded at the end of the school day. Ted asked Jack if he could stay and address the unit after school but that would have made Jack late to collect his dad so he had to decline. At that, Ted asked him to stay to lunch – the school lunches were marginally better than those he had eaten in the various cookhouses in the Army so accepting was not arduous. Ted then set-up for the Cadets to parade after lunch and for Jack to address them then – getting his hands on a real live success as an officer was too good an opportunity to miss! In the time before lunch Jack asked to meet the Headmaster and much enjoyed showing off the uniform and the medal ribbon he wore to rub his face in it. Jack enjoyed speaking to the Cadets and even more showing off the Jag to Ted whilst managing to give the impression it was his without actually saying it was. He collected his dad on time and returned home having had an excellent day which had laid a few ghosts to rest.

Chapter 13

Jack, on the Monday, was entering the world of a Commissioned Officer and as such, in due course, he would receive from Buckingham Palace, his Commission from his Monarch, on fine parchment/vellum, he wasn't sure which, which started with all Her Majesty's titles and then said,

"Our trusty and well beloved...Greetings..."

Jack was to be proud of that forever; it is what gave him his authority to act as an Officer. Non Commissioned Officers, i.e., those up to the rank of Staff Sergeant (or equivalent) received nothing and those holding the rank of Warrant Officer Class 1 (normally RSMs) and Class 11 (normally CSMs) held warrants from the Monarch.

So on Monday, Jack drove to the Officers' Mess and parked his car there. He had written to the Adjutant (Adj) asking for permission to live out, at his parents', initially until he could obtain his own accommodation. The Adj refused on the grounds that as a newly commissioned officer, he needed to live in the Mess for a while to learn its rules. Jack was not happy at this as he was well aware of how that Mess operated having worked in it as ordered by the CSM at that time, but he did not feel it appropriate to bring that up at this stage so stay in the Mess he would for a short time. In fact it would be for quite a long time but the future is never known to us.

Walking back from the Mess to the offices, he passed a couple of soldiers travelling in the opposite direction and enjoyed the thrill of returning their salutes for the very first time as an officer. As he approached the building, a Sergeant was coming out. Jack recognized him immediately, it was Sgt Ellis, 'bullshit Charlie' as he was known and the first NCO to train Jack when he joined the Army four years before. Charlie realised an officer was standing there but it took a few moments to recognise Jack.

"It's Private Hughes that was," said Charlie. "Well, blow me down if you didn't make it." At this he threw up a magnificent salute and then offered his hand to shake. Jack was happy to return the salute and shake the proffered hand. They both were under pressure of time but Charlie had sufficient time to explain that he was leaving the Army on retirement at the end of the following week, as was CSM Bidmead, soon to be the subject of action taken by Jack, and they were both having a bash on the Thursday night, next week, in the Sergeants' Mess.

"You will come won't you, Sir, I'll arrange an invite for you, but I would love for you to come and tell me the secret of those bloody boots." Jack laughed.

"I wouldn't miss it for the world," said Jack and they split up.

Jack walked down a long corridor, past the RSM's office, the Colonel's office and almost to the Adj's office. He was bothered. Standing facing him at the end of the corridor, outside the Adjutant's office, was a full Lieutenant. That wasn't the problem. The problem was that both their Sam Brown cross shoulder belts pointed to the outside of the building. That couldn't be right, one should point one way and the other should point the other. Jack started to panic that he had his on the wrong way, but then he thought Charlie would surely have said something but he didn't. Just then, the door was thrown open and the Adjutant stood there.

"Right, you two, come in." Jack saluted when the Lieutenant didn't do so – it was the senior's job to salute but Jack knew this Adjutant and took no chances. Belatedly, the Lieutenant saluted but in the manner of an American, palm to the floor rather than vertically. *Very strange*, thought Jack.

He wasn't to be left in puzzlement for long. "Have you two met?" On receiving a negative, he said, "Mr Wade, meet Mr Hughes; Mr Hughes, meet Mr Wade. Mr Wade joins us having achieved a mighty 3rd class degree in music. Mr Hughes joins us having served four years in the ranks. Mr Hughes, you are Duty Officer today and Mr Wade will accompany you as officer under instruction. You don't have a problem with that do you, Mr Hughes?" Jack did have a problem and said so.

"Sir, Lieutenant Wade outranks me, how can he take instruction from me and how do I give him orders?"

"I have great faith in your abilities, Mr Hughes, so I am sure you will manage." As he said the last, he removed a cloth bag from a drawer of his desk offering the mouth of it to Jack. Jack said,

"I don't think that will be necessary, Sir, do you? You will already have had a clerk remove the good times and the only ones remaining are those around two to three am so why don't you just tell me one of them?" The bag contained Housey Housey numbers which equated to times. The Duty Officer on picking one from the bag would hand it to the Adjutant, who would consult his list and say what time had been chosen. It was meant to be a random system but Hersham used to have all the good time numbers removed for Lieutenants and 2nd Lieutenants. Good times were those up to midnight and after 05.30 hours so that it was possible to achieve a relatively good night's sleep. The bad ones were those from 0100 hrs to 05.00 hours when your sleep was bound to be interrupted by the need to carry out a surprise inspection of the Guard. When Jack had been here at the Holding Company prior to going to Mons, he had had to carry out this task out for Hersham so it came as no surprise that he was still the same little shit he had been then. Jack would have expected to be invited to sit once the introductions were over but they weren't. Although Hersham was a Captain and Jack only two ranks below him, they were both junior officers (senior officers were Majors and above); therefore, playing the seniority card was somewhat unacceptable. Certainly, he was the Commanding Officer's (a Lt Col) right hand man but he was more of a gopher and runner than an important officer and this emphasis of the differences in their ranks was very unusual. For Jack, used to working for Generals when he was a Staff Clerk, Hersham's attitude, for a mere Captain, was pathetic. Hersham, his enjoyment ruined simply said,

"Why don't we make it 02.30 hrs then? For now, make your way to the Mess and get settled in. Be back here at 14.00 hrs to meet the Colonel, he's travelling back from a shooting weekend in Scotland this morning and will meet you then. Remember, Mr Hughes, you have Guard Mount at 18.00 hrs and will need to inspect one of the mealtimes. I expect you to be immaculately turned out at all times. At that, he handed Jack a red sash and said, "As Duty Officer you will need to wear that. You know about Guard Mount, meals inspections and a night-time inspection of the Guard, don't you? Carry on." At that Jack saluted, Wade did a shuffle and they walked out. Jack was buggered if he was going to march out. They passed the CO's office in silence but as they approached the RSM's door, he appeared in the doorway and gestured that they should come in. When they did so, he greeted Jack with a huge smile and said,

"So you made it, Sir, I felt sure you would. I was posted to Mons for a couple of years, years ago, only in an admin role and I know how hard it is to pass that course. Very well done, Sir, if I may say so." He ignored Mr Wade. "May I ask if you would be willing to shoot for the team again, Sir?" Jack, knowing what side his bread was buttered and the importance of remaining on the good side of the RSM said,

"Of course Mr Lightfoot, I'd be delighted. When do you want me to shoot?"

"Well, Sir, the first round of targets have to be sent off tomorrow pm so is there any chance you could shoot tomorrow at 08.30 hrs?"

"That's fine as far as I'm concerned so long as Captain Hersham hasn't got something lined up for me then."

"He won't, Sir, I will speak to him about that." Even Adjutants knew not to mess RSMs about!

Picking up a cardboard box from the corner, the RSM said,

"Perhaps this officer would like to carry this box over to the Mess so that it will be you returning compliments Mr Hughes." At that, he handed it to Wade and shook Jack's hand.

"Once more, Sir, very well done, I look forward to you being part of the team again and you might go via the Museum to the Mess to pick up a sword, necessary wear for the Officer of the Day which I am sure the Adjutant probably forgot to mention." At that, Jack saluted – not strictly correct but a polite acknowledgement of the RSM's courtesy and they walked out with Jack fuming at the duplicity of Hersham; he had handed the Orderly Officer's sash to Jack but made no mention of the sword. *Someday I'll get that little shit*, he thought. Little did he know it would only be a few weeks away.

"Why am I carrying an empty box?" asked Wade.

"Because if your arms are full and you cannot return salutes, which you should do as the senior of the two of us, it will be for me to salute and you to carry on. Have you had no training at all in saluting, marching, drill etc.?"

"Well, most of the time at uni, I managed to dodge it. Is it really that important?" Jack couldn't believe what he was hearing. He, Jack had had to go through six months of hell at Mons and this complete arsehole was senior to him by virtue of a 3rd, yes 3rd class degree in music, and not only that, but Jack was also going to have to teach him and the shit would land on Jack every time this prat made a mistake. And that was down to that shit Hersham, who Jack knew had all the complexes associated with a short man no taller than a horse's arsehole. "I think you made an enormous mistake dodging your training. For a minor victory then, you are going to pay an enormous price now. Hersham will be out to get you and me, too, if he can, but he won't get me because I won't let him. So, for a start, you will parade every morning behind the Mess at 0530 hrs, that's 5.30 am to you, and I'll pound as much drill into you as I can every morning, Saturdays included, until you have at least mastered the basics. If you don't want to follow my orders, then you can always complain to the Adjutant but if you were to think about how the RSM treated you and then me you should have a good idea of the contempt in which you are held."

Signing into the Mess was quite pleasant. The Mess Manager, Mr. O'Halloran, remembered Jack from when Jack worked there under the 'punishment' of CSM Bidmead who had made his life a complete misery whilst Jack waited to go to Mons – based on his own, Bidsmead's failure to obtain a recommendation for a commission and thereby the creation of a jealous hatred of any soldier competent enough to earn a place at Mons. Jack had threatened Bidsmead that he would get him back when he was commissioned but Bidsmead had just laughed at the idea of a brand new, junior, 2nd Lieutenant being able to 'get' a senior CSM. Jack had learned from Bullshit Charlie that Bidsmead was leaving the Army on the week Friday, the same time as Charlie, and had noted that he had very little time in which to get him.

The allocation of rooms in the Mess was normally done on the basis of seniority, the more senior the officer the bigger and better the room. Lt Wade had been allocated the smallest and pokiest room above the kitchens, with all its attendant smells and early morning noise cooking the breakfasts. Jack had been given a smallish but comfortable room to the side and back of the mess with a pleasant view over the woods and right by a back door and steps, not normally used, but immensely useful for Jack if he wanted to come and go unobserved. Jack made a point of effusively thanking Mr. O'Halloran.

It took very little time to unpack, Jack had only brought a minimum of kit with him, not expecting to be long in residence. Grabbing Lt Wade he took him out to the back of the Mess and put him through a good hour of drill, with particular emphasis on saluting, He gave him another half hour after lunch so that Wade was able to more or less competently salute the Adjutant when they paraded at his office at 13.55hrs. He inspected them thoroughly, noting that Jack was carrying a sword with, Jack thought, disappointment. The Colonel was friendly and welcoming. He did not spend much time with Lt Wade, he had, after all, little of military interest to say. Jack, on the other hand, went through a thorough grilling. From the questions he asked, it was obvious that he had read Jack's documents as he particularly asked questions about the shooting of the terrorist in Aden, throwing in an aside that he could see why the RSM had snaffled him for the shooting team! He finished by saying that he wished Jack had been posted permanently to the Depot rather than only temporarily whilst waiting for the next Junior Officers' Course.

He laid out for Wade that he would be in charge of the band's diary and appointments until the course starting on 2 January – it was amazing how the Army could make use of even the most useless prats – a 3rd in music was obviously the qualification necessary to run the band's diary! Jack, however, was facing a mixed bag. He was to be the Platoon Commander for a platoon now forming, with effect from 9 November. For the intervening two weeks or so, he had a number of jobs lined up for him starting the following day when he was to head a Barrack's Inventory Team checking on the contents of the Royal Army Chaplains Department headquarters in Bagshot only a few miles down the road from Deepcut. It was not known how long that would take so once he returned he would be allocated duties as necessary. The Royal Army Ordnance Corps had built a large centre made up of the Junior Leaders Regt RAOC, the Depot which was responsible for Recruit Training and the passage on posting for soldiers moving unit, the Officers' School, the riding school stables – Jack was not looking forward to the compulsory riding training – and a small Royal Military Police unit to police the area given its huge size. The buildings were mainly old and decrepit but money was not to be spent on them because, being built against their southern boundary, was a huge new replacement area for all the units. It was scheduled to be opened by the Queen, in about a years' time, as she was the royal Colonel of the Ordnance Corps. Little did Jack know that he would be commanding the lead platoon on the March past. Jack requested permission to speak, which was immediately given, so he said,

"Sir, I have arranged to shoot for the team tomorrow morning, will I still be able to do that?"

"Yes, indeed," said the Colonel, "The RSM has already told me of your agreement to shoot for the team and I wouldn't dream of interfering with anything the RSM has set up. You do not need to be at the Chaplains until 11.30 hrs so you will have plenty of time. Any further questions from either of you?" Receiving no replies, he welcomed them to the Depot, wished them well with their careers and dismissed them.

Hersham sent Wade off to the band's offices and spoke to Jack for a few minutes. He gave him the glad tidings that as he would be the senior of all the officers attending the Young Officers' Course he would be responsible for their behaviour and attendance at the various training sessions. Jack knew the importance of commissioning dates controlling seniority and asked,

"What about Lieutenant Wade? By that time he will have been in the Army quite a while and was a Lieutenant who could ignore the instructions from a 2nd Lieutenant?"

"You will make sure he doesn't, Mr Hughes, now I suggest you familiarise yourself with the duties of the Duty Officer in the Manual over there, you may take it to the Mess to study if you wish, and Mr. Wade will join you there in ample time to inspect tea in the Cookhouse. Make sure the Guard Mounting is on time and correctly carried through, I shall be watching. Good day to you." Jack picked up the Manual, saluted and walked out – he was buggered if he was going to march.

Chapter 14

Wade turned up at the Mess just after 15.00 hrs – in time for a cup of tea. Jack gave him the Guard Mount section of the Manual to read and said,

"Read and inwardly digest that lot. I am not going to have you on the square with me; you don't know how to march and turn properly nor do you know the orders to give and when to give them. If you stand there, the soldiers will look to you because you would be the senior officer present and they would, quite properly, ignore me. So you can stand just off the side of the square on the side that has bushes near it and hide yourself in them. I don't know what that little shit Hersham will do but he's already told me he will be watching me and he's likely to ask you questions about the Mount and the sequences even though you aren't on the square."

Jack and Wade inspected the evening tea and as there were no complaints, the Mess Sergeant having ensured that there would not be, Jack signed the book and made sure Wade did as well. The first stages of the Guard Mount went through as normal if a few minutes late. The reason became clear when the Guard Commander, a Sergeant, reported 12 of the guard present and one absentee. Just as he reported this, the missing Guard ran onto the square and took up position on the left of the line. The Sergeant bawled out,

"Where have you been, you horrible little man you?"

"Sorry, Sir, the CSM kept me on a job until just five minutes ago and I had to change and get here and that's why I am late, Sir." As the man spoke Jack realised that he knew him. Jack cut off the Sergeant by asking,

"Were you digging trenches by any chance?"

"Yes, Sir."

"Right Private Wilmott, it is Wilmott, isn't it?"

"Yes, Sir."

"Report to me at the Officers' Mess at 08.00 hrs tomorrow morning. Clear?"

"Yes, Sir."

"Right, Sergeant, carry on I will deal with Wilmott tomorrow." And at that the guard mounting continued, band blaring away and all. Jack picked out the Stick Man, not Wilmott, and dismissed the Guard and the band to their duties.

Jack collected Wade from the edge of the square and took him along to the guardroom to sign the necessary paperwork there. Wade blurted out, in front of the Sergeant and the Corporal Guard Commander (the Sergeant was in overall charge of events throughout the night but the actual Guard was commanded by the Corporal) and a few of the Guards who were moving around,

"I thought we were to inspect the Guard at 02.30 hrs?" Jack could not believe what he had just said. He replied,

"You have just announced to just about everyone around us the confidential time we were to inspect the Guard." Looking at the Sergeant he said,

"That will now have to be changed won't it, Sergeant?"

"YES, SIR!" answered the Sergeant with a big smile on his face.

Jack waited until they were on their way back to the Mess to explain to Wade, in words of one syllable or less, just what a prat he was. Wade asked Jack why he was intending to see Wilmott in the morning. Jack, not wishing to reveal what he was doing, simply passed it off as something not to do with the guard mounting and it therefore did not concern Wade. In the event, Jack inspected the alertness of the Guard at 02.30 hrs on the basis that they would not have been expecting them at that time. Nothing was amiss and Jack got Wade to sign the log as well as himself as he was sure Hersham would check.

Chapter 15

Wilmott turned up promptly at 08.00 hrs just as Jack dismissed Wade from his drill lesson and Jack took him into a small anteroom come office and shook hands with him. Wilmott had been a close friend of Jack's in Aden and had been the first soldier Jack had ever put on a charge not more than five minutes after he had been promoted to Lance Corporal. He did not intend to do the same thing on appointment as an officer. After a brief catching up chat, Jack asked Ken,

"Have you been digging lots of trenches which have then had piping laid in them by civvy contractors and which you have then had to fill in?"

"How the hell do you know that; you've only just arrived at the Depot?"

"Were you chosen for this duty by CSM Bidsmead?"

"Yes."

"Was that because you had fallen foul of him in some way?"

"I don't know what I did but he certainly had it in for me from the word go."

"Right, I want you to write down the history of your trench digging, how much of it you have done, where and when. I think he's on a fiddle with the contractor getting soldiers to dig the trenches for nothing and then splitting the money saved on the contract by using soldiers to dig and fill in the trenches saving considerable sums of money which would have had to be paid to unionised civvy labour so that bastard Bidsmead would have been picking up a tidy sum in backhanders. He is due out of the Army at the end of next week so I need to move fast if I'm to stop him retiring with his ill-gotten gains. Sign the statement but leave it undated for the time being and leave it here for me in my pigeonhole. I have to be on the range in 10 mins and I can't be late for the RSM even though I am a 2nd Lieutenant now! Keep this strictly between us. If it gets out, I will know where to come. I have to do that formal warning bit. Sorry, I know you to be a good soldier and I know Bidmead's habit of keeping soldiers so late that they arrive late for Guard Mount and if it were up to me, I would speak out and drop him in the shit but given how this will hit the fan, I need to protect you and I can't do that if you go blabbing your mouth off everywhere and he gets wind of it before I am ready to act. OK?"

"You know you can trust me and there's nothing more I would like than to see that bastard shafted."

"You will probably be interviewed by the 'Monkeys', that's not a problem, is it?"

"No, Sir."

"Good man. Get that statement done as soon as you can and then get back to your duties. If anyone asks, you've just had a bollocking from the Duty Officer and the bastard has put you on a charge. I'll catch up with you later. By the way, where will you be?"

"Digging another fucking trench behind the cookhouse." They parted laughing.

When Jack arrived at the indoor range, it was to discover the RSM already there unlocking the weapons safe. Reaching in, he passed Jack a Mk3 Lee Enfield with his, Jack's, name on it. Taking it, Jack said,

"Have you kept this expecting me back or was it just in the safe?"

"I knew you would make it through Mons, Sir, so I kept it. Just in case it's been knocked over or something, it might be prudent to fire a group just to check the zeroing." Jack said,

"Well, you had more faith in me than I did at times at Mons." And they both laughed. Jack fired five rounds for grouping, putting them all in the bull!

"I think that zeroings OK," said Jack, with a big smile.

"So do I, Sir," said the RSM, writing Jack's name, rank and date on it. "As you can't do any better than that it can stand as your entry. See you next week at the same time?"

"Yes, sure." And with that Jack set off for his big job of the day with a little smile on his face just having been saluted by the RSM. He paused, turned and said to the RSM,

"I'm not very happy about one of the Guard arriving late on Parade last night. He had been kept up until Guard Mount time and only then released by the CSM. He had no chance of changing into clean kit and parading at the correct time. When I was here, the CSM used the same trick with me and it's not on. Can I ask you to have a quiet word with him to ensure he stops this though he only has a few days left there will still be a few poor sods being jumped on in that time."

"Quiet word, Sir, it'll be so quiet that it will be heard in Istanbul!" Jack walked away knowing it would not be a good thing to be in the CSM's boots for a while. *Revenge might be the Lord's,* thought Jack, *but it's nice to be his messenger.*

He called in the Mess to collect Ken's statement which was absolutely fine, and then drove over to the Royal Military Police Guardroom.

He stopped at their anteroom and asked who the senior rank in charge of the unit was.

"WOI Stevens is in charge, Sir," said the Corporal behind the counter.

"I need to speak to him on a very serious matter; will you tell him I'm here?" The Corporal disappeared. Jack wondered, *the RMP guy I had the dealings with in Aden was Stevens but he was a WOII – could it be the same man?* The WOI came through the door and stopped, taking a very long look at Jack he said,

"I don't believe it; Lance Corporal Hughes as was," and at that he turned around and walked back through the door through which he had just entered. Before Jack could decide what he should do at such extraordinary behaviour, the WOI re-appeared wearing his hat. He called out,

"Attention," at which the Corporal stood to attention and he then threw up a very smart salute which Jack returned with a huge smile on his face. "This man, this officer I should say, Corporal Smithers, made my stay in Aden a fucking great experience, the best posting of my career to date and now seeing him standing there with a message that he has a very serious matter to speak to me about means that life is going to get interesting again – is it, Sir?" At that he ushered Jack into a tiny little office at the back of the guardroom and taking off his hat, shook Jack by the hand warmly congratulating him on his promotion,

"But you are now only one rank above me so be careful," with a big smile on his face.

Jack explained his history with CSM Bidsmead and produced the statement from Ken Wilmott that he had obtained that morning. He handed over a piece of paper with the details of Private Cliff Hudson on, he being the provider of the details of the meeting between CSM Bidsmead and the civvy contractor when the brown envelope changed hands. Jack also handed over the diary he had kept of the trenches he had dug, where and when and the notes of any conversations he had had with Bidsmead. Of the latter, he said he didn't want his notebook to be used if at all possible as he would like his involvement not to come out if at all possible. WOI Stevens looked at him for several moments and then said,

"You wouldn't like a transfer to the RMP I suppose? You've certainly stitched up that bastard Bidsmead. I have always had a nasty, slimy feeling about him. We'll need to get a couple of MPs in plainclothes into the Dog and Duck for this Friday as it's his last one; he won't be going there next week as he will be out of the Army by that day so he'll be wanting to collect his dues."

"I was just about to suggest that," said Jack, "and if an envelope is passed over they can—"

"Please leave some police work for us to do, Sir, so far you've done it all and I'll be out of a job if you carry on at this rate," and they both laughed.

"I have to get on my way to the Godbotherers at Bagshot; if I'm late the Adjutant will have my goolies—"

"No he won't, Sir, I'll tell him you were helping with the arrest of an arch criminal who has stolen thousands from the Army and since I know one or two small matters not to his credit I don't believe there will be any problems at all."

"Nevertheless I would prefer that Captain Hersham knows nothing about my involvement…"

"A confidential informant like?"

"Exactly and I would appreciate it if you could unofficially keep me informed as your investigation progresses. I need to find a way for him to discover it was me that done for him without it appearing in the official records."

"There's no problem with that at all, mum's the word." At that, Jack left hearing as he did so Mr Stevens warning the desk Corporal, Corporal Smithers, that he had not seen a 2nd Lieutenant in the building that morning.

Chapter 16

The Royal Army Chaplains' Department was based in a Victorian house modelled on a Tudor Mansion without the black and white appearance. Set in its own grounds the driveway was imposing and designed so that those approaching the house were greeted with an imposing view of it as the driveway straightened for the last 50 yards or so.

Inside was even more spectacular. Jack entered through the front door, no tradesmen's entrance for him now – there was a sign indicating this – to be greeted with a huge hall going up to the rafters of the house. Around the four walls on the first floor was a veranda with a door on each wall, as Jack was to discover, into four majestic bedrooms, described as the North, South, East and West rooms – so original. Not obviously to view were some 70 smaller, far less grand, bedrooms for the servants and others not fit for the four master bedrooms. The four master bedrooms were set up as bedrooms as were about half of the smaller bedrooms. The others were now used as offices, learning or study rooms, storage rooms or for any dam thing for which they wanted them.

Built at the side of the entrance was a reception desk manned by a tiny receptionist who immediately said,

"You must be Mr Hughes, we have been expecting you. Two of your team are already here and are taking tea in the library, which I will take you to. When the other two members of your team arrive, I will let the Chaplain know and he will come and meet you there. That's all right I trust."

"Fine," said Jack. The two already in the library were a WOII in uniform of the RAOC and a civvy who was introduced as a Barracks Inventory Officer a Ministry of Defence Civil Servant. It was clear these two had worked together before and the two soldiers who had not yet arrived were part of a team of four whose permanent job was to carry out these sorts of inventories. Jack had no idea why he was attached to the team and nor did the team although they had had Junior Officers attached to them in the past. None had ever worked on such a grand building which made Jack smell a rat as to why he was there.

It was only a few moments before the other two arrived and the Chaplain joined them. A full colonel with rows of ribbons on his uniform he announced that he would prefer to be addressed as 'Padre' and did not expect to be saluted. He explained that he had recently been promoted to be in charge but had been there for many years in the Headquarters and although he had signed the books for the contents, he was not at all happy that a proper inventory had in fact been carried out for many years, hence his request for an in-depth investigation and audit. Jack could definitely smell a rat starting and finishing with a certain Captain Peter Hersham.

The WOII, holding the position of a Barracks Inventory Accountant, Ken Barrington, suggested that the Padre show Jack over the property whilst he got the team set-up in the office they had been shown as theirs for the time of the audit. Jack thought, *I am going to need to have a very serious off the record conversation with this chap and finding out what they had to audit was a good idea.*

The Padre was obviously very proud of the building and what went on there. They ran religious courses for all denominations. Some of the soldiers were there because they had a genuine interest in religion, a calling almost, whilst some of them were there as a skive from Regimental duties. The Padre seemed to take them all at face value which might explain a lot about why the earlier inventories had not been done properly. He talked about a visit that had taken place there just two months earlier when the Queen visited. The house had been built for the Duke of Connaught, a son of Queen Victoria, and had been taken over by the Chaplains just after the war. The more the Padre talked the more Jack thought it likely that no proper inventory had been done since then. Normally every Army unit had an Annual Administration Inspection every year where everything in the unit was counted or accounted for, inspected and reported on. They were hated by every commanding officer and could indeed break a commander if the standards were not high enough. Careful questioning of the Padre revealed that there had never been an annual audit carried out by an outside unit – they seemed to have been forgotten by authority and Jack thought the Padre might regret asking for an outside audit – still he could always pray for a good result since he had a head start on the inside rail!

The building was mightily impressive. A truly grand building for a member of royalty which had fallen on slightly poor times. There was, of course, a chapel and some various odd building closely scattered around the house used as classrooms and for various other purposes. The most impressive feature of all as far as Jack was concerned was the billiards/snooker table in the basement of the house. Forming a games room, the table was simply beautiful. It had been given to the Duke of Connaught by the people of India on his wedding. It was constructed mainly of teak exquisitely carved and decorated with a slate base covered by first class felt on the playing surface. It was so perfect, flat and even with a proper nap to the felt, that professional snooker players booked time to practice on it. Use by soldiers and junior NCOs was banned. Senior NCOs and Warrant Officers rarely if ever attended any of the courses but did they do so they might have been given permission to play. The Padre made this all clear and finished by saying to Jack,

"You, of course old chap, can use it whenever you like." Jack thanked him and they got on with the work. Every room had, or should have had, an inventory form which listed every single item in that room. In theory, an audit was easy, the auditor simply identified and counted all the items and then compared the findings to the room inventory list. If they matched, it was just a question of

move on to the next room. If they didn't, and during this audit not one single room was correct, then it was a question of listing the missing items which would then be charged to the responsible person or written off to the taxpayer.

Jack spoke to Ken Barrington, the WOII BIA and they agreed on how and where they would start. Ken was surprised that Jack indicated that he would carry out audits; it was the first time an officer had offered to do so in his experience, they normally found a paper they had to read and avoided doing any of the work.

Jack did enjoy playing a game on the snooker table. Ken Barrington introduced him to it as a quick little game when time was limited like at lunchtime. Jack ate with the team in the cookhouse, there being nowhere else! Eating normally took 35 mins or so leaving 25 for a game, but no way could Jack play a full frame of snooker in that time. The game involved placing two balls over every pocket and potting them with as few strokes as possible. *This should be easy,* thought Jack, *one pot for each pocket and the two balls would drop in.* Oh no they didn't, one would drop in, the one closest to the pocket, but the outer one would run off down the table. Ken soon showed him that there was a way to cannon of the outer and run down to a corner pocket knocking the closest one in but then it was a matter of who could pocket the scattered balls in the fewest shots. Jack enjoyed it so much, even though he lost every game, that he introduced it to the Officers' Mess back in Deepcut because there was the same problem there of limited time at lunch time in which to play a frame.

Jack started inventorying in one of the master bedrooms. Rarely if ever used, no one of rank senior enough had ever stayed there! They had had a visit from the Queen some two months before when many items had been washed, scrubbed, painted or replaced but as she hadn't stayed overnight no-one had used the bedrooms although the Queen had used one of the dressing rooms to freshen up. It was very quickly apparent that there were serious discrepancies. The room should have had all manner of things that were not there. Jack checked with the Padre if they were packed away somewhere for safety or some other reason(s). As far as the Padre was concerned, they should have been there and he had no explanation for their absence. When Jack checked with the team, a serious number of items were missing from all four master bedrooms.

The most difficult room to audit was the kitchen. Many of the items in use could have several names, some of the items were unidentifiable on the inventory account and to top it all there were many items not there – teaspoons being a classic. One of the items caused Jack to roll up. Printed on the inventory form was,

'*Pots, tea or piss.*'

Jack assumed that if they were in the kitchen it was tea!

The count took five days and the writing of the list of missing items amounted to four and a half A4 pages. These were very serious deficiencies. The day after Jack returned to the Depot, Peter Hersham, the Adjutant, sent for him.

Marching in properly and saluting immaculately, all Hersham said was, no greeting, no welcome back, no how did you get on but,

"Are you sure these discrepancies are right, there are no items tucked away in storerooms somewhere?"

"I'm sure, Sir, we checked every building and I did personally tell the Padre of the serious amount that was missing and could it be in storage somewhere that we had missed. He said no and I left it at that."

"Carry on with your duties." And that was that. Jack never did hear anything officially but odd whispers went around that all hell had been let loose once the audit report had been received with no end of disciplinary meetings being held.

Jack was then used as a dog's body for the few days before he took command of his Recruit Platoon.

Chapter 17

Jack's platoon numbered 26 soldiers, some of whom had been in the Army for nearly three weeks and some only three days. The first few days were a bit of organised chaos. Some had already had some medical jabs and others hadn't so conducting any instruction with the whole platoon was impossible. Jack made use of that time to interview the lot of them. Taking only about 10 mins apiece, Jack was primarily interested in the skills they had acquired before joining the Army and their reasons for doing so. Most fell into the "there was no work where I live" or "I want to see the world like the adverts say" and/or "I like sport". The odd one out was a man called Terry Boardman.

Boardman had been, according to him, a very successful car salesman and had been a high earner. This had made him attractive to women and he found dating and mating with them, many of them, very easy. Then one morning one of them had turned up at the garage where he worked to tell him that she was pregnant and he was the father. At that time, it meant a swift wedding and a later explanation that the baby was a little premature. He told Jack that he had said to the girl, who he could barely remember, that he could not talk there and then, because he was at work, but he would meet her that evening and sort it out. Once she had left, he had driven home in one of the cars for sale, packed a suitcase, dropped the car off at the garage and had walked into the nearest recruiting office, which happened to be the Army one, and had insisted on joining there and then. Later that day, he had found himself on a train to Bordon to join, after a few days, the RAOC at Deepcut.

Jack was somewhat stunned by this. To allow himself time to think, he asked a few nebulous questions about his education and determined that although he had taken five GCEs he had only passed one, Art. Jack finished the interview by saying something that was to come back and haunt him and probably destroy his Army career although he was not aware of it at the time. He did not say anything about doing the runner but did point out that he was quite well educated compared to most of his fellow soldiers and if he was prepared to work hard, and with a little bit of luck, he could go far in the Army, even achieving commissioned rank as Jack had done. Pretty innocuous stuff you might think but it turned out to have been the worst possible thing to say.

As the weeks progressed, so the platoon gradually came together. Their basic military training was scheduled to last for six weeks. Their trade training at different places for different skills would follow on and last at least six weeks long and maybe up to 18 depending on the skill. The programme was in existence and had been for years. Each new platoon followed it with only minor changes driven by holidays such as Christmas and minor changes to update it such as when the Lee Enfield was phased out and the SLR phased in.

For Jack although it was his first platoon command in the Army it differed very little from his time in the Army Cadet Force or the training he had been through in the RASC or at Mons. It was therefore quite boring and he could not get out of his mind that he had another year of this at the Junior Leaders Regiment. He noticed, during the morning and afternoon tea breaks that the platoon commanders from other platoons were already in the Mess when he got there and were still there when he left. Carefully asked questions solicited the answers that most of the training was left to the NCOs and the officers kept out of the way. Jack wondered if that explained the absence of the platoon commanders when he joined the Army and at Mons. Even more careful questions of his platoon sergeant elicited the answers that he too would like to see less of Jack.

Before Jack could react to that the Sergeant, Sergeant Terry Reilly, came to Jack with a problem. Boardman was proving a nuisance and had refused an order from one of the Corporals, Corporal Dash. Dash was a Drill Pig. The drill instructors were normally not popular. Their job was to instil discipline and drill and the way of doing it necessarily involved shouting. Jack had noticed that Dash was more than somewhat heavy. He had been a Drill Pig during National Service when the treatment of soldiers was hard – many of them, if not most of them, were in the Army unwillingly and had to be carefully watched and trained. Those days had gone and the all-volunteer Army demanded a different approach to the soldiers. Dash had not taken on the new rules, indeed he revelled in the old ones and Jack had made a note that he needed to do something about him. Now he had to do something now. It turned out that Dash had been giving Boardman a particularly hard time because he was one of those, rare, individuals, who was quite uncoordinated and marched with his left arm swinging forward with his left foot and his right arm with his right leg. It gave him a very peculiar gait, a bit like a waddling duck, and it had to be got rid of. Practice of the correct way to march was the only way to deal with it but when Dash had had a go at him, a la old Army, and told him to report for extra drill after tea, Boardman had said to him something like, "No I won't. When I am an officer and Mr Hughes says I will be, I'll get you, you bastard." Sgt Reilly then told Jack that Boardman had been using this 'I will be an officer, Mr Hughes says so', almost as a mantra and all the NCOs, including him, were fed up with it.

Jack's first action was to get Boardman in and teach him the facts of life. NCOs gave him orders and he would obey them, like them or not. His one GCE pass entitled him to nothing – certainly not to be treated as officer material that would have to be earned the hard way by showing exemplary performance of his duties and bloody hard work. So far he was going backwards and had much catching up to be done. He could start by volunteering to work in the cookhouse washing up every evening for the rest of the week and on Saturday. A very crestfallen Boardman marched out.

Cpl Dash was next. Jack deliberately left a few minutes to pass so that word of what had happened to Boardman could get about. As he expected, Dash came into his office with a smile on his face and a very casual salute. Jack immediately said,

"It is customary for an NCO to knock on an officer's door and to wait to be told to enter. Get out and enter properly." The smile was wiped off Dash's face instantly. He was slow to react. "Now," said Jack in a loud voice. Dash went. He knocked on the door and Jack called, "Enter." He did, crashing to a halt, as only a Drill Pig could and saluted. He remained standing to attention and Jack did not tell him to stand at ease. "What use do you think is an NCO who cannot get a recruit to obey an order from him?" Dash did not answer. "Well?" said Jack.

"Nothing to say, Sir," the typical answer of a soldier to an irate officer.

"Cpl Dash, I have been watching your performance very carefully. It seems to me that you are having trouble adjusting to an all-volunteer Army. Would that be true?"

"Don't know, Sir. I drill them like what I've always done."

"Doesn't that prove my point?"

"You have to shout at them to get them to move. That's a proper command voice."

"Do you have to swear at them, as you were just this morning when you called them a lazy load of bastards?"

"I didn't—" Jack interrupted,

"I hope you aren't going to say that you didn't swear at them thus calling me a liar to my face because I was at the edge of the square watching the drilling of the three sections and I distinctly heard you doing so?" Dash did what all soldiers in trouble did again. He said nothing. Jack said, "You are aware are you not that swearing at soldiers by NCOs is now absolutely forbidden by Army Orders?" Dash was stuck. He could not admit to knowing without getting into trouble and he could not avoid trouble by saying he did not know because the introduction of that order had caused considerable discussion and some dissent when it was introduced. He once again remained silent. Jack let the silence go on for a couple of minutes, it seemed much longer to Dash, and he then said, "If I hear you swear at a soldier ever again, I will march you straight to the Guardroom and lock you up. Is that clear?"

"Yes, Sir."

"March out." Dash did. Once he had gone, Jack turned to Sgt Reilly and said, "He's not going to change. I think I saw something about NCOs unable to adapt to a volunteer Army being sent on a rehabilitation or retraining course at the Army School of Education. Would you have a look in the Orderly Room and see if you can find out about it? He's a good soldier but his ways have to change or we'll be inundated by recruits asking to buy themselves out because of his bullying. There is a fine line between driving and bullying and at the moment, he's on the wrong side of it."

Friday night was bull night. Officially bull night had been eliminated as soldiers hated it and it was thought to put civilians off joining the Army so they changed the name to interior economy and carried on exactly as before. There really was no option to doing it. A large number of soldiers in a room had to keep it clean to prevent disease and other nasties. Friday night was interior economy night and everyone had a job to do to clean up. The floor had to be polished, everything dusted, windows cleaned and the ablutions cleaned to the umpteenth degree. On Saturday morning, the barracks would be inspected by the Corporals, then the Sergeant then Jack and three Saturdays per month by the Company Commander. The fourth one would be an inspection by the Colonel accompanied by the RSM. This was the serious one and the standards had to be immaculate or everyone in the command structure would pay for it; in Jack's case by extra Duty Officers days. Jack and his NCOs managed to avoid penalties for the period Jack had the platoon which he regarded as a miracle with a whole platoon of Guardian Angels looking after him.

The Saturday penance by Boardman took place on the middle Saturday. Jack discovered what had happened when he arrived on the Monday morning. As chance would have it, he had been listed as Duty Officer for the day so had collected his sash and sword on the way in. He was greeted by Sgt Reilly who immediately took him into the office. Apparently on the Saturday afternoon, about 1600 hrs when his cookhouse duties had finished, Boardman returned to the Barracks and, having collected something had made his way upstairs to the empty barrack room. Jack's platoon did not even fill the three rooms over which they were spread. The fourth room contained the basic furniture, beds, wardrobes, footlockers etc. ready for more soldiers should they appear. Shortly Boardman reappeared with the ends of a leather bootlace around his neck, collected a woollen tie from his wardrobe and went back upstairs. He reappeared a second time with the ends of the tie hanging around his neck and called out,

"Has anyone got a length of rope I could have?" On receiving no answer he had disappeared upstairs again carrying something he took from his wardrobe. Fortunately the soldiers in his room had enough sense to realise that something was wrong and one of them reported to the Guardroom. The Corporal of the Guard quickly arrived on the scene and went looking for Boardman. He found him inside one of the metal wardrobes, crouched up with the door shut. He had slashed the back of one wrist with the smallest cut it was possible to make and, he said, was waiting for himself to bleed to death. In fact, according to the Corporal, the cut had already started to heal over and had stopped bleeding. Boardman was taken to the Guardroom and locked up for the rest of the weekend. The procedures for handling attempted suicide were well established, it being something that did happen from time to time during not long past National Service.

Jack immediately made his way to the Guardroom. He was furious. He knew this would go on his record and count against him for the rest of his career. The Sergeant of the Guard did not want to let Jack into the cell containing Boardman because Jack was unwilling to remove his sword. After a short discussion which ended in Jack giving the Sergeant a direct order, he was admitted to the cell.

Drawing the sword, he reversed it and proffered it to Boardman. Boardman took it gingerly between two fingers. Jack let rip.

"You yellow-bellied little bastard. You did not intend to kill yourself; you were only pretending. Well, now you have a sword, all you have to do is fall on it and the job's done. Do it." The Sergeant, who had followed Jack into the cell had a fit, but Jack believed Boardman's attempts to kill himself were so feeble that he had no intention of doing so – he was just a cry baby who, having been told off by Jack and punished with the extra duties had just gone off on a big sulk. Sort of as he had done a runner when the girl told him she was pregnant.

As Jack retrieved his sword from a despondent-looking Boardman, the Corporal stuck his head around the cell door and said,

"The Adjutant's on the phone for you, Sir." Jack took the call.

"My office now," was all that was said. Jack went. The Adjutant said, "Tell me," so Jack did. At the end of Jack's tale, the Adjutant said, "Well, he's not the first to try and I don't think he'll be the last. You do believe that this is an attempt to get out of the Army for free, don't you?"

"Yes, Sir."

"Carry on." Jack officially heard no more although he was sure a record of it would have been made on his record – unfavourably. Boardman was released from custody into the care of the Padre and could be seen running errands etc. for him for about 10 days when he was discharged from the Army as being medically unfit.

Chapter 18

The last 10 days of the training period were very busy. The platoon was to spend two days camped out in a defensive position they prepared themselves from which they would carry out the range of skills a soldier needed. The first day and night were horrendous. The rain poured down and it was bitingly cold. They were two men to a two-man bivvy. Jack had had a two-man bivvy to himself during battle camp at the end of Mons and even so it was too small for one man let alone two. The most important point when in one of these canvas tents, old and thin as they were, was not to touch the inside of the tent when it rained. With two men to a bivvy, this was absolutely impossible with the result that all the soldiers were wet through as was all their spare kit.

Two of them were shivering uncontrollably and Jack was bothered that it might be hypothermia. Two Cadets at Mons had died from hypothermia just a week or so before – it was a major press story and as both of them were overseas Cadets, and even though they were issued with more cold weather kit than the Brits, they had been caught out in atrocious weather on Dartmoor, snow, blizzards and freezing rain and had died before help could reach them. Jack was damn sure he wasn't going to be making the headlines only a week or two after the previous incident so he called off the exercise and returned to camp. There he faced a grilling from Peter Hersham about why he had done so. In a war, they couldn't just pack up and go home; they were soldiers, weren't they? And on and on he went. Jack did, in turn, what he had learnt to do as a private soldier when faced with an angry officer and said nothing. The Adjutant eventually ran out of breath and words and with nothing said from Jack to feed on dismissed him.

It so happened that that day the officers had been invited to the Sergeants' Mess for Christmas drinks. Jack had been expecting to miss it, because he would have been out on the exercise. Having seen to the dispatch of the two shiverers to the MI Room and the sorting out of the rest of the platoon and how the rest of the day could be filled in with training Jack thought he might just let the Sergeants treat him to a drink or two. As he arrived at the Mess doors the RSM, the President of the Mess, was just welcoming the Colonel when the Colonel, hearing Jack coming up behind him, turned to identify who it was. Seeing Jack in his combat kit, rather than Service Dress, he went ape. It gradually became clear that the Colonel expected him to be in Service Dress and for him to arrive in combat kit showed the deepest disrespect to the Sergeants. Once again Jack never said a word because, this time, he was given no chance to if he had wanted to but was ordered to go and change into Service Dress. Jack was thinking, *Fuck it, this isn't worth it for a free drink.* He too, was somewhat cold and pissed off by the weather so he wasn't going to come back; it was likely to have finished before he could do so anyway, but as he turned away, deliberately failing to salute the Colonel, the Colonel said,

"Report to me when you return and apologise to the RSM for your rudeness when you do."

Jack just walked away. He walked over to the Officers' Mess, showered leisurely and dressed. He had no intention of getting wet again walking back to the Sergeants' Mess so drove there. As he arrived some of the officers were already leaving. The RSM met him at the door and escorted him to the Bar and ordered Jack a pint. He said,

"The Colonel was quite wrong to give you a bollocking about your dress. This is the Sergeants' Mess and we decide what dress visitors are expected to wear, not the Colonel. You do not owe me an apology. I will make that clear to the Colonel in due course. In the meantime, get that down you. If I might also say, Sir, I think that was a right and brave decision you took to cancel the exercise and bring your platoon back. Ex-Sergeant Ellis will look after you, please enjoy yourself and be sure that you are welcome in this Sergeants' Mess anytime."

While Jack and the RSM had been talking, Bullshit Charlie, Jack's first training sergeant and who had retired just a few weeks before, had crept up behind Jack with a pint in one hand and his right hand outstretched to shake Jack's hand. Having done so vigorously, he handed Jack the pint he was carrying. Jack's Platoon Sergeant, Terry Reilly arrived with two pints, one obviously for Jack and WOI Stevens, RMP also appeared at Jack's elbow clearly with yet another pint for Jack. Somehow, the RSM manoeuvred the Colonel so that he could see the scenario of Jack, surrounded by senior NCOs all intent on buying him a drink. It is said that a picture is worth a thousand words and this scenario proved the point. The Colonel never referred to the matter again and Jack did not report to him. He did regret it the next day when the effects of all those pints made themselves felt, however. Interestingly, nothing was said about Bidsmead not being there.

The passing out parade, with band, went off flawlessly. Jack, as the Platoon Commander, was out front and the visiting Brigadier, with the Colonel by his side, took the salute. He made the customary speech and handed out a small cup to the Best Recruit. Afterwards, in the NAAFI, Jack circulated amongst the families who had travelled to see their loved ones pass out. A few asked Jack to pose with them to have their photographs taken and the most common comment made by the families was, "I can't believe the change that you have made in my son/brother/nephew and even one husband." Jack felt glad to have successfully completed his first real task as an officer in turning a bunch of scruffy, untidy and even downright dirty individuals into a smart, trained and valuable assets to the Army, themselves, the country and, with the Army committed to tasks worldwide, to the world. He was looking forward to his Young Officers' Course but he faced it with a small glow of satisfaction at what he and his small team of

NCOs had achieved. However he wasn't looking forward to a platoon command at the Junior Leaders Regiment at the end of it!

The joining instructions for the Course had come through a few days before the Platoon passed out and contained the programme for the six week course. For most of the time they would be based at Deepcut Mess so Peter Hersham's order that Jack should live in the Mess for a couple of weeks to learn Mess etiquette had spread from the two weeks to eight by Christmas and another six following it.

During the six weeks of the course, Jack would have to find a place for him and Janet to live as they did not wish to continue imposing themselves on Jack's parents.

And Peter Hersham slipped in the final unpleasantness by putting Jack on duty, as the Duty Officer on Boxing Day. Jack was at least spared the waiting on soldiers on Christmas day and to all intents and purposes the Depot, and all the other units, closed down just before Christmas and didn't start up again until 2 January. The place was a ghost town on Boxing Day with almost no one in the Depot, only the smallest of meals to inspect, and the Guard mount was a much-reduced affair. Talk about shades of Pearl Harbour when the Japanese attacked on the Sunday morning when no one was on duty, the Russians had the best part of a fortnight in which the British Army was away on leave!

Chapter 19

When the Junior Officers' Course assembled on 2 January, there were 11 of them. They were fell in in two ranks to be welcomed by the Colonel, brief and perfunctory, before being handed over to the Adjutant, Hersham, again. One of the group was a full lieutenant, by virtue of quite long other rank service as a Sergeant in the Royal Engineers, and Jack expected that he would be the senior of the group and responsible for marshalling them about etc. Jack was therefore thrown when Hersham announced that he, Jack, was to perform the role. Jack had already come to despise and hate Hersham so he did not hesitate to point out to him that there was a full lieutenant, besides Lt Wade, amongst them, who outranked Jack and should therefore be the one responsible. Hersham's reaction was to say that we have been here before Mr Hughes with Mr Wade, "This Lieutenant has only been an officer for a couple of weeks, you more than three months so you are clearly the most senior and will fill that role." Jack knew when not to argue with Hersham.

As it turned out, the lieutenant, Lieutenant John Wight, and Jack were to become good friends. At the first break, John Wight approached Jack and introduced himself. He made it clear that he would not question any instruction Jack gave and he stuck to that. It was the other eight who were to prove problematic– Wade was still so new that he just did as Jack told him. All of them from Sandhurst they were to a man, immature, had unearned attitudes of superiority and were absolutely convinced that they knew and understood how soldiers should be managed as they knew how soldiers thought and behaved. John Wight was ex-Mons and had been a Sergeant for eight years. The other eight had already passed snide remarks meant for John to hear and once they discovered that Jack was also an ex-ranker they included him as clearly being inferior. Jack tolerated it for about ten days. They would arrive late on parade, pretend not to hear instructions and generally mess Jack about. They were careful not to do it when there were witnesses like the RSM or Hersham, a skill they had learned and developed over the years of harassing those less fortunate than themselves. Jack was fairly sure that the RSM would know what was going on but he said nothing. Hersham, of course, being one of them said and did nothing even if he did know. Jack let it go at first having learned that one of the best ways to deal with this type was to ignore them entirely but then, after a gym session instructed by Jack when they really did piss him off, he was still smarting from the would-be suicide which he felt would influence adversely his career, to the point that he felt that if he could not control these upper class little shits his career would be over anyway. He decided on a course of action that he would not normally have contemplated but if he didn't fix this himself the word of him being mocked and unable to command these little shits would spread with Terence-Darby, the ringleader, bragging about their superiority over ex-ranker officers. So he waited after the showers when there were no witnesses around. He found the weapon he wanted in an Indian Club from a pair in the Gym and he hit Solomon Terence-Darby, as hard as he could, with it between the shoulder blades and when he went down he put the boot into him a couple of times in the belly and balls such that he needed minor treatment in the MI Room. Before he had him carried off to the MI Room he whispered in his ear,

"There are nearly six hundred soldiers in this Camp; every one of whom hates stuck-up snots like you. If you say to anyone anything other than you slipped in the showers, I, being one of those unintelligent, working class nobodies, will ensure that every one of my pals, all six hundred of them, will have you in their sites, or maybe a mistake with a hand grenade. You have heard about the sorting out of unpopular American officers by their troops fragging them in Vietnam, haven't you? You may not have heard that they learned it from us in Aden, in Korea, in the Second World War where officers hated as much as you little shits are, keen to send their men forward, usually hanging back themselves, seeking glory for themselves, were sent to meet their maker a little early." Jack knew Terence-Darby was the ringleader and had guessed that he was all talk and no action. He also knew that there had been talk about the terrorist that Jack had shot and killed in Aden *(found in 'It must have been the Compo – book one of this trilogy)* Jack did not believe in bluffing, and he wasn't too sure if he was or not, but he wasn't going to stand any more nonsense from these elitist, stuck up, Hooray Henrys – especially now that he outranked them. Terence-Darby did not reveal the truth of what had happened to him but said that he had slipped in the showers. Quite proper of him to not grass on Jack of course, but he clammed up to his confreres, as Jack had half expected, expected, since he could not admit to being bested by one of these lower-class peasants such as Jack and John represented.

At the start of the Second World War many 'upper class' officers had been found to be severely wanting. When the Army, after the First World War, had largely reverted to the social club it had been pre-war, it even largely got rid of its tanks and reverted to being donkey wallopers with a 'good seat, good family and the right sort of chap' being the most important requirement to become an officer and qualify for promotion; all these terribly nice but severely lacking in professional soldiering had been quickly exposed by the very professional German Army. Throughout the war, considerable numbers of officers had been promoted from the ranks, as indeed had happened in the First World War and exactly the same as after the First World War, the Army reintroduced their right sort of social class chap and the professionalism started disappearing again. Jack had served many of these, older, qualified by war officers in HQ MEC, and their replacement by Hooray Henrys coming up through the more junior ranks was very evident – one could not be commissioned into the Guards Regiments without considerable private means; those men identified in the ranks as being officer material, such as Charles Telford, who had passed through Mons with Jack, were never offered commissions in a Guards Regiment, but in Charles' case was offered a commission in the Royal Army Pioneer Corps. Perhaps fortunately for the Army, there were not enough of these Hooray Henrys to fill all the commissioned vacancies and men from lesser social levels in society and even worse, men from the ranks, were being commissioned.

Jack was even told by one of the Sandhurst entry that soldiers preferred being led by officers who were clearly gentlemen rather than more common ex-rankers! Oh boy have you got a surprise coming when you first come up against real soldiers thought Jack. As it happened the course split into two, seven from Sandhurst, and two of the Sandhurst entry, who were from working class backgrounds and who had already been subjected throughout their two years at Sandhurst to the upper-class snobbery of the Hooray Henrys, plus the two ex-Mons officers. The leader of the Hooray Henrys, Solomon Terence-Darby, was to reappear later in Jack's life but that was the best part of two years away.

The course was programmed to last six weeks. It soon became clear that the course was well padded with subjects which related not at all to their role in the RAOC. There were a huge number of drill and PT lessons, so many that if they had been removed the course could have been easily covered in four weeks. No explanation was ever forthcoming for this. One thing which did delight Jack was that between the time Jack went off to Mons and came back the necessity for officers to learn to ride horses had been dropped. He had been victimised by CSM Bidsmead and had been sent to the stables every morning, Sundays included, to muck out. With the introduction of all-terrain vehicles, and especially helicopters, the need for horse and mule transport had largely disappeared. Certainly it would have taken more than two weeks to learn to ride properly but with that subject deleted from the programme, rather than shorten the course, the powers that be had decided that drill and PT should take its place. All the course members were pissed off with those two subjects having had more than enough of them at Mons and Sandhurst. Jack did enjoy the sword drill, conducted by the RSM, which had not been covered at Mons on the basis that officers didn't carry swords anymore, which was pretty well universal, but at the Depot and the Junior Leaders' parades, sword drill took place and it was essential for officers there to be competent in it. With the rest of the drill, repetitious of what they had been through before Jack found himself being excused quite frequently to shoot a card for the team. Jack didn't know if Hersham knew that he was being excused but if he did he never said anything.

The course involved learning all about how the RAOC carried out its role in supplying the Army so it involved visits to different types of depots throughout the country. Transport was by the ubiquitous Bedford chassis coaches, good for only about 40–45 mph and therefore slow in travelling anywhere. Only three of the visits registered in Jack's conscience. CAD Kineton, an ammunition depot where the design and attention to safety was very impressive; the stores depot in

Nottingham where they were shown the computer and CVD Ludgershall where Jack was to be posted.

At the time the RAOC was the biggest operator of computers in Europe – they had three! In appearance, they were simply lots and lots of grey cabinets, a bit like their Army issue wardrobes. They didn't even have loads of flashing lights as per the science fiction films. The rooms in which they were situated were air-conditioned, not a luxury for the staff working there but a necessity to keep the computers from overheating although the conditioning could create heating if necessary. The computer was fed by 800 Comptometer Operators – a fancy name for typists whose typewriter did not turn out print on paper but punch cards which would be stacked and fed to the machine which produced rolls of punched tape with which to feed the computer. The most impressive part was the sight of 800 pretty, some very pretty, young ladies (Nottingham ladies were reputed to be some of the best looking in the country at that time) who were subjected to largely stupid questions by randy young officers! It would not have been surprising if all the left boots were sent to Singapore and the right boots to Hong Kong as a result of their questions, comments and visit!

CVD Ludgershall was the only 'A' vehicle depot left to the Army. It occupied an old, ex-American airfield. The 'A' vehicles were those whose normal place of use was in and about the front line. People erroneously thought that the 'A' stood for armoured but it didn't as was pointed out to them during their visit. Located between Andover and Tidworth, it covered a huge site, the distance around the perimeter of the old airfield was a good couple of miles – some of the land had been fenced off and was used for another purpose now. The old hangers were ideal for the storage of large vehicles, mainly tanks and armoured personnel carriers or versions of them like mortar carriers, armoured ambulances and other funnies.

The Depot took in brand new vehicles from the manufacturers and married them up with kit coming from other suppliers; the gun optics for example were ordered years ahead to fit a specific vehicle when it arrived at the Depot. Orders would be received to issue vehicles, some to units returning from overseas, some to UK-based units, who were handing in old vehicles to be replaced with new. The vehicles passed through a number of processes on receipt, inspection, maintenance, repair if necessary and then into storage. Some of the vehicles were maintained as a war reserve whilst others passed through either to units, to purchasers or for disposal. Jack was fascinated by the whole process and the sheer presence of the armoured vehicles and could not wait for his time to be up at the Junior Leaders.

The course actually finished on the Thursday with a dining-in night in the mess in the evening to dine the young officers into the Corps. On Friday, they would make their way to their new units. As Jack was staying at Deepcut but moving from the Depot to the Junior Leaders, he would still be a member of the Mess which housed officers from all the units in Deepcut. He discovered a few days into the course that John Wight had received a posting to the Junior Leaders, also as a Platoon Commander, and this had naturally drawn them together so he had no move to make either. As he was over 25, he qualified for Officers' Married Quarters but Jack, at 23 did not. Both of them had made their number with the Adjutant of the Junior Leaders and what a different character to Hersham. Captain Jeremy Woodhouse had welcomed them effusively into his office, invited them to sit, offered them a coffee and said that salutes were only necessary on first meeting in the morning and in public if more junior ranks were around. They had met him to introduce themselves and to ask for permission to live out of Mess. He knew Jack's situation would be difficult as not only did he not qualify for Officers' Quarters he only received Other Ranks married pay until he was 25 so paying for private accommodation, Mess Bills and all the other bills an officer incurred would be difficult. In fact Jack had found a flat, in Frimley Green, the nearest village to Deepcut, which had been part of the village GP's house which was far too large for the widow so that a flat of a lounge, kitchen, bedroom and bathroom had been created. With its own, outside, stairs it provided exactly what Jack and Janet wanted. At eight guineas per week, it would have been too dear for Jack but Janet had obtained a clerical job just along the road at Johnsons Factory and with the two incomes they could just manage although they would need to be careful. Fortunately, the service in Aden had allowed both of them to put a few pounds by and they were confident they would manage.

John Wight had arranged to move into quarters on the Friday and Jack was moving into the flat on the Saturday. In the event, that Thursday turned out to be somewhat epic and saw Jack obtain some little revenge on that bastard Hersham.

Hersham had rostered Jack as Duty Officer for that Thursday, his last day at the Depot and, as he had been Duty Officer on his first day there, it did seem to be a little consistent. During the day, they had been given their marks for their performance on the course and had spent some time handing in kit, like their swords – apart from Jack who needed his for Guard Mount – and saying goodbye to various people with whom they had come into contact.

The dining-in of the new officers into the Corps was a glittering affair. They all wore their Mess Kit for the first time, except Jack, who as Duty Officer, was required to wear Service Dress and the Duty Officer's red sash. A small section of the Band was playing in the foyer and aperitifs were served in the Ante Room. Mainly sherry was circulating on trays held by waiters, but a few more senior officers had ordered shorts and Jack had to order orange juice as alcohol was forbidden the Duty Officer and he just knew that Hersham would check, and he did. The Dining Room was spectacular when the doors were thrown open; a blaze of light from dozens of candles, loads of silver trophies and impressive silverware, cutlery it really was a picture of elegance and finery. Place names had even been set out and Jack was dismayed to find his name was at the bottom of the table. This meant that when the Colonel called out,

"Mr Vice, the Queen," Jack would have to offer the toast to the Queen who was not only the Queen but also the Colonel in Chief of the Corps. This pissed Jack off no end. The Mr Vice role was traditionally allotted to the most junior officer and Hersham had loaded Jack with the most senior role throughout his time at the Depot and now was stuffing Jack again. Jack wasn't prepared to accept it so he spoke quietly to the Mess Manager, a friend and confidant since he had served there in the ranks, and he swapped Jack's name for the little shit that Jack had had to teach one or two facts of life to at the beginning of the course. When they all sat down, Jack deliberately made eye contact with Hersham and stared at him until he looked away. *One to me,* thought Jack, *he isn't quite so brave in public.*

The dinner progressed through the courses and after the toast cigars and cigarettes were lit and some serious drinking started. It was not long before the junior officers were being encouraged to play games, mess rugby, British bulldog and others. Jack went for a pee and then, rather than returning to the main part of the Mess sat in the Anteroom and chatted to the retired Brigadier who somehow had wangled it that he lived in the Mess. Strictly he should have found his own accommodation on retiring from the Army and somehow that had not happened and he had become a permanent fixture in the Mess. They had been chatting for only a few minutes when a Lt Col, the brother of a famous Field Marshall, and probably only a Lt Col because of it, passed by on his way to the lavatory. On his way back, he stopped and spoke to Jack. It was very evident that he had imbibed too much already. No one actually knew what he did; he had an office in one of the office buildings and a Corporal Clerk worked for him but he wasn't attached to any of the units at Deepcut so his role was a mystery.

He accused Jack of being a coward because he was not taking part in the rowdiness going on. Before Jack could respond and ruin his career before it had even started, the Brigadier intervened and said,

"Colonel, if you were to engage your brain rather than your foul mouth, you would notice that this young officer is the Duty Officer; it should be obvious enough by his SD and Sash, and for him to be drunk and involved in those shenanigans would be a serious dereliction of duty. I think an apology might be appropriate, don't you?" The drunk turned away with what might have been an apology and staggered away. Jack went to thank the Brigadier but before he could speak the Brigadier said, "He's been a waste of space all his career. His brother is one of the best Field Marshalls we've ever had. Such a pity. Now where were we?" and they carried on their conversation.

Jack decided to try and get his head down for a few hours before he was to inspect the Guard, at a horrible 03.45hrs, so he made his way to the Duty Officer's bedroom about 00.45 hrs. On his way, he noticed four or five officers struggling with someone who had a blanket draped over him. Shortly before they had all been trying to de-bag one another, so Jack thought it was something to do with that. In fact several of them had decided to get their own back on Hersham for being such a little shit and Jack had seen them as they were forcibly taking him to the Basingstoke Canal in Camberley where they stripped him to his underdungers and chucked him in. So the ex-Sandhurst lot were not all bad! The canal by that time had become quite overgrown and full of mud and weeds; it wasn't deep but it was bloody cold, it was the middle of February and trying to get out covered him in mud and God knows what else. The officers who had done it had cleared off back to the Mess and, having leapt on him from behind with the blanket, Hersham was unable to identify them. He had an even greater problem identifying who he was to the police who picked him up only a few minutes later. They at least gave him a blanket to cover himself – if he had been left for much longer he could have been in considerable danger of hypothermia.

Jack was unaware of any of this. The culprits had kept it very close to themselves and had, in fact, carried out a very successful exercise. About 02.00 hrs, the police rang the Mess and one of the culprits answered the phone. It was a short conversation with a denial that this individual could be their Adjutant because he was in the Mess.

Jack inspected the Guard at 03.45hrs as detailed by Hersham and was returning to the Mess about 20mins later when the phone rang as Jack passed through the Anteroom. Picking it up he answered,

"Officers' Mess, Deepcut," to be answered with,

"This is the Camberley Police here again. This chap we picked up at the Canal is absolutely adamant that he is Peter Hersham, your Adjutant and..." at that point, realising what had been going on Jack said,

"He can't be. I'm Peter Hersham," and put the phone down. *Get out of that, you bastard*, he thought and just as he turned to go back to bed for whatever time remained to him he was caught up with a group of officers heading for one of the pair of brass cannons which graced the entrance. One of them had discovered a few days before that tins of processed cheese from the Composite Rations fitted pretty well perfectly down the barrel. That discovery was quickly followed with the discovery that tinned jam and tinned beans also fitted extremely well. That being the case only a supply of gunpowder and a suitable target was needed. Gunpowder came from stripping down a number of Thunder Flashes. The suitable target took a little more thought and it was only when someone realised that over the crest behind the Mess the ground dropped, covered with trees, to the Guards' Training depot at Pirbright. It was probably about ¾ of a mile away, and it probably was out of reach but it was worth a try.

The bang was enormous. The first tin of cheese disappeared into the night to be followed by a tin of strawberry jam. They only had enough powder for one more shot so they doubled up the load by loading a tin of cheese and one of jam and sent that off following the others.

Checks at dawn showed cheese and jam splattered all across the Guards' square! But it looked like the third shot had fallen short in the woods much to the delight of the forest animals who were not normally the recipients of compo cheese and jam.

Several days later the Guards raided the RAOC Mess and removed one of the cannons. Unfortunately for them, fired from their square, the shot could not clear the hilltop and the cheese and beans that they fired splattered all through the woods – again to the delight of the forest animals even if it did frighten them initially by the bangs and the arrival of the beans and cheese by airmail! This could not go on, it was far too dangerous, and sure enough word came down from on high that 'enough was enough and it was to end now!'

Jack had to be up at 06.30 hrs to carry out various inspections and so was leaving the Mess at 07.00 hrs when a police car pulled up and Hersham got out. As he was wrapped in a blanket, Jack did not have to salute him, but he would probably not have done so even if he had been in uniform if he could somehow have avoided it. It turned out that Hersham had persuaded the police to ring the Colonel at home and after suitable questions to establish his identity he had been released. Hersham glared at him as he walked past but he said nothing. Jack could not stop smiling all the way to dismiss the Guard. He was not to escape that easy. Having handed over to the new Duty Officer, he was just finishing packing his kit into his car when Hersham, espying Jack, came over. Jack saw him coming in his door mirror and was just able to remove his hat and toss it onto the seat when Hersham arrived.

"I don't suppose you could tell me who the individuals were who grabbed me and threw me into the canal," he asked. Jack replied,

"As I was out of the Mess inspecting the Guard when it happened I did not see who did it, but, even if I had, I would not tell you," said Jack feeling just too much pissed off with Hersham and the way he had behaved to Jack since he first met him when he was just a soldier waiting to go to Mons. Hersham did not look pleased but he said,

"Well, perhaps one day we may find that you are posted to a unit where I am in command and you might want to change your mind," clearly indicating that he did not believe that Jack didn't know who the individuals were. Jack looked at him for a long moment and then, tossing all care to the winds said,

"If I were ever posted to serve under you, I'd walk down to the Basingstoke canal, find a deep bit and throw myself in." He then got into his car and drove off.

He was to see Hersham around the Deepcut area and Mess but never again had any direct contact with him.

Chapter 20

That Saturday, he and Janet moved into their flat. It was fully furnished, a necessity for them as they owned almost nothing in the way of furniture but they did get to open some of the wedding presents they had received in November 1966 and which had remained in storage at Jack's parents until now, February 1968! His father brought the boxes over for them and some sandwiches and cake that his mother had put together for them. They went down well so it wasn't until the evening when Jack and Janet sat down to the easy meal Janet had knocked up they discovered that 'fully furnished' meant that there was lots of catering equipment, large ladles, pots and pans etc. but no cutlery! As they sat down to eat, Janet went to lay the table and discovered it. Fortunately, Jack had a knife, fork and spoon set issued to him and another set, which clipped together for camping, which he had bought when he first joined the Cubs – about 16 years before. So they used these two sets for the first week until they could go shopping on the following Saturday afternoon, Jack having to work on the Saturday morning.

On Sunday, it snowed and settled and then froze so that it was quite dangerous. On Monday morning, he drove to the Junior Leaders Regiment with no trouble, if somewhat slowly, and met John Wight there before they went in to the Adjutant's office to receive a warm welcome. Captain Jeremy Woodhouse explained that the Colonel, Lt Col Christopher Ridgeback had telephoned for the Duty Driver, in a four wheel drive Landrover, to come and get him since he couldn't get his Rover out of his drive. Both of them were to go to B Company with Jack taking over a platoon of 36 boy soldiers most of whom were towards the end of their Boy Service and most of whom would be passing out to Man Service in July when the Regiment broke up for the summer. It was run very much like a school with three terms per year with 10 weeks of leave between the terms. The bad news was that the officers did not get 10 weeks leave, nor did the NCOs, only their customary four and during the remaining six weeks they would be attending training courses, preparing their training programmes for the rest of the year, would be going on speaking tours to schools etc., in an attempt to attract more recruits. John Wight's platoon was made up of 34 boy soldiers who were a year younger on average than Jack's platoon. Jack's first thoughts were that he had been stuffed again but the Adjutant explained it had been done that way as Jack was only going to be with them for the rest of the year and they wanted to maintain continuity as far as possible with John having his platoon for their almost two years.

Each platoon was structured with boy NCOs so they both had a boy Sergeant, three boy Corporals and three Lance Corporals. They also had an adult Sergeant each. The boy NCOs were chosen from the Platoon, so were really no more senior or experienced than the soldiers they commanded. As the future leaders of the adult soldiers when they reached man service; it was important that they had all the necessary qualifications needed for the job, so all of them needed to have passed their third and second drill certificates and if possible their first. They could not be NCOs in man service unless they had at least their second-class education certificates and again, preferably, their first-class ones – equivalent to a good GCSE pass which were just being introduced to the academic world. It was said that a GCSE Grade 1 was equivalent to a GSE pass. In fact, it became clear over the years that grade inflation increasingly gave higher marks for lower standards. For purely academic subjects like history or English, it probably didn't matter too much but for those of a technical nature for vehicle technicians it was vital to maintain standards – if a mechanic couldn't get an engine to start, he was bloody useless no matter how many GCSEs he had to his name. Jack thoroughly approved of the boys having to spend half of every day in the Education Centre being taught by Royal Army Education Corps officers and NCOs – most of the boys didn't, they had joined the Army to get away from school and the first thing the Army did was to stick them into school for half of every day!

It emerged later that there was a very much more serious problem to morale. The schooling issue could be dealt with by communication and training. The practice adopted by the Colonel, for those boys who had decided that the Army was not for them, was a much bigger and harder to deal with problem. It turned out that six of Jack's platoon had paid the money necessary to buy themselves out of the Army, there were four in John's platoon and about the same numbers in all the other platoons – nine platoons in all through the three companies so about 40 boys in all. Soldiers buying themselves out was said to reflect badly on the Commanding Officer. So he had adopted a policy to deliberately slow everything down – the longest lad had been waiting nearly six months to be discharged. The Col did it in the hope that during this time they would come to like being in the Army and withdraw their request to be discharged. Not only did this not work, not one had ever withdrawn their application, but far more seriously, their presence in the platoon was causing havoc with them disobeying orders, turning themselves out badly for parades and generally causing mayhem.

Jack was also given further bad news by the Adjutant. The Colonel had decided to make him the Wines Officer. It went from bad to worse. Not only did Jack know absolutely nothing about wines but his predecessor in the role, a senior Captain, along with the President of the Mess, a Major were under arrest for missing monies and wines amounting to thousands of pounds and were awaiting Courts Martial. Jack was stunned. The Adjutant made light of it. He advised that Jack get himself over to the Mess and meet the civilian Mess Manager, a man who in fact Jack knew quite well, and spend the next couple of days taking an inventory of the stocks. He should compare that to the inventory taken by the RMP when they investigated the accounts and determine a hard starting amount for all the wines, beers, spirits, soft drinks, cigarettes and tobacco, and cash.

Jack made his way to the Mess and sat down with the Manager. When Jack announced he was the new Wines Officer, the Manager let rip, starting with bastards, then cheating bastards and then fucking cheating bastards. Apparently, he did not regard the Colonel and other officers with much esteem. He then explained to Jack how he thought most of the stock had gone missing. When officers ordered drinks from a Steward, they were presented with the drink(s) ordered and offered a chitty which they were supposed to sign indicating that the cost should be added to their Mess Bill at the end of the month. One favourite trick was to refuse to sign the chitty on the grounds that it should be kept open for further rounds of drinks later on. They would then leave the bar conveniently forgetting to sign the chitty. Without the signature, it was impossible to identify who the recipient of the drinks was – no names were written on the chitty. Jack knew that chitties were kept open because he had heard officers doing it but the failure to sign the loaded chitty was new to him. *Even so*, thought Jack, *that couldn't account for such large losses.*

The first step was to count the stock. It took three days and then the total was less than the RMPs had identified indicating that theft was still going on. Jack had to take stock again a few days later at the end of the month and three bottles of red, two of an expensive Claret and one of an expensive Burgundy, had gone missing. Jack had introduced the policy that officers had to write out their own chitties with their name clearly on the top and, despite lots of grumbling, that had stopped the unsigned open chitty abuse stone dead.

Talking to the Mess Manager Jack was suspicious of him. The Civil Service Pay was pretty poor and Managers had a few perks, illegal, but generally ignored, when they received back handers from suppliers for placing orders with them. Jack started to say to him,

"As only you and I have keys to the cellar—" before Jim said,

"No, that's not true. The Colonel has one. The Adjutant has one. Several ex-Wines Officers and Presidents of the Mess have one." Jack was astonished. *Then we have no security at all*, thought Jack. He considered his options. Asking that lot for their key back was a non-starter. They were all senior to him and such a request would be regarded as a personal slur on their honesty. What to do? Getting up he said to Jim,

"Come with me." He made his way down to the cellar and put his key in the lock – it was a lock which had been installed in the house in the late 1800s and was quite substantial, so it took Jack a couple of hefty kicks against the protruding handle of the key before it snapped off. "Fit a new lock, keep one of the new keys for yourself, give one to me, lock the third one in a lockable cash box and ask the Adjutant to keep the box in his safe along with the key to the cash box which is to be signed out if used."

"Yes, Sir," said Jim with a big smile on his face. Jack put a notice up on the Notice Board in the Mess saying that unfortunately the lock to the cellar had broken and had had to be replaced. Anyone needing access to the cellar could obtain such access by signing for a key from the Mess Manager who would accompany that person into the cellar so that an accurate record of items removed could be kept. Jack expected to have some problems but not one key holder ever came to the Mess Manager or him for access. The losses also stopped dead.

Jack received a message from the Adjutant that the CO wanted to see him, with the Cellar Book, the following Thursday. It was to be a Ladies Night on the Friday and Jack assumed that it was something to do with that. It was, but Jack was a little surprised at first at how pleasant the Colonel was to him. Beckoning Jack into his office with a welcoming smile on his face he gestured to Jack to sit at the table in his office and he then stood up and moved over to sit by Jack. Taking the Cellar Book from Jack, he opened it on the table between them.

"Now let me see," he said and started turning over the pages. "The starter tomorrow night is a fillet of Dover Sole in a Parsley sauce. What would you recommend to go with that?" Jack knew the pleasant smile was too much. He had no idea about wines. They had almost never been drunk at home and his other rank service had involved beers, lots of beers but no wines. Jack had had a brief conversation with Major Scagg in Aden about Mess etiquette and Scagg had said things were changing and that if Jack fancied a beer, he could have one. That did not help at all in this situation. He had bought a bottle of wine the first time he took Janet out to the Chinese in Aden. Now what was that called because he quite liked it. It took a moment to recall the name, Piesporter Michelsberg that was it. It was white, fruity and not at all sour or sharp which most wines Jack had tried, all six of them, two whites and four reds, especially the reds were to Jack's taste like drinking vinegar, so, knowing that whites should be drunk with fish or chicken, he looked down the cellar book for it. The CO started to fidget but Jack wasn't sure if they had any in the cellar and was bloody sure he wasn't going to name something they did not have. They did! So Jack pointed it out.

"I don't believe I have ever tasted that one," said the CO. "We'll try it. Tell the Manager that we need enough for 62 guests and have a couple of bottles of another white ready in case someone says they don't want the Piesporter. The main course was beef and whilst the Colonel had been talking, Jack had had just enough time to think about what red he would recommend if he was asked. He was. Jack had long thought about who could have taken the two Clarets and the one Burgundy that had gone missing. He had no actual evidence that pointed at the CO and it seemed utterly impossible that he would have taken it – perhaps he had a habit of listing his purchases at the end of the month but, thinking about those missing wines, Jack replied when asked,

"Well, Sir, we have two very good Clarets in the cellar and an exceptional Burgundy, what about one of them?" The CO looked at him and said,

"I think that's an excellent choice, we'll have the Burgundy and open a couple of one of the Clarets for those who don't like the Burgundy." The aperitifs and the sweet wines to accompany the sweet, followed by the Port and Madeira to go with and after the cheese were chosen by the CO and Jack was rapidly dismissed. Jack made sure in future that he discussed the menu and the wines with the Mess Manager before all the rest of the dinners so that he would not be exposed as ignorant. He had been lucky that time and knew it.

Chapter 21

Jack had yet to meet his platoon. The frozen snow was still causing havoc. It had been cleared from most of the footpaths but huge areas still remained to be cleared. One of them was the area outside Jack's platoon barrack block. As he drove up, his platoon was fallen in about 10 yards from the car parking area. Sizing it up quickly, Jack, in second gear, gave a quick prod of the accelerator intending to swing the back out a bit before catching it and then pulling into the space next to what turned out to be the Sergeant's car. His experience of controlling skids on ice had all been learned in his little Ford 8. His Morris Isis was a very different beast, much, much heavier with very low-geared steering. He couldn't catch it when the back swung out, the swing was faster and stronger than he was expecting and the steering did not respond as expected because he could not turn the steering wheel quick enough. The result was that the car performed a full 360-degree spin ending up perfectly parked next to the Sergeant's car. *Christ,* thought Jack, *that was too close – I don't need any more problems than I already have; I'd better tone it down for a while.* He opened the door, got out, reached back for his hat and cane, put the hat on and walked over to the platoon as though nothing unusual had happened. The platoon started clapping. Jack stopped, took a bow and saluted them. *Sometimes you get lucky,* he thought. He certainly never told anyone the truth!

He got an even bigger surprise when he saw the adult Sergeant. Jack knew him. They had served together in Aden although the Sergeant had been a Corporal then and going out with a WRAC girl. She was one of Janet's best friends and had attended their wedding.

"Corporal Rota as was, now Sergeant Rota as is. That's a surprise," said Jack, "I had no idea who was to be the Platoon Sergeant and look who it isn't."

"I did hear a couple of days ago that you were to be the Platoon Commander and I heard that you were already causing a bit of a stir in the Mess over wines chitties or something…?"

"Long story," said Jack, "I'll fill you in later for now introduce me to what I've got."

Chapter 22

The problem with the boys who had paid their money and wanted to be leavers and their bad behaviour caused Jack to get fed up with this situation very quickly. Discreet questions to some of the longer serving Platoon Commanders showed that they too were unhappy with it but none of them showed any inclination to do anything about it. Jack did. He kept thinking about the Potential Officer Cadet Wing he had joined in the RASC when he joined the Army. It seemed to him that if all the leavers were placed together in a unit under a strong Sergeant they could be used for all the odds and sods jobs that always needed doing around any Army unit. That way they would be kept away from the other lads but would still be performing a useful role until their discharge came through. He then made one of the worst mistakes of his Army career. He put the idea down in a letter to the Colonel.

His proposed solution solved the problem for the Platoon Commanders but did nothing for the Colonel's idea of keeping them in the Army in the hope they would change their minds; in fact being 'gophers' would make them even more likely to want to leave. Jack had not understood the Colonel's fear of a bad report, loss of his, to be given to him at the completion of his time at the Junior Leaders (a foregone conclusion of course) OBE (which stood for Other Buggers Efforts) almost guaranteed if he kept his nose clean; and the loss of promotion and the OBE for a poor showing in retaining recruits in his unit. Consequently, Jack was not expecting the shit storm that was about to engulf him.

It started with a message to report to the Adjutant. The Adjutant just had time to whisper to Jack,

"Keep your mouth shut and agree with everything he says," before the Colonel realised that Jack had arrived.

"Come in here." Jack marched into the CO's office and saluted. The Colonel let rip. "When I want advice from a wet-behind-the-ears subaltern, I'll bloody well ask for it. Do you think...?" Jack let the rest pass over his head, a trick all Other Ranks rapidly learned when they joined the Army when dealing with an irate officer. Jack realised the CO had paused but had no idea what he should say. Remembering what the Adjutant had whispered, he said,

"You are absolutely right, Sir, and I apologise for my letter." At that, the Colonel wrote 'BALLS' across it and flung it back at him. Jack picked it up, saluted and marched out. He winked at the Adjutant as he went past with it being returned by a slight smile from the Adjutant.

It went badly downhill from there. That night was Jack's second dining in night in the Mess – a ladies night. There was a dining in night more or less every month for the officers in the Regiment. There was a ladies' dining in night roughly once every three months for the officers to show their appreciation of the support the ladies gave them but this one was early because of an early Easter messing up the training programme. Jack and John Wight and both wives were looking forward to it with excitement and less trepidation than the first one when they had all been very nervous as the newbies. Gathered in the Ante Room was a glittering array. The ladies all dressed in their finest long frocks and the men in their Mess kit with miniature medals on display. First problem. Jack wore the GSM for his service in Aden. The Colonel, along with about half the senior officers had no medals clearly indicating to anyone familiar with medals that Jack had served in a war theatre and the Colonel hadn't.

Second mistake. Jack and Janet, and John Wight and his wife, Jac, were gathered in a small group drinking Sherries, chatting and taking in all around them. Shortly a more mature lady arrived and introduced herself as Henrietta, the Colonel's wife. She had not attended the previous Ladies' Night. She was pleasant, welcomed the two, Janet and Jac, to the Regiment and described coffee mornings she held every week in her quarters for all the wives. It was quite clear that although she said, "You would be welcome any time you wished to come along," what she was really saying was, "You will come along, an order, rather than an invitation."

Third mistake. Janet had no intention of attending the coffee mornings. Jack and Janet could not afford for Janet to lose a day's pay every week. John was in receipt of a full Lieutenant's pay and married allowance, had a married quarter and a wife who was earning more than him as a Librarian. Jac could probably have managed to take the morning off each week as the staff worked to rosters in the Library but Janet could not take that sort of time off and still retain her job. It was to remain a bugbear for the rest of Jack's service at the Junior Leaders with the CO's wife badgering the CO, the CO badgering the Adjutant and the Adjutant badgering Jack. Each time Jack would say,

"If I can have some money from the imprest (an account the Regiment had to pay for non-routine costs and expenses), I can afford for Janet to come but if no money – no can do. It's not because we don't wish to take part we do – but the Army treats me unfairly because I am married and under 25, so we cannot afford to do it. As you are aware, to get into debt as an officer is a very serious offence, resigning even, so thank you for the invitation but my wife is unable to accept it," or words similar every time Jack was put under pressure.

The final mistake was a beauty. A piano had been playing in the background. The CO's wife referring to it said,

"Isn't he playing beautifully?" Janet, who knew something about music said,

"He's missed a few notes and the timing and rhythm are a bit out but it's very nice in the background." The player was the CO who fancied himself and was accustomed to fulsome praise from his officers and their wives. Jack found himself doing Duty Officer for a week with no explanation as to why. And Jack had been at the Regiment for less than two months. Still Duty Officer was not as onerous as the Depot, they were responsible for the security of the whole camp which was a nightmare given that a public road ran through the assortment of buildings and units with no perimeter fence of any kind. Years later, the security had been considerably enhanced due to the threats of the IRA with a substantial perimeter fence, gates into the various units with RPs (Regimental Police) during the day and Unit Guards at night. But for just the Junior Leaders, the role involved checking the cookhouse and that lights went out at 22.00 hrs and not much else.

When Jack arrived at his Platoon Barrack block on the following Monday morning, it was clear that something was on. The place was swarming with Military Police and Sergeant Rota, in public conversations between them was always formal but in private it was Jack and Stan, managed to whisper that there had been a robbery and his 6 'leavers' had been caught and arrested before Jack was peremptorily ordered to the Adjutant's office by an RMP Captain who looked at Jack as though he was the condemned man about to face execution.

Marched immediately in front of the Colonel he was surprised to find a Brigadier sitting at the CO's desk and the CO standing to the side. Jack saluted and remained standing at attention.

"What have you got to say for yourself?" was the Brigadier's opening remark. Jack felt that ignorance was the best opening response so he said,

"Regarding what, Sir?"

"The robbery carried out by your platoon not to say about the assault on the sentries."

"Sir, I have no idea what you are talking about. As soon as I arrived, five minutes ago, at my Platoon Office, an RMP Captain marched me over here and told me nothing. I know nothing of a robbery or assault on sentries." The Brigadier stared at Jack. Jack had worked for considerably more senior officers than the Brigadier and was not frightened as he was supposed to be. However, he was puzzled and thinking about, how he could be blamed, and escape from under, something which must have happened on the weekend when he was not in the Camp. Jack waited out the Brigadier who eventually said,

"Six soldiers from your platoon ambushed the two sentries whose stags covered the NAAFI and stole a considerable quantity of cigarettes and alcohol from the NAAFI, to the approximate value of £6,000 which they hid in the empty, spare lockers in the unoccupied room in your Barrack Block where it was found by the Military Police. So, now you know, what have you to say for yourself?"

"Nothing, Sir. I was not in the Camp at that time and know nothing about it. May I ask who the six boy soldiers are?" Good to get in that these were boy soldiers not adults and who could be expected to get up to mischief. The Colonel said immediately,

"I don't see the need for you to know their names, the fact that they are from your platoon is quite enough." Jack smelt a rat. Why would the CO not want him to know who they were? Jack could only think of one reason, it was the six who had paid their money to be discharged and had been such a nuisance to Jack. That would explain why the CO did not want it to come out. *Fuck that,* thought Jack, *he's not getting away with that.* So taking the bull by the horns, he looked at the Brigadier and said,

"Are their names, Abbot, Wilson, Corbyn, McConnell, Mandelson and Foot by any chance, Sir?" The Brigadier looked at a piece of paper he had in front of him and took a long time before confirming that they were. "They are the six boys who have paid their money to buy themselves out of the Army. Abbot paid his money nine months ago and the shortest, Corbyn, paid his money six months ago. There are boys in the same position in almost all the platoons. They are like a rotten apple in the barrel and the idea that, if they are kept in long enough, they will change their mind is patently wrong since not even one boy has done so during the time this practice has been followed; what they have done is lower the morale of all the other keen boys; they turn up late and dirty for parades and generally cause mayhem."

"Well what have you done about it?" asked the Brigadier believing that this was a killer question and Jack would not be able to provide an acceptable answer.

"I wrote to the Colonel, about two weeks ago suggesting that a special platoon should be formed of these boys and they should be put under the charge of a strong Sergeant. I suggested that they could be used as a special duties platoon to work on all the odd jobs that need doing around the place until their discharges came through." Whilst Jack was speaking, the Brigadier looked at the Colonel and Jack caught the barest suggestion of a shake of his head. *You bastard,* thought Jack, *he's going to deny I wrote that letter or that he received it. Bastard. Bastard. Bastard.* It was now clear to Jack that he was to be offered up as the sacrificial lamb whilst the Colonel would be cleared by his mate the Brigadier. *Bastard. Bastard. Bastard.* There was no way Jack was going to go down without a fight when the Brigadier asked,

"Is it right you personally taught them sentry ambushes just last Friday?"

"Yes, Sir."

"Why did you do it and why last Friday?"

"Because my adult Platoon Sergeant was on a day's leave attending his mother's funeral and because it was listed on the Regimental Training Programme for that day."

"What programme?"

"The boys spend 50% of their time in the Education Centre, mostly mornings; of the remaining time, 30% is set out by HQ controlling the allocation of platoons to the ranges, gym, training areas, the square etc. so that there are no clashes with platoons wanting the same area at the same time and the remaining 20% is planned out by the Platoon Commander to carry out any other training needing doing or refresher training for those lessons which need it. Because the ambush and anti-ambush training uses the small training area which is wooded and behind and around the NAAFI, that's where it is done by every Platoon doing ambush training. HQ dictates when it is done by each platoon and my platoon was designated for last Friday." During this explanation, the Brigadier started fidgeting and throwing dark looks at the Colonel. Probably this was not going as he had anticipated at all; Jack was showing no evidence of being cowed or scared and certainly wasn't accepting any blame. The Brigadier then made the biggest mistake of all. He asked,

"And what happened to this alleged letter?"

Bastard, again thought Jack. No, in fact he thought, *Cunt, you aren't going to get me with your 'alleged'.*

"Sir, the Colonel sent for me and gave me a bollocking. He told me that when he wanted advice on how to run his Regiment from a wet-behind-the-ears, just-out-of-the-ranks subaltern, he would ask for it. Until then, I was to keep my mouth shut, my eyes open and to leave letter writing to my betters also to shut up. He then wrote balls in capital letters across the letter and flung it back at me telling me to get back to my platoon and do some proper work."

There was a pause. The Brigadier had clearly just heard something he did not like at all. By now, he was glaring daggers at the Colonel who looked decidedly green and wishing that he was anywhere but in that room, even though it was his own office. The Brigadier then brought in a metaphorical digger and enlarged the hole.

"And where is this alleged letter now?" he asked.

Yes, definitely cunt is right, thought Jack. Reaching into the left breast pocket of his tunic, he pulled out the 'alleged' letter and handed it to the Brigadier, saying,

"Here, Sir." Jack could not have explained why he had kept the letter in his pocket. He had not anticipated anything like this happening and had just left it in there from the meeting two weeks before and forgotten about it. He had worn combat kit for most of the intervening period so that the letter was just in his SD uniform pocket. The Brigadier read the letter, looked at the Colonel and tore the letter up dropping it into the waste bin. *Fucking cunt,* thought Jack; *definitely a fucking cunt,* and Jack's career was just about to go into the bin with it.

"May I say something, Sir?"

"Go on."

"When I described what the Colonel said to me, I referred to the fact that he referred to my Other Rank service; that was below the belt. I am sure my records will show that I was a Chief Clerk. I was serving in HQ MEC when my recommendation for promotion to commissioned rank was made. That recommendation was signed by my OC, a Major, the department SO1, a Lieutenant Colonel, the BGS, the Army Commander, a Major General and finally by the Theatre Commander, a full Admiral. The point I am trying to make is that I was a bloody good clerk and it was my custom and practice to keep copies of any important documents for those three officers. I could hardly fail to follow that practice with documents important to me and the document you have just torn up is a Xerox copy of the original which is carefully and safely filed away." There were clear looks of consternation on the faces of the Brigadier and the Colonel. The Adjutant, who was standing behind them, had a glorious smile on his face. *Gotcha,* thought Jack; *explain destroying evidence to the Board that tries you*, he certainly hoped so. The silence seemed to stretch for eternity. The Brigadier's day was not going well or as planned at all. He should have known that no plan survives the first encounter with the enemy and he was not facing a wet-behind-the-ears subaltern but one prepared to fight. The direct implied threat of the original letter being elsewhere was bad enough, the Brigadier could be accused of destroying evidence and if that wasn't bad enough, the reference to a Brigadier General Staff, an Army Commander and a Theatre Commander all being called as character witnesses didn't bear thinking about. Abruptly, the Brigadier said,

"Thank you for your assistance, Mr Hughes, please carry on." Jack gave a poor salute and walked rather than marched out. All day he was expecting to become a civilian but nothing happened. The rest of the day was a bit of a mystery to him later on when he thought back to it. What he did remember when he appeared for duty the following morning was to discover a new Commanding Officer with Lt Col Christopher Ridgeback consigned to history. The day after that a platoon of 'leavers' was formed and the boys who had paid their money discovered themselves civilians the day after that. Except for Fridays when they had to wait until the Monday.

It was almost 51 years later when, in one of those reminiscing moments during a family get together, Janet said to Jack, "By the way whatever happened to that copy of the letter that lousy Colonel wrote balls all over, I don't think I remember ever seeing it?"

"What copy?" said Jack.

It was a moment or two before Janet took in the smile on his face and said, "You never had a copy did you?"

Jack smiled and said, "I very rarely bluff because you look such a prat if the bluff is called but when that Brigadier tore the original letter up in front of me I knew I had to come up with something good and quick or I would have been the ex-2nd Lieutenant J. Hughes minutes later, so I bluffed and guessed that he would not know what a Xerox copy looked like. And he didn't and I got away with the bluff."

Janet looked at him for a second and then leaned over and kissed him on the cheek saying, "I knew you were a good 'un when I decided to marry you."

Shortly after the letter incident WOI Stevens RMP who had sort of adopted Jack as his lucky mascot just happened to walk by Jack's Platoon Office. Popping his head around the office door and giving the biggest of smiles rather than any form of salute, he said,

"I just thought I would let you know that a certain ex-WOII, lately of the Depot, pleaded guilty at his Court Martial yesterday to receiving illicit payments, fraudulently carrying out work for a certain civilian contractor and misuse of Army personnel, property and time and is now a Private Soldier who will be transported from our Guardroom at 14.00 hrs this afternoon to Colchester (the Army prison with a fearsome reputation and an almost nil re-offending rate) for a period of ten years. After which he will be dishonourably discharged with the loss of his pension. If you happened to be in the area at the time, you might wish to wave him goodbye or something. Oh and one other thing, Sir, a certain RMP Captain who accompanied you to the Colonel's office did seem to think you were indeed the worthy individual I have always known you to be; in fact, he said something like you served the Colonel up like a chicken all trussed and stuffed." And with that he disappeared.

Jack could not resist. He turned up at the Guardroom just before 14.00 hrs and, as his ex-tormentor was marched out, he stopped him and the escort and said,

"I told you, on my last day as a Private Soldier here, that I would get you, you bastard, and I did. If you have wondered how the Monkeys found out about what you were up to I can tell you. It was me who told them. OK escort, take him away," and with that Jack spent the rest of the afternoon smiling.

Chapter 23

The following few months were probably the happiest of his commissioned life. There were events going on which provided amusement like the Treasure Hunts arranged by the 2i/c of the Regiment. They happened most months on the first Saturday of the month starting at 16.00 hrs and finishing back at the Officers' Club at 20.00 hrs in time for a curry supper. At first, Jack and Janet made up a twosome and John and Jac did the same in their car, a three-cylinder, two-stroke SAAB. Neither of the couples did very well and their first three or four hunts, they never found the treasure, not even coming close. The cost was also an issue for Jack, his Morris Isis did 25 mpg at the very best when driven gently; the hunt wasn't supposed to be a race and the Treasure Hunt notes handed out at the start absolutely forbad racing. That was also to prevent problems with insurance companies who took a dim view of racing and would not pay out for any damage so caused, but the average speed was quite high and the miles per gallon quite low!

So they paired up using John's car for one hunt and Jack's for the next. Their four brains combined did mean that they did do a little better in the hunt but not much and they only made it to the finishing point twice in all the attempts they made.

The friendship with John and Jac developed into quite a close one. They spent a couple of afternoons on the nearby River Wey drifting along through lovely undisturbed countryside with idyllic pastoral scenes including a ruined Abbey or Monastery clearly visible from the river but not quite accessible from the river it shallowing off but offering no safe landing stage. It was one of those sites where they intended to visit by land someday but never quite got around to.

The military side of life was not really demanding. The problem of paid-up leavers causing misery for all and sundry had disappeared, the amount of work needed to be carried out by the Platoon Commanders was quite small with most of the training programme dictated by the Education Centre and 30% of the remainder filled in by programming from Regt HQ. The only irksome bit was having to work on Saturdays and Sundays, for the inspections on a Saturday morning and sports in the afternoon, church and sports on Sundays.

John Wight one day suggested to Jack that they should organise a night-time exercise. It was clear that thought in the Army was moving towards night fighting as a force multiplier. Most of the places where fighting was going on around the world, Borneo, for example, was being fought by insurgents, terrorists or liberation armies. The Russians with their huge forces could not be resisted for long by the Brits alone, but with the sophisticated night fighting equipment becoming available to act as a considerable force multiplier that must be the road to go; Jack had typed a report on the introduction of the first night sights to the Army when he was a Staff Clerk in Aden (*It must have been the Compo'*) and knew that there had been many advantages to using the light intensifiers at night. Infra-red sights, had first been invented during the second world war, but were not widely used probably because there needed to be an infra-red light source; red cellophane paper covering a torch or headlight would provide a crude infra-red source but you also needed a piece of kit, normally special binoculars which could see infra-red light. The problem was that if the other side had an infrared viewer you became a target as soon as you switched on your infrared light! Not a good idea. The light intensifiers then in use in the American and British Armies gathered whatever light there was available and intensified it by bouncing it up and down cathodes to produce an image in the dark. Its chief advantage was that you did not have to shine a light to use it. Armies with it could dominate armies without simply by attacking at night.

Of course the boys' Regiment didn't have any such kit and probably would never get some, expensive and rare as it was but nevertheless night training had become a passion of John Wight and he kept bringing it up. Jack, to get some peace eventually said,

"Well, come up with some ideas and we'll see if they are viable." John really went to town on his plan. Part of it involved the two platoons because exercises of more than platoon size never happened and the Company Commander, when he was told about the plan thought that was an excellent idea and full Company exercises involving the three platoons in the Company went onto the training programme. When word of this spread to Regt HQ there started appearing on the Training Programme exercises for all three Companies in the Regt.

As John explained his plan to Jack, Jack had trouble keeping a straight face. John's plan involved his platoon attacking an old, ruined house shown on the Ordnance Survey Map as being right at the edge of the Deepcut Camp, with Jack's platoon defending it, and once John's platoon had attacked and taken it the two platoons would swop over positions and Jack's would attack the property and John's would defend it.

"What time do you envisage the exercise kicking off?" asked Jack.

"About 22.00 hrs because it doesn't really get dark until then at this time of the year."

"How long do you envisage the whole exercise taking with both platoons attacking and defending?"

"Well, it's hard to be precise but probably three to four hours in total."

"So finishing by about 02.00 hrs or a little later. So how are we going to get around Regimental Orders which state Boy Soldiers must not take part in night exercises after midnight?" John looked at him for a long time and then said,

"Are you sure?"

"Damn sure."

"Shit and double shit. Well, what we'll have to do is have my platoon defend the house one night, making sure we finish by midnight and then your platoon can defend it the next night. Any problems with that?" Jack paused for effect and then said,

"I don't think we will be around the second night."

"What the hell are you talking about, of course we'll be around the second night. You're not going to tell me that there is some rule about not having two nights exercise on two consecutive nights are you?"

"Oh no," said Jack, "at least I don't know of any such prohibition it's just that I think after the first night the Brigadier Commandant whose house that is might have had us locked up for disturbing his sleep." John's mouth fell open and he started stuttering,

"The Brigadier's house, it can't be, you're winding me up; you've never been keen on night exercises…" and so on. Jack started laughing. He had difficulty wheezing out that when he had been at Deepcut before going to Mons the Commandant's house was one of the places where the CSM had sent him to do fatigues. Strictly soldiers should not have been used to carry out work on what was in reality married quarters and thus the responsibility of the Ministry of Defence. But the CSM always crawled around the Brigadier and he was prepared to turn a blind eye if it got the problem sorted far quicker than an application form for repairs to the Barracks people would have dealt with it.

John was mortified. "Fuck, double fuck and triple fuck," was heard to be said with considerable feeling and he picked up all the ops orders, the map and threw them in the bin. The fuck, double and even triple fuck could still be heard as he disappeared into the distance. A few days later, he approached Jack and said,

"I have learned two things about night attacks. One I need to be more careful in my preparation of the proposed geography of any exercise I plan and secondly to ask you, smart arse, if you know any problems that could arise from my plan. I am so glad this was not just for my platoon or I am sure that you were right again that it would have been me that was locked up" Jack took this as their relationship was back in place.

The truth was that there was no area in the Deepcut camp that offered a building, old or new that could serve for the purposes they wanted. But there was quite a lot of ground which could be used for platoon attacks against a defended position with trenches and some wire. So Jack proposed this. The first attack would be made by Jack's platoon against John's dug in platoon and then they would swap over and John would attack Jack's platoon. The same basic plan as John had proposed before but in daylight and a dug-in position rather than a building. If it all went well, they could repeat it a little later into the autumn when it got dark earlier and they could carry out an attack and defence the same evening. Even though they did not have night sight equipment, they could practice in the dark and discover at what a disadvantage operating at night could generate. Having agreed the plan for the following week, the two platoon commanders went their separate ways in the meantime.

Jack, however, was not happy. In all the exercises Jack had so far seen, the boy soldiers had been running around shouting "bang, bang" and "you're dead" or similar. They had no blank ammunition, or if they did the Armourer would not issue any. Jack kept thinking about this and then one morning, about 03.00 hrs, as would become a normal event, the answer came to him.

When he arrived for parade at 08.00 hrs, he carried out the inspection as normal and then dismissed the platoon to the Education Centre. Telling Sergeant Rota to cover for him if anyone came looking for him, he said he would be back in a couple of hours. He had remembered that Sgt Dewey at Mons had a store of ammunition and other whizz bangs in a lock-up at the end of his Spider. So he drove there and found him. The Sergeant seemed pleased to see Jack, at least he saluted Jack which did not always happen to returning junior officers. After a general catching up, Jack explained about the boy soldiers running around shouting bang, bang and how pathetic and demeaning that was and he wanted, if it was possible, to give the platoon a full issue of ammunition along with some whizz bangs, smoke grenades and Very pistol flares etc. to give them experience of proper kitting out. Dewey asked,

"How many in your platoon, Sir?" Jack replied,

"Thirty soldiers, therefore 3,000 rounds for them plus a few dozen for the three Brens plus whatever else you can spare – I know you'll be rewarded in Heaven for all this but that's all you'll get because I haven't anything else." Dewey laughed and said,

"You were a cheeky bugger when you were here and those pips on your shoulders have given you aspirations to be even more so." Saying that, he led Jack to his store and counted out a number of ammunition boxes giving Jack a total of 4,500 rounds. Jack looked at the pile and said,

"I can start a full-scale war with that lot – I'll get my car." By the time he returned, the pile had grown enormously with enough thunder flashes to give everyone two each, two smoke grenades each and 30 Very pistol cartridges. He also handed Jack five tripwire mines (they only gave a loud bang to announce that someone had tripped the wire) which could be set-up at a defensive position to imitate Claymore anti-personnel mines which were horribly effective and lethal against an approaching enemy. Helping Jack to load all the munitions into Jack's boot, Dewey said,

"You know, Sir, they still talk about how you rescued the General and hijacked his car to get away."

"Well," said Jack, "I did have to make a second lot of coffee after I boiled his balls with the first lot so he owed me something." Dewey laughed and said,

"Just one more thing, Sir. Don't come back again for more stuff because I'll not be here – I'm posted in two weeks to Hong Kong. But I am glad you did turn up because I was wondering what I was going to do with all this stuff and then heaven or the other place sent me you! I can easily use up the rest so thank you very much and good luck with your exercise."

"And good luck to you, Staff." They shook hands and Jack drove off with a big smile on his face. He never did meet Sgt Dewey again although he continued to remember him with affection.

When he got back to the Junior Leaders, he showed Sgt Rota what he had managed to acquire without telling him where it had come from. Rota was amazed. They discussed where they could store it until the following week when the exercise was scheduled to happen. The only safe place they could think of which would not be found by any inquisitive sod was to leave it in the boot of Jack's car. They were both determined that when they attacked John Wight's platoon there would be a wall of noise and complete pandemonium when Jack's platoon charged in.

On the day of the exercise, both platoons fell in at 21.00 hrs, it wasn't completely dark but it was dark enough and they still needed to have finished the exercise by mid-night. Both platoons were briefed on their roles and then John Wight's platoon marched off to set up their defensive position – most of the trenches of which had been dug during the day. Sgt Rota briefed Cpl Allen, 1 Section Commander to take a recce patrol of three to find out where they were setting-up and what their layout was to be. Jack fetched his car and stopped by the platoon. The looks on their faces when they realised that they were to be issued with a hundred rounds per man and five magazines for each of the Brens was unbelievable. Jack had to issue strong warnings about the use and misuse of blank rounds and the use and misuse of the Thunder flashes. Jack intended to keep the smoke grenades, Very pistol flares and the mines for their defence of the position. Three boys were detailed to load the magazines for Cpl Allen and his recce patrol so that they would be ready to move the moment they returned.

When Cpl Allen returned, he described the enemy position and location. It was pretty much where Jack expected it to be. He had walked the area in the morning whilst the boys were at Education and the area, being very small, only offered a couple of potentially good positions and John had chosen the best one.

Jack sent No 1 Section off in front with orders that once they were spotted by the enemy they were to go to ground and crawl away, standard practice, but they were to pretend to return fire by shouting bang, bang as the enemy would expect. In the meantime, Jack would lead the rest of the platoon off to the right to go right flanking. When he was in position, he would detonate a Thunder flash at which point, Sgt Rota would order the three Brens to let rip along with the rest of the riflemen of No1 Section.

It worked like a charm. The blast of noise from the three Brens and the four riflemen dominated everything. As Jack gave the order to advance, his two Sections advanced firing round after round. When they charged the last few yards, it was to find the enemy platoon in complete disarray and John Wight shouting "you bastard" at Jack as loud as he could. Jack's platoon swept through the site and took up position a few yards beyond it whilst selected detailed soldiers made their way back through the site dealing with any enemy still alive.

John caught up with Jack and asked quite impolitely, loudly and angrily,

"Where the hell did you get all that ammunition?" Jack savoured the moment.

"That's for me to know and you to wonder," said Jack and that was all he would ever say on the matter.

When they swapped roles, Jack ordered a different approach. He had most of his platoon preparing a defensive position on the other side of the site to the one John had chosen for his platoon. Jack had the boys pulling up bushes and rearranging them to disguise the site as there was no time to dig new trenches. They camouflaged the site such that they were virtually invisible until you got within 20 yds or so of them. He had the five trip wire mines set out on the approaches but about 50 yds from the position on the side he guessed they would attack from – he hoped this would throw them out of balance and mess up the attack. He arranged one of the existing trenches to show up slightly and the ground and track was such that it invited any attacker to attack right flanking. He then hid the three Bren gun teams so that they would fire along the assaulting sections, a classic enfilade, catching them in the open with the troops in the new positions firing at their front and the machine gunners from their flank. He also issued smoke grenades and the remaining thunder flashes to both positions so that there would be absolute mayhem and a ruined attack.

No plan survives the first contact with the enemy but Jack's almost did. The enemy spotted his position quicker than he thought they would and, at first it looked like they were just going to charge full frontal at his position but their boy Sergeant shouted at them to halt and then withdrew the front of their platoon to adopt a fire position ready for the flanking attack. The rest went exactly to plan. As the two sections swept in from the right, they hit the mines which stopped them dead – they had never come across these before and paused to work out what to do. Jack's boy Sergeant, whom he had placed in charge of the three Bren teams, timed opening fire, beautifully doing so, just as they paused, confused, by the mines exploding. The boys in both positions went into a bit of a frenzy throwing thunder flashes, smoke grenades and firing blanks as fast as they could.

Apparently, Jack was a bastard again – at least that was what John called him when his attack collapsed and Jack called that he had defeated the attack. Cleaning up the site and returning it to its original condition took a while but the buzz from the boys, especially of course Jack's platoon, lasted over several days.

One thing Jack had to do was get rid of the Isis. It was a relatively luxurious car but it was showing its age. The engine was making a slight rumbling which Jack's dad diagnosed as the big ends being on their way out – a potentially very expensive problem. All the slack, and more, in the steering box adjuster had been taken up and there was a lot of slack in the steering. The brakes were pretty well shot so that with the engine, steering and brakes all needing doing it was better to get rid of it rather than spend more money on a beast that was past its normal sell by date. He exchanged it for an HA Vauxhall Viva. Much smaller than the Isis but returning over 40 miles per gallon compared to the Isis's best of 25. The Viva was fitted with radial ply tires which were a revelation in the wet compared to the cross-plies on the Isis. He enjoyed scaring the shit out of his father, the first time he was a passenger, when he approached a bend in the wet at a speed which would have been suicidal in the Isis. Such was progress!

Chapter 24

The Ministry of Defence announced that the boys' barracks were to be fitted with central heating. This came as a complete surprise. Nothing had ever been said about it before and the Regiment had never raised a query with the MOD because just at the edge of the current site a whole new camp was being built. Modern, up to date with central heating, smaller barrack rooms housing four rather than sixteen soldiers, much better ablution facilities etc. the new barracks promised heaven so why then, only three months before the old barracks were due to be knocked down had they decided to spend a fortune fitting central heating and better showers, sinks etc. to the old barracks nobody knew – it was just typically mad.

Friday night was bull night. The Army denied to anyone who asked that bull existed anymore. They now called it Interior Economy but it was bull. Bull. Bull. Jack had to put in an appearance every Friday night. One Saturday per month was the Colonel's Inspection where, accompanied by the RSM and the Company Commander, he carried out a detailed inspection of the barrack block. Woe betide any Platoon Commander whose block was not up to standard; extra Duty Officers were handed out like sweets to kids on Christmas, which although Duty Officer was not as onerous as at the Depot it was still a pain in the arse and hated by everyone. The other Saturdays, the inspection was carried out by the Company Commander. Jack had avoided any extras for a few months but then one morning he thought he was for it. The second boy soldier in the first room was a lad called Festwick. Small for his age and weak with it, it was a wonder he was still in the platoon. Any one more unsuited to be a soldier was difficult to imagine. Only a few days after taking over the Platoon, Jack had gone into the Gym where his Platoon was undergoing fitness training. Jack wanted to check on the fitness of his new Platoon but he also wanted to check on the PTIs to ensure that they were not bullying as was their wont according to Jack's experience of them.

The Platoon were spread around the Gym working on difference items of Gym furniture. It so happened that Festwick was attempting to climb a rope and was failing miserably. At first Jack tried encouragement but that had no effect. Festwick was apparently using the right technique, his feet and knees were gripping the rope properly but, combined with his arms, he simply seemed to lack the strength to pull himself up. Since he probably didn't even weigh eight stone, his weakness was very worrying. He clearly wouldn't pass the Gym tests that were coming up and then his future would be in doubt. There was the possibility that he would simply be back squadded and given longer time to improve, or even sent to the PTI school where unfit, recovering from injuries, wounds etc. soldiers were put through special fitness training, but this was for adult soldiers and Jack simply didn't know what might happen. Jack really did not want Festwick to be given to the mercy of the PT people – he held them in very low esteem and did not trust them an inch. Turning to Sgt Rota, he passed him his hat and cane. Then, just using his arms, he pulled himself to the top of the rope, hung there for just a second or two and then let himself down hand over hand.

"See it's not difficult. I am a lot heavier than you, and I can do that without using my feet which makes it much easier. I want you to work with Sgt Rota here and build up your strength. I know you can do it, he knows you can do it and you know you can do it so get on it." He took back his cap from the Sgt, straightened his uniform, took back his cane and walked out. He hoped that Festwick would respond, he wanted to stay in the Army and could only do so if he passed the physical fitness tests. He also hoped that his demonstration had impressed the Platoon with his arm strength and create one of those little legends that go around the place.

It didn't actually work. Two weeks later, Jack and Janet were driving up to the Officers' Club on the Saturday afternoon and who should be walking down the road to Frimley Green, which was the only place the soldiers could catch buses or trains, but Pte Festwick. That wasn't a problem. What was a problem was that he was carrying a kit bag and suitcase indicating he was going somewhere. Since he hadn't applied for leave, the chances were that he was going AWOL so Jack stopped.

"Hello, Festwick, where are you off to?" At which Festwick burst into tears. Jack calmed him down as best he could and told him to get into his car. In bursts of sobs, phrases and cries, it came out that he had had enough of the Army, he was constantly being teased by the other boys for being a wimp and he had come to the conclusion that the Army was not for him. Jack had a problem. He had come to the conclusion, following the Gym visit and subsequent reports by Sgt Rota that Festwick was not suitable for the Army – some men were and some men weren't. The issue was what to do about it? Technically, Festwick hadn't left the area of the Camp when Jack stopped him and walking along carrying all your civvy kit might be good evidence of an intention to desert but who knew if he might have changed his mind before he left the barracks and even then he probably wasn't technically absent until he failed to turn up for lights out, when, without a leave slip, he would definitely have been absent.

Jack found the boy Sergeant, told him what had happened and ordered him to arrange a roster of junior NCOs to keep their eyes on Festwick for the rest of the weekend. He told Festwick that he would talk to the Company Commander first thing on the Monday morning to set in motion the steps to buy him out. At that Festwick burst into tears again and it took a while to get out of him that he had talked to his mum about that but, as a single mum, she simply didn't have the money. Jack knew, but not for publication, that there was a discharge process for boys in Festwick's position which did not involve any cost to Festwick, but all he could say was, "Don't worry about that, there's bound to be a way around that; we'll look at that on Monday."

Following the debacle when the previous Colonel had been so hastily transferred, the Army, especially the Junior Leaders, had become much more sensitive and within 10 days, Festwick was out of the Army and Jack had one less weak link in his platoon. Jack had a personal policy of getting rid of weak links in the team but Festwick had been trying and he had hoped that he would somehow turn into a good soldier.

Jack had one more horrible problem at the Junior Leaders. All of the exercises Jack had undertaken with his Platoon involved the boy NCOs carrying out the duties applicable to their rank. But all of the boys were supposed to be leader material and designated for accelerated promotion when they entered man service. Like so many things, the theory was fine but the practice simply didn't work. The first problem was that for six months to a year on entering man service the ex-boys were pretty useless. Whilst in the Junior Leaders pretty well all day every day, seven days a week were mapped out for them. Very little leave was allowed, other than that at the end of each term; they were not given freedom at the weekend when dismissed at Saturday lunchtime; they were scheduled for sports, Sunday mornings were Church and the afternoon taken up with organised games, hobbies etc. This was all organised by the adult Sergeant and Officer so it was no surprise that a posting to the Regiment was so hated; no one had any free time during term time and then for the adults the breaks were filled with courses, either on or planning for. The few times Jack and his wife had been able to socialise with John or other officers was when the Sergeants were on duty on the Saturday or Sunday. The boys were also only allowed to draw a small sum of their pay each week so that they did not have enough money to sneak out to the nearest pub, the NAAFI being well aware of the boy's ages and their attempts to obtain alcohol. It meant that many of them went wild on joining man service, they suddenly had lots of money, lots of freedom and made the most of it so that on a Monday morning when reporting for duty, they were well hungover and in a right state following wild weekends. Also, although, initially they were better trained than the just out of recruit training soldiers they were mixing with, they did not have the maturity or leadership authority to show themselves as being suitable for promotion. Some did, of course, but on balance they just became another soldier and far from the motivated and trained leaders they were supposed to be. Most of the adult Sergeants and Officers were well aware of this but none were prepared to stick their heads over the parapet and say so, least of all Jack who had had the painful experience of once having done so and nearly lost his head as a result.

Jack had the thought one day, that perhaps he ought to carry out a little role swapping, as had been common at Mons, and give some of the non-NCO lads, the brighter ones, a bit of practice as NCOs. The first of these exercises took place in July, shortly before the end of term, and involved a simple platoon attack but with the boy NCOs playing the part of the enemy defending the position John

Wight's platoon had done when Jack had blown them to bits, with other boys playing the roles of Sgt, Cpl and L/Cpl.

Everything had gone off pretty well, the boys had carried out so many attacks that they knew off by heart how to do it but those playing the role of NCOs had had some practice of command and had done quite well. It wasn't until they were gathered on the objective that someone pointed out that the heath behind them, where they had started out from for the attack, was on fire. The wind was not very strong so that the fire was advancing quite slowly although it was widely spread and of substantial proportions – it hadn't rained for three weeks and the heath was very dry.

The boys had been practiced in regular fire drills so one boy was sent at the run to the Guardroom to alert the Fire Piquet and the civvy Fire Brigade and the rest grabbed fire beater equipment and started trying to beat out the fire. The Fire Piquet were quickly on the scene with their hoses and fire engine on two wheels and pulled by the Piquet. Jack organised a small squad to back burn the vegetation, at the edge of the exercise area, to try and create a firebreak up to the edge of the little lane which led to the car park. The lane was little more than a car wide and the far side of it from the fire was the Officers' Club side wall. The Club was a much more popular venue than the Officers' Mess. Although it was only made up of two or three old wooden huts knocked into one, there was a dining room, bar, a billiard room with two billiard tables, a dart board and a few other table games. It was run by an informal committee of officers and was a far cry from the pomposity of the Mess. Jack could not imagine just how deep in the shit he would be if he burnt it down. When it became clear that burning embers were being blown on the roof of the Club, which could not be reached by any of the boys with their beaters Jack pulled the Fire Piquet from the heath fire and ordered them to start wetting the roof. The Piquet rapidly ran out of water – the cart only held enough to deal with small fires but fortunately just around the corner of the Club was a stand of two fire buckets and two sand buckets. The sand buckets were of no use because no-one could throw it onto the roof and would probably be of no use if it could have been gotten there. So they just dumped the sand and used the four buckets, filled from the kitchen in the Club, to keep filling up the Piquet's' little fire engine. It required a considerable effort to pump the water high enough to land on the roof and Jack had to organise a relay of pumpers to keep the roof wetted. Fortunately, the civvy Fire Brigade were on the scene in just over 10mins and with the Regimental Fire Piquet and the boys beating the hell out of it the fire was soon brought under control. The Officers' Club had a few scorch marks but was not damaged and was in full use that evening.

Jack and the Senior Fire Officer took a walk back over the burned heath, only 70 yds or so to where the fire had appeared to have started. The wind had carried it, in fact easterly, and there was quite a clear delineation as to where it started. The SFO swooped and picked up a hand-rolled cigarette stub. Nothing else appeared to be a likely candidate and, unlike the previous time Jack had used the heath, no ammunition or pyrotechnics of any kind had been issued to the boys so they could not be the cause. Jack returned to the Platoon and ordered them to adopt the formation they had used for the attack. There appeared to be three likely candidates for the cigarette and Jack ordered all three to turn out their pockets. Two had nothing of significance but the third boy pulled out a cigarette-rolling machine, a packet of filters and a packet of Rizla cigarette papers. At first, he acted as soldiers always do and denied everything but faced with the cigarette butt and a persistent Jack he admitted that he had been having a discreet fag but was adamant that he had extinguished the butt before he had moved from the position. Jack had a word with the boy and adult Sergeants and the miscreant found himself on all sorts of fatigues for the next week.

Jack wasn't entirely surprised to be sent for by the Colonel the next morning. The Colonel seemed to think that the fire had been caused by the use of something loud and spectacular by Jack which he regarded as being entirely stupid given the state and dryness of the heath. Jack was unable to get a word in for a while. He was a little surprised that his activities in obtaining ammunition and explosive devices had reached the Colonel's ears and was, at the same time, quite pleased that his enterprise appeared to have been recognised even if nothing in the way of praise had been said. When the Colonel eventually stopped, Jack said,

"The fire was caused by one of the boy soldiers smoking, against the rules, rules that I had iterated to them before the exercise because I had recognised the dryness of the heath. The culprit was found and has now been suitably dealt with." The Colonel simply looked at Jack. He then said,

"If you had burned down the Officers' Club, cigarette or not, boy soldier or not, I would have had you roasted over the embers and served for Sunday lunch." Jack thought that's quite colourful but as nothing had been said about extra duties he assumed that the meeting was over and said,

"I can understand that, Sir." He saluted and marched out.

That was not the end of it; the Club had not finished with him. The fire happened on the Friday afternoon. On the following Tuesday, three men turned up from the insurance company that insured the Club. They were there to assess the damage, if any, and to produce a quote for the next year's insurance fee which was due shortly. The inspection took a while with their faces getting longer and longer by the minute. Jack was entirely unaware of all of this and was sitting in his Platoon office when a runner arrived and said that he was required in the Colonel's office immediately. As he made his way across, the Club was not on his mind. He had had his bollocking for that and was busy running all of the other things he had been up to which might need explaining away and could not find anything that struck his mind by the time he arrived. Sent straight in by the Adjutant, it was to be addressed by a clearly cross Colonel. He started,

"The Officers' Club has just been examined for insurance etc. They have reported that the fire caused no significant damage." *Thank God for that,* thought Jack but, in that case, why was he here and why was the Colonel so mad? He was soon to find out.

"The examination has determined that the premises are in a very poor, even dangerous state. There's wet rot, dry rot, cockroaches, silverfish, woodlice, mice, rats and just about every other creature known to mankind infesting the place. It is to be condemned and demolished. That is all to be at the cost of the officers; the insurance does not cover these problems. If, however, you had burned the bloody place down, that would have been covered and we would have had a nice new club paid for by the insurers. Why, oh why, did you not burn it down?" Jack looked at him for a moment, then saluted and marched out. There was nothing he could say, indeed there was nothing to say. He could feel eyes on him from the other officers during the rest of his time there. It was not a comfortable feeling. Had he known the situation, he would have happily staged a fire and burnt the bloody place down deliberately but now it was too late. He was always to feel a little pissed off that his valiant efforts to save the place were never recognised although he could understand why!

Chapter 25

During the Easter break, he had been sent on an 'How to Instruct Instructors' course at the Army School of Education in Beaconsfield. As the boy soldiers were to be the future NCOs of the Army, they would spend lots of their time instructing. Jack went reluctantly, partly because he would be away from home, albeit waited on hand and foot in an Officers' Mess, but mainly because the programme for the course seemed to be about instructing, which he knew how to do, indeed his first Colonel had been so impressed by his ability to teach the Stirling SMG without notes or aides that he had been taken out of basic training and sent on to the next stage; he could see nothing that said 'instructing instructors' only 'instructing' and felt sure it would be a complete waste of time.

It was; not only that, although it was quite good in showing methods by which the lesson(s) could be made more interesting much of this was done with overhead projectors, 8mm cine film and other modern training aids just appearing in the training world – there wasn't a hope in hell of them appearing in the Junior Leaders. The most they had was chalkboards, flip charts and manuals. As the course progressed there was constant reference to preparing for a presentation that was to be given on the last day of the course by each of the course members. The presentations were to be for at least 20 mins and they were expected to make full use of the equipment in the training rooms. The course was due to finish at lunchtime. They were to be marked on their presentation and this mark would be included in the report on their performance sent to their units. Given that each speaker would have to set up the room to be able to do their presentation and remove any kit used afterwards, it was highly unlikely, therefore, that they could get through more than two presentations per hour; starting at 09.00 hrs, break for tea at 10.00 hrs for 20 mins officially, more like 30 mins in reality, and finish at 12.00 hrs meant that it was highly unlikely they could get through more than five at the absolute maximum. With ten of them on the course, five would not do a presentation. In that case, how were they to be measured, marked etc.? Jack was one who was not called on and he had no idea what the report on him said – his performance on the course was never mentioned when he returned to the Junior Leaders nor was he asked if he felt if it had been useful attending it.

The one thing he did do at the course was to meet an old enemy. He had been walking from the Mess to the classroom when, coming the other way, was a large squad being marched by a Sergeant. The Sergeant ordered an 'eyes right' as he passed Jack which the squad did and the Sergeant gave a smart salute which Jack returned. The squad carried on, on its way, and Jack headed for the classroom. However, he quickly became aware that he could hear running footsteps behind him and a voice calling, "Sir, Sir." Looking back, he saw a very small soldier running after him. He took in the uniform of Service Dress and then realised that the uniform had white patches on the collar – the sign of an officer cadet. Looking closer, he realised that it was Mohammed Mohammed who had disappeared from Mons mysteriously and who had tried to kill Jack in Aden to which Jack had responded by trying to kill Mohammed. *(See 'It must have been the Compo')*

"Sir, so nice to see you," crashing up an exemplary salute, "I am here at Beaconsfield to learn English and it is now very good, is it not?"

"Hello, Mohammed. We wondered where you had gone, so how much longer will you be here?"

"Oh for another three or four weeks if I pass my exams." The Sergeant had halted the squad and was now making his way back to where Jack was standing. Seeing him coming and the look on his face, and that Mohammed had done his best, not a very good best, but nevertheless his best to kill Jack, Jack was happy to cut short the conversation by saying,

"Well best of luck with that," and turning to the Sergeant he said, "Carry on please," returned the salute and walked away. He did not intend to spend all the summer break on courses so he booked three weeks annual leave for the break.

The period towards the end of the term was hectic. Firstly was the drill rehearsals for the passing-out parade for those boys leaving for man service. Normally that would be the last day of the term but there was a problem – the Queen was coming to open the new Barracks on that day and there was to be a parade of all the units at Deepcut for this ceremony. Then the very bad news came. The Junior Leaders Regiment was the only one which could muster a large number of bodies, about 600, for the parade. The Depot could only produce two recruit platoons, each of just over 20 soldiers, and a rag and tag platoon of soldiers passing through on posting to somewhere else or for discharge as time served. For Jack, it got worse and worse. For reasons never explained to him, his platoon was to head the Junior Leaders Regiment which meant that Jack was the front officer for most of the time and in reality controlling the parade. The Colonel was not taking part, he had to be in the Queen's party, so the 2i/c should have been in the lead. He went sick with an injured ankle which left Jack at the front leading the parade and giving the marching off orders. In his role of Wines Officer, he was sent for three times by the Colonel who changed his mind each time as to which wines were to be served with the lunch. Then, having worked out the amounts and placed the orders with the suppliers, the Commandant got involved, sent for Jack and the Cellar Book and changed it all over again. The worst problem from Jack's viewpoint was not changing the order with the supplier but the fact that the Brigadier had chosen all the most expensive wines in the cellar. As the cost of the wine was spread amongst all the officers, albeit on a shares basis i.e. 1 share for a 2nd Lieutenant, 2 shares for a Lieutenant, 3 shares for a Captain and so on upwards, it still meant that Jack would receive a hefty Mess Bill at the end of July, which with a holiday coming up he could ill afford.

Complaining to the Mess Manager about it he looked to see that they would not be overheard and said,

"There is a way that the bills could be lowered a little bit if you want to chance it."

"Tell me," said Jack.

"Well, at the lunch on the boys' passing-out parade the day before, we could fill a load of empties of the Clarets the Brigadier has chosen and put them out on the sideboard for the bottom end of the tables. The expensive stuff for the top table would be set out at the top end of the sideboard. Since the red wines are opened at least an hour before the meal to allow them to breathe the fact that none of the bottles will have corks in them will not be noticed – if someone should look at them, it will be as it should be." Jack thought about it for all of two seconds.

"Let's do it." And that's what they did. However, as Jack well knew, no plan survives the first encounter with the enemy. The boys' parade had gone off very well and the Colonel and the visitors, including the Brigadier and several high ups from the MOD, had retired to the bar in the Mess early so that by the time they were due to sit down to lunch the CO was well lubricated. As they were about to enter the dining room the Mess Manager approached the Colonel, and said,

"Sir, there is a call for General McCartney and it is extremely important, so says the caller." The General was guided to the phone, in more ways than one. Answering it he could be seen to visibly be sobering up. Turning to the two Brigadiers who had accompanied him, he said,

"We're returning to the MoD now." His driver was dragged out of the kitchen where he was about to enjoy a very nice meal, intended for the officers, and was on his way with the three passengers in less than five minutes. The Colonel then, with some difficulty, made his way, followed by everybody else, into the dining room. However he could not make it to the top table and collapsed onto Jack's chair at the bottom, Junior Officer's, table. Laughing uproariously, he indicated that Jack should take his place at the top table, with the Brigadier to his right, and he ordered the Mess Manager to start serving. There was no problem with that, the first course and white wine was served and the meal progressed. The Mess Manager and Jack kept some eye contact but there was no way that the expensive Claret could be picked up by one of the waiters who were not in the know, from the far end of the sideboard, and carried to the Colonel at the bottom of the table; it would be obvious that something was going on and even the CO in his well lubricated state could not miss it. Jack and the Mess Manager shared a shrug and the cheap red was served to the Colonel. Having gone through the sniffing, holding up to the light rigmarole, the CO then took a noisy slurp and described the wine as being top notch. Jack and the Mess Manager started breathing again and discovered that once well under the influence an aficionado could not tell piss from fine wine.

Jack frequently received invitations to weekend house parties from people he did not know, indeed he had never heard of them. So he spoke to the Adjutant who burst out laughing.

"That's our Royal chasers. They will know that you will have four tickets for the Queen's visit. An ambitious mother will want her daughter to marry well and the chances of meeting someone of the right sort of class and background will be immeasurably increased when the Queen is here. If you go to the weekend, you will be right royally treated, maybe even a visit to your bed at night in return for which you will be expected to invite the mother and daughter to be your guests at the lunch."

"But I'm married," said Jack.

"Ah, well, they will have assumed that as a 2nd Lieutenant, you will not be married hence the invitation. Mind you, if you wrote to them telling them you were married so long as they got the invitation, it would not matter as there's bound to be some other available prize to hook onto – maybe even you." Jack had heard of dissolute behaviour in the upper classes but he had not expected to be invited to take part. He turned the invitations down but they still kept coming.

The parade went off well; it should have done they practiced it often enough. Jack was still the most junior officer so it fell to him to propose the Royal Toast, which he managed without stuttering and all the best wine was served! Jack was not prepared to try it again.

Chapter 26

Jack borrowed two, two-man bivvies' for him and Janet to sleep in plus a bigger tent to use as a cooking, dining and living area along with all the necessary petrol cooker, pots, pans and utensils. They planned to go camping in Wales starting at Towyn, where he had attended the Army Outward Bound School (*Fully detailed in 'It must have been the Compo'*). He had read over a number of years about the rebuilding of the narrow-gauge steam railway there and wanted to visit it. They had been allowed no private time at the AOBS so he had not been able to see it then. As they were camping, they intended to move around Wales visiting Snowdon and that narrow gauge mountain railway and finally over to Blaenau Ffestiniog to see the progress with that railway, also narrow gauge. In the event driving to Towyn on the Saturday, they were blessed with good weather but as soon as they got the tents up, it started raining and it didn't stop. On Sunday, they drove to Snowdon on the basis that there was a café at the bottom and the top of the mountain to shelter from the rain and, of course, they would be dry in the train. The problem was that they entered cloud about halfway up and couldn't see a damn thing. Jack took a picture of Janet standing on the top but with cloud all around her the only good thing about the photo was her orange coat stood out against the cloud.

By Monday morning, they were thoroughly pissed off by the weather. They couldn't access a TV or radio for a weather forecast and going by the one in the paper they bought, the rain was going to carry on for at least three or four more days. So they packed up and went home! The only interesting point was that Jack noticed what he thought at first was a leaf hanging on his radiator grill but on closer examination, it turned out to be a bat. He carefully removed it from the car and hooked it onto the underside of a large oak tree branch. It was to be many years before Jack and Janet returned to Wales to see all the sites they had wanted to see.

Jack's Platoon was 10 boys fewer for the rest of the Autumn Term, they had passed into man service at the July parade. Nothing of note occurred, except at the end of September; Jack took the Platoon, along with the other two platoons from B Company to a firepower demonstration on Salisbury Plain. He had seen one before when he had been taken to one whilst he was at Mons. If you like big bangs and lots of them, then this is the place to be. The spot chosen was on the top of quite a steep cliff which curved to make a half circle. Dug in at the bottom of the cliff was an infantry company with various targets set out up to three miles away. The loudspeaker system explained that the purpose was to show the power of the weapons available to a normal infantry company. It started with just a Section of 10 firing at man-sized targets about 200 yards away. As they were hit, the targets fell down. They were all down in just seconds. Then the exercise was repeated with the whole company firing rifles, light and medium machine guns. Then the three-inch mortars joined in followed by a Wombat anti-tank gun firing at car hulks up to a mile away. The last weapon to be shown was a Vigilant anti-tank missile, wire guided, which was fired at a moving tank more than two miles away. That was absolutely amazing seeing the rocket track the tank and then hit it – only a puff of smoke showed, they weren't actually allowed to fire live rockets and kill off a tank crew! Jack just thought that it was a pity that they didn't use a live head and blow the tank away as it might have contained the two mad Irish buggers with whom he had ended up in jail in Mombasa. The finish was where the audience were asked to imagine an enemy approaching from over the horizon and being engaged by all the weapons as they came into range of each one. The noise was fantastic and the dust, smoke and flashes vastly entertaining. It certainly made it appear to be a lot safer to be dug in facing an attack than to be in an attacking force.

At that stage, they broke for lunch – very few of the boys having any food left by that time. They had each been issued with a brown paper bag containing a sandwich, apple and sweets or chocolates; most of which had been consumed before they had left the environs of Deepcut!

After lunch, they made their way to a different viewpoint, about half a mile away, where they were to view a tank firepower demonstration. Jack vaguely noticed a company of Mons Officer Cadets marching parallel to them but he certainly noticed when one of them broke free and ran over to Jack calling out, "Sir, sir," as he came. Jack was astonished that it was Mohammed Mohammed again. Rushing up, he halted, threw up a salute and said,

"I am so happy to see you again, Sir, as you can see I am now back at Mons and should pass out at Christmas time." His English was now very good but Jack did not want to know; he just wished he had shot more accurately and killed the sod in Aden. He was saved from a conversation by one of the Staff arriving and ordering Mohammed to get fell in. He saluted Jack without saying anything and marched away.

What a weird world, thought Jack as he followed his Platoon. Such coincidences seemed hardly likely but they had happened. More was to come. At the tank firepower site, there was a set of tiers of seats rapidly filling up. Jack made his way up and sat at an end seat on the second row. He didn't notice the people behind him. He had been sat there for only a few moments when a voice behind him said,

"You made it then?" Turning around, he was astonished to see Major Scagg who he had worked for in Aden and who had recommended him for a commission. He didn't know whether to salute or shake his hand which was resolved by the Major offering his hand which Jack heartily shook. There was only time for a very brief conversation before the loudspeaker sprang to life.

The tanks, in the main Chieftains, showed what they could do. Once again they were highish above a re-entrant into the cliff line and there was a Chieftain directly below them. Its first target was so far away that it only appeared as a dot on the horizon. Jack, having been before had taken the precaution of borrowing a pair of binoculars from the QM stores so he could see the target, a battered old Fiat Panda, disappear in a flash of light and smoke.

They then put on a story of an enemy appearing over the far horizon and advancing on their position. The worrying part, for those infanteers who had watched a tank being destroyed by a Vigilant missile, was that a Chieftain driving across the front of their position swung its gun around and made a first round hit on the horizon and way outside the range of the Vigilant. It meant their position could be shot to pieces by a moving tank, outside the range of their own weapons, and a very difficult target, therefore, for them to hit or destroy. When additional armoured vehicles, with large guns, some multi-barrelled, some mounting large missile launchers, drove across in front of them unleashing a storm, an absolute storm of shells and missiles miles away at, in effect, defenceless targets, literally miles away it destroyed the comfort installed by the effectiveness of the infantry firepower presentation and created a strong wish in everyone present to be in the armoured regiments and not the poor bloody infantry. Major Scagg leaned forward and said,

"I don't know about you, Jack, but that little lot makes me think that being back in HQ MEC would be no bad thing when the fighting starts." At that he shook Jack's hand and said, "So very nice to see you made it through. Mrs Scagg will be delighted when I tell her because you were always her favourite amongst the clerks when she had to be driven around. Good luck to you." At that, he shook Jack's hand again and walked away. That made Jack's day although the thought of Mohammed being trained to be an efficient killer did haunt him a bit for the rest of his days.

Chapter 27

As the end of October drew nearer, he started to think of Christmas and finding a flat somewhere in Andover. Andover was about 13 miles from the depot but they needed to be in Andover for work for Janet – she couldn't drive and in any event they couldn't afford a second car.

They drove down to Andover on the middle Saturday in October to make their number with a number of estate agents and start them looking for somewhere suitable. They were not an impressive lot; generally untidy and non-reactive when Jack and Janet walked in, so much so that they only gave their details to one of them. They arranged for the local Andover paper to be sent to them so they could make their own appointments to view but the first Saturday they saw three properties in the morning and two in the afternoon and the best that could be said of them was that they were the highest priced slums Jack had ever seen including some of the huts in Aden. They arranged a set of visits on the third Saturday in November with Jack getting very worried that he was going to have to move into a Mess in Tidworth and Janet into his parents' or sister's, so difficult was it proving to be to find a flat.

They had three viewings in the morning; in the last one the wallpaper was actually hanging from the wall and as the agent shut the door, the draft caused two strips to fall down peeling away from the wall altogether and landing up in a heap on the floor. It was clear from even the most cursory of glances that the place was full of damp and the agent's statement that a good fire going in the grate would soon sort that out was hollow in the extreme. The first one after lunch wasn't even worth viewing, the path up to the front door and the garden, which had clearly been used as a dumping ground, was enough for Jack to say, "No," to the agent as he went to open the door. The agent, who at least had the grace to look ashamed, said,

"Well, the last one we have on our books is a lovely little property but it is in Kimpton, which is about halfway between Andover and Ludgershall. It therefore doesn't meet your criteria for being in Andover but there is a bus service, in fact the bus stop is outside the property and it is a good service." With heavy heart and the feeling that they were wasting their time, after all he had described some of the slums they had viewed as 'lovely little properties', they drove out to Kimpton to be greeted by an archetypal thatched cottage; painted pink, it was idyllic, at least from the outside. It was side on to the road with no path; looking at it from the front, it was like a child's drawing, two windows upstairs, two downstairs but the door was at the right-hand end opening through an extension. It opened into a kitchen dining room with a door through to the lounge. At the far end of the lounge was a wooden door which shut off access to the wooden staircase leading to upstairs. Up there was a bathroom, small bedroom and master bedroom. It was all in good order and ideal for them. The price was the same as Frimley Green flat and was lower than the properties they had been shown in Andover because it was a bit in the wild. The drawbacks to living there didn't become apparent until they moved in which they did on 31 December. Their leaving the Junior Leaders was a fairly low-key affair mainly because the movement of people between postings was quite common and meeting up again quite frequent.

The only people Jack and Janet would really miss was John and Jac. Their friendship had grown steadily. They made each other assurances of meeting, after all Kimpton wasn't too far to make a visit for the day impossible and indeed John and Jac visited a couple of times through the summer as did Jack's family and Janet's, although Jack had to drive over to Newbury and collect Janet's mum and brother as they had no transport of their own. They even had a visit from Jean, his cousin who had emigrated to America, when she returned to the UK for a visit. But that was all for the summer – before then they had to get through the winter and boy was it cold. The only heating point in the whole of the cottage was an open fire grate in the lounge. The walls of the cottage were over a foot thick and, as it had been empty for a month or two, it had absorbed the cold and trying to get any heat into it was a mammoth task. As soon as he returned in the evening, Jack lit the fire. It would be only just beginning to take the cold off the room when it was time for bed. It wasn't safe, even with a narrow mesh fireguard to leave it built up when they went to bed so it had to be damped down. Opening the door to the stairs let some of the heat go upstairs but it wasn't very much and that made the lounge colder. They had to buy two electric fires, one for the bedroom and one for the kitchen and even so it was bloody cold. As the spring came, they were to discover all the lovely wildlife that lived in the thatch but preferred to come into the cottage. Virtually every day, Janet discovered the spiders like those that were used in horror films waiting in the bath for her! They were huge and turning on the taps did no good; they were perfectly able to swim and as the water level rose, so the closer to the rim of the bath and escape they came, so they had to be battered with the loofah or bath brush, whichever was the handiest, until their splattered remains could be washed down the plug hole. The birds loved nesting in the thatch, which was supposed to be sealed by being netted, and being early risers, their scratching around and tweeting did not receive a welcome at 04.30 hrs! Then there were the horses, they trotted past at about 06.00 hrs on their way to the gallops and the fact that one of them, Highland Wedding, was the winner of the Grand National that year did not make the noise any the more welcome. And then there were the ghosts. The church was right across the road but the cemetery was the other side of their cottage meaning they had to float through the cottage, across the road and into the church; whilst they were quite quiet the sight of them floating through was a little disturbing! They celebrated Christmas and New Year with their families and travelled to Kimpton on 2 January.

On the 3rd, Jack reported for duty just before 08.30 hrs as ordered. His welcome was not exactly what he expected. The Officer Commanding, a Major, opened by saying that as there was no actual establishment position for a Subaltern; they were not entirely sure what to do with him or what use he could be. He said that they would start by showing him around the Depot and then he would work in each of the departments for as long as necessary to get to know the workings. He would be added to the Duty Officer Roster and would stand in for any officer on leave, on a course or sick. The OC said he prided himself on running an efficient unit with physically fit soldiers. This last started warning bells ringing in Jack's mind. The OC had a set of parachute wings sown onto his SD and hanging on a peg in the corner was a red beret. Not everyone who wore a red beret was a qualified parachutist but since Major Burton wore the wings, he clearly was. The issue was, what was he doing in the RAOC? The RAOC was a peculiar organisation in that the most common officer rank was that of Major. This was because that level of seniority was needed to sign authorisations for kit purchase or disposal etc. There were only about 80 posts for Subalterns, 250 for Captains so that the 450 or so posts for Majors could not be filled from within the Corps even if every junior officer was promoted to Major. So that meant transfers in from other units, mainly the infantry, of Majors who were becoming too old for running around the woods but were fine for desk jobs. Jack quickly came to the conclusion that Burton was an ex-para and probably was going to be a problem. Even at the short introduction, it was clear that he thought the RAOC soldiers should be up to the fitness standards of Paras when he told Jack that in addition to the normal Wednesday afternoon being given over to sport he had introduced PT for Tuesday and Thursday mornings – at 07.15 hours so that they could get in an hours PT without it interfering with work and that Jack would be expected to attend as well as taking the sessions when he was unavailable. *Oh let joy be unconfined*, thought Jack. He wasn't surprised to discover in due course that the older soldiers, nearing demob and on their last posting in the Army, had a sickness rate far higher than the norm and the absence always coincided with Tuesday and Thursday. Jack was always surprised at the inability of senior officers to spot cause and effect and his knowledge of the results of the personality profiles that he had typed in Aden of the Parachute Bn tested for the guided missile assessments had shown a distinct propensity to illegal and unintelligent activity and he thought he could see some more of it here.

There were about 350 people employed in the Depot he was to discover. Eighty of them were soldiers and the rest were Ministry of Defence Civil Servants. Jack had worked with some Civil Servants in HQ MEC in Aden and had formed a strong opinion of their value – about as much use as a chocolate teapot. The soldiers were mainly vehicle specialists, a military term for mechanics and their role was to work on receipt, storage, servicing, maintenance, kitting out and issue of the 'A' vehicles in the Depot. There had to be a cadre of soldiers able to carry out all the functions in the event of war when the availability of civvies might be too low. With the vehicles, some of them were brand new and arrived from the manufacturer as a basic vehicle and needed kitting out, some were in storage for emergency issue if necessary, some were for sale and some were for training. The civvies would have much preferred that the soldiers were not there and it soon became apparent that the feeling was reciprocated in spades.

Jack's first job was to work in Reception. New vehicles coming in still had to be minutely inspected – the manufacturers were not above leaving jobs unfinished or pieces missing altogether – and this work was carried out mainly by the Royal Electrical and Mechanical Engineers (REME) so that when the vehicles were released to the depot, there was not too much work to be done to them. The ones that were a problem were the 'second hand' vehicles coming back from the units. They were dangerous, frequently a vehicle would arrive with ammunition in one or more of the guns fitted to it. The staff took great glee pointing out to Jack the repair marks to surrounding buildings caused by someone playing the tank commander and squeezing the trigger only to find that the hanger and the one next door had just been instantly fitted with non-working air conditioning!

The returns from units vehicles were supposed to be cleaned before return. To be fair most of them had had a bit of a wash and brush up on top and inside but none of them were properly clean, particularly underneath where mud, oil, vegetation and all sorts of muck had become securely lodged in all the nooks and crannies. This meant that items like bearings and other moving parts could not be properly examined. This meant that all the underneath had to be scrubbed clean using brushes and liquids made up mainly of paraffin, penetrating oils and detergents. The people who did the cleaning, official job title, Scrubbers, were all women. It was a filthy job working in pits under the vehicles and Jack was to discover just how filthy for himself. He collected a clean pair of overalls every day for the first five days he worked there. It was bitterly cold so he wore heavyweight underwear, jumpers and rubber gloves. The physical exercise of scrubbing generated some warmth but for the most part it was bitterly cold and disgusting work – and someone had to do it; Jack's experiences in the ranks had taught him a 'bugger them, let's get on with it' attitude which carried him through that week. What also helped were the Scrubbers themselves. They weren't the daintiest of creatures which they proved very quickly. The first afternoon, after they had got a bit used to Jack and he them, he became aware that something was touching his bottom as he worked. The space in the pits was very limited and bumping into one another a not uncommon experience but this was different. Concentrating, it seemed to him that a hand was having a quick pat of his bum. The third time it happened it was a definite pinch! Turning around as quick as he could he was still too slow to identify the culprit. They were all, the three of them, innocently scrubbing away. The next time he was quick enough and caught the hand. It belonged to the oldest one among them, a woman in her late 40s or early 50s.

"Next time, I'll give you an hour to stop," he said, letting go of her hand. After that, there were no more pinches and his acceptance by them was demonstrated by their inclusion of him in their conversations. Nevertheless, he was very glad to finish his week with the Scrubbers. Moving through the rest of the departments took the next six weeks and he applied himself fully to learning as much as he could as he did so.

At every opportunity, Jack bagged driving lessons on the various vehicles. Some, like the Centurion tanks, were monsters to drive. They had three-foot pedals like ordinary cars, brake clutch and accelerator. Where they were very different was in the steering. There was no such thing as a steering wheel, instead there were two enormous levers so that to turn left one pulled, very hard, on the left lever which would brake the left track and the vehicle would veer left. Completely locking the left brake, or right, would make the tank spin around within its own length to the left or right depending on which lever was pulled. This wasn't encouraged because the tracks would really chew up the ground and there was a risk, albeit small, of shedding a track. Best, or worst of all, was the gear lever. Centrally positioned, it was an enormously long rod with a huge black knob on the top. The problem with changing gear was that the clutch was extremely stiff with the result that after only 20 mins or so, Jack's left leg started trembling – probably explained why all tank drivers had massive left thighs!

The Saladins and Saracens were six-wheel drive armoured vehicles, one with a turret and 76mm quick firing gun and one a personnel carrier normally carrying eight soldiers which were really on their way out to be replaced by the 430 series of vehicles which ran on tracks. The six wheelers had steering wheels attached to the forward, sloping bulkhead and required a peculiar shovelling motion to turn. The problem with these was there was not self-centring action so that once having turned the wheels to turn left they stayed there and would complete a circle and would continue doing so until it was shovelled back to the central position bloody quick or up the pavement you went. They were, however, much easier to drive than the Centurion. They could also be driven on the normal roads where the tanks were limited to the training areas.

After familiarising with a Saladin, the Corporal training him suggested that they go out on the main roads. Eventually they ended up squeezing through some very narrow roads in Salisbury. They reached an impasse with a parked lorry blocking the lane coming the other way and a double decker bus starting to overtake it. Jack, driving, had right of way but the bus driver believing the in the bus drivers' holy commandment, 'might is right', decided he was coming through. They met, nose to nose, alongside the lorry. The bus driver, knowing he could never hold his head up again in the drivers' league tables if he reversed, leaned out of his cab and gestured for Jack to back up. Not a good idea. Speaking over the intercom he ordered the Corporal to swivel the 76mm gun, main armament, which was resting pointing to the rear on its travelling cradle, to raise it from the cradle and swivel it so that it pointed directly at the bus driver. That having been done Jack climbed out of the Saladin and walked up to the driver.

"Three things," he said, "I have right of way, this Saladin doesn't have a reverse but I do have a great long barrel which, when I stick it up your arse, will certainly encourage you and your crappy fucking bus to move backwards at a rate of knots. So which is it to be?" Just then a policeman came walking up and Jack, polite as ever said,

"Good afternoon, Officer. As you can clearly see, I have the right of way, I do not have a reverse gear so unless we are to stay here all day may I ask you to direct this bus driver chappy to reverse his omnibus back to allow me to pass?" The driver started to speak but, probably because the constable had also been the recipient of the bus drivers' code of might is right, cut him off and said,

"If you aren't moving back in the next thirty seconds, sunshine, you will be spending a lot longer than that down the station explaining why you blocked a member of Her Majesty's Armed Forces going about their lawful business." The driver reversed. As Jack drove past, ensuring that no one could see, he gave the driver the finger. He enjoyed that drive although the Constable's last comment, "I used to drive one of them when I was in," did reveal that he knew Jack did have a reverse but only one unlike the Italians who had five fitted to theirs.

He didn't enjoy the next time he drove a Centurion; well, not very much. He had been driving around the Depot when the Corporal instructing him ordered him to stop. He did. The Corporal climbed down from the turret and said to Jack,

"Would you like to try out across country now, Sir?"

"Yes please, if you think I'm ready for it."

"Oh, yes, Sir – back you go." Jack selected reverse, built up the revs, pretty well to maximum, something over 2000rpm for the Meteor engine, banged out the clutch and backwards lurched the tank.

Two or three weeks before, the OC had got a bee in his bonnet about civvy cars in the depot. There was a staff car park at the gatehouse where the staff were supposed to park, but with the depot being spread out over a huge area parking there could mean a walk of half a mile or so to their particular workplace and in the winter with a howling gale blowing across Salisbury Plain such a walk could resemble Scott's trek to the Pole. So, over time, people had started driving to their hanger and parking nearby or indeed in some cases, actually inside their hanger. These cars were sharing space with very heavy armoured vehicles wherein the driver had very poor visibility. Technically, they should be escorted by a walking guide who would ensure safe movement, but for the same bad weather reason the walkers had disappeared and the drivers often drove shut down peering through little more than a letterbox-sized flap. Near misses were common, so much so that no one took any notice anymore. The OC having witnessed such a near miss threw a mighty wobbler and had put up everywhere notices absolutely forbidding any civvy cars in the depot past the car park and threatening dismissal or worse for any miscreants.

Officers Commanding the Depot had for years agitated for a staff car for the OC to be used to meet and transport visitors rather than tatty old, dirty and well-worn Landrovers. Miracle of miracles the Vehicle Org relented and authorised the issue of a Mini for the Depot. The OC determined that no heavy booted,

Paddy Hopkirk wannabe, was going to thrash his brand new Mini for damn nearly 70 miles had himself driven there in a Landrover and drove the Mini back himself. The plan worked well but for two problems; the first was the Mini was not new, it had over 50,000 hard miles on the clock, squeaked, rattled, groaned and shuddered at anything over 40 mph and was generally worse than the Landrover in which he had travelled to Ashchurch.

The second problem was just about unbelievable. He had taken just about three hours to get back and was busting for a pee. He stopped just outside the toilets and rushed in to do his business. He took no notice of the fact that he had driven right up behind a Centurion with its engine running – the smoke belching out of it should have been a good clue. Jack maxed the revs, something over 2,000, selected the lower of the two reverse gears and banged out the clutch. The Cent lurched with the back lifting up a bit and then travelled backwards. It was a bit of a shock for the Corporal and Jack to see a very, very flat Mini appearing from under the tank. The OC's face was a picture – if Jack could have taken one, he would have won any photographic competition for the next ten years. Through Jack's and the Corporal's minds exploded the thought, *is there somebody, a very flat dead somebody, in there?* The OC's thoughts were somewhat different, he knew there wasn't anyone in it but he had parked it there, against the instructions he had written and he was now going to have to do some explaining about his actions. He also had a Mini that was no longer fit for purpose and how long would it take to get another one this time? There was also the issue of the failure of the Corporal to check behind the tank before sending Jack back. Jack was, of course, the driver who had reversed over the Mini but of the three of them he was the only totally innocent one; the OC should not have stopped there and the Corporal should have looked behind the tank before sending the tank backwards but the timing of events was such that shit happens!

He need not have worried about how long it would take to get another one, the Army being the Army, if you had a piece of kit and it became worn out you turned it in for another one so long as you had the right chitty signed by a senior officer. The OC was a senior officer and signing the right chitty was a matter of moments. Explaining the accident was a bit more difficult but Jack was never party to the investigation and its outcome so he never knew how that was dealt with but he did find out how the replacement was dealt with. The next day, the newly modified Mini, for posting under doors, was loaded onto a three-ton Bedford and it was sent back to Ashchurch. Jack went with it; the OC having decided that he wasn't going to waste another whole day travelling there and back, in a Bedford going and a clapped out Mini coming back – Jack could do that. The OC held it against Jack as the one who had driven over his car but he couldn't officially blame him but he could ensure shitty little jobs ensued.

Jack was subjected so an unpleasant few minutes with the Lieutenant Colonel in Command but falling back on his experience as an Other Rank faced by angry authority lots of "Don't know, Sir; all I know is I was ordered to come here and pick up a replacement; you'll have to ask the OC, Sir" kept the conversation short and harmless as far as he was concerned. He was, however, surprised when he collected the replacement; it was new, brand spanking new. He found out from the Sergeant ordered to deal with him that they only had two and they had off loaded the crap one onto the OC yesterday, but now they had to issue the new one!

Jack enjoyed driving it back. The milometer showed 000007 miles! Jack had just started reading *Casino Royale* by Ian Fleming and it tickled him that he had 007 as the mileage. The extra two zeros could be ignored. Jack was normally very simpatico with things mechanical. His dad on his cars and Jack on his motor bikes and cars had taken the proper procedures to run in new or re-bored engines but he couldn't resist the temptation to see what she would do on a couple of long, downhill stretches on the way back. It wouldn't quite reach 70 mph but that was quite exciting on a roughish road and a bit of a bouncy ride. He didn't tell the OC about that bit though. He did tell him that he had stopped after an hour to let the not-yet run in engine cool down, and he had then stopped after a further hour to do the same thing again. He said he had driven most of the way at about 40 mph with the occasional lift to 50 mph when going down long downhill stretches. All of that was true, he did not want to get back to the Depot quickly so he was happy to poodle along and take his time apart from one or two travels into James Bond territory – about which he did not, of course, tell the OC. In fact, so surprised and pleased was the OC that he allowed Jack to be the only other driver authorised to drive the Mini; mainly for collecting visitors from the station and returning them at the end of their visit. It was ironic that Jack, who was the one who drove the Cent over the first Mini, was the only one who was allowed, besides the OC, to drive the second, new one. Once again, Jack's luck had held.

Chapter 28

Visitors to the Depot varied enormously from very interesting to the absolute pain in the arse. The first category included a company which was trying to sell the Army its power/pressure washers. They turned up with the Sales Manager, their General Manager, a couple of Operators and a PR girl who was absolutely gorgeous and obviously intended to charm the OC. They turned up in a fleet of vehicles so Jack had had no chance to collect them from the station.

They off loaded their machine near the Reception shed and proceeded to spray water in a jet at a dirty Centurion which had been parked there for them. The jet could certainly shift the muck, in fact on full power and narrow jet it was extremely dangerous and could cut through metal as they discovered later. Jack was to the forefront having only recently spent a week with the Scrubbers. He wasn't prepared to slide under the Cent as he was wearing his best uniform but it was obvious from the demonstration that it had a weakness. The jet of water, enhanced with chemicals if desired, could not reach behind anything; if it was in full view, it could be sprayed but the back of anything would not be cleaned if the spray could not be directly at it – something which would be quite common when cleaning under a vehicle. The company personnel were visibly dismayed when Jack made this comment but they brightened up when Jack said it would certainly speed up and ease the job of scrubbing but it would still need Scrubbers to reach those areas the spray could not reach.

At that point, the OC ordered Jack to ring the Officers' Mess in Tidworth, where he lived, and warn them that there would be three visitors for lunch plus him and Jack. The two Operators could have dinner in the Cookhouse if they wished – they were obviously not senior enough to rank as officers and be invited to the mess.

When they returned from lunch, they discovered just how powerful the washer jet could be. A three-tonner driver faced with the job of cleaning his lorry and seeing the kit sitting there had decided to take a short cut and use it to wash the three-tonner while the visitors were away. Turning everything to maximum he switched on and out came a spray. A few days before he had been to see Zorro and what better way to start than to wash a 'Z' on the door. He was more than dismayed, but very impressed, to discover that the jet cut a beautiful 'Z' right through the driver's door. The visitors discovered that their kit probably needed a key for security to switch it on and off and the driver discovered just how much a replacement door cost for a Bedford RL.

MOD Sales were so efficient that they arranged for the Jordanians and the Israelis to visit the Depot on the same day to buy tanks. Since they were actually engaged in a war at the time, one had to wonder if they could assemble even one brain cell between them but it made the organisation of the two visits extremely interesting! However, as the Jordanians wanted to buy battle-ready, latest mark, Centurions and the Israelis wanted to buy stripped hulks, they were able to keep them apart in the Depot without too much trouble. The difficulty was when it came to lunch; they could not both be taken to the Mess as they might start fighting over the hors d'oeuvres so the Israelis were taken to the Mess and the Jordanians to the swankiest restaurant in Andover. Jack understood that when the OC complained the Colonel, to whom he answered, dismissed it out of hand as he was the idiot that planned it. The Israeli Colonel was to re-appear again in the future.

Perhaps the worst visit was that of the Brigadier who commanded Vehicle Organisation. He was due to retire and was making a 'leaving' visit tour to each of the units. The visits were spread out over quite a long period of time and Jack's Depot was one of the first in April. Jack accompanied the OC and the Brigadier as they toured the Depot, not for any reason other than to act as a Gopher should something be needed. The tour was going well, they had had lots of notice of him coming so the Depot was as spick and span as it was possible to be but, and there is always a but, the civvies, or one particular one, cocked it up literally. They entered one of the hangars where a vehicle just coming into service in the Army was being readied for issue. The Army had recognized years before that most if not all of the infantry needed to be far more mobile than plodding on two feet and they also needed protection from nuclear or other chemical or biological elements. The current Saracen, Saladin range, six-wheeled vehicles, mobile across rough ground and fitted with rudimentary air cleaning equipment, were not suitable for modern war. They were being replaced by the AFV 430 series – the 432 capable of carrying ten troops closed down for several days, Ambulances, Mortar carriers and lots more not yet built. Facing the Brigadier were 50 432s, a very imposing sight.

The Brigadier exclaimed that these must be the new 432s which the OC confirmed. Walking up to the back of the nearest one, he opened the back door, which was just about the same width as the vehicle to give quick and easy access and egress. There facing them was a bare ginger-haired arse belonging to a male who was positioned between the spread legs of a female and giving her what for! Quickly shutting the door, the Brigadier walked on. The OC whispered in Jack's ear,

"I want him in my office the minute the Brigadier leaves."

"What about the woman?"

"Just take her name." Word of what had happened rocketed around the Depot, rapidly reaching the ears of the Whitley Council Rep (shop steward to normal people) who demanded to see the OC. Such was the OC's rage that he wouldn't see him first which was a pity for the OC because, having given the bloke an enormous bollocking and telling him he would face disciplinary action the following day, the Whitley Council Rep pointed out that both individuals were on their tea breaks, they were in their normal place of work and there wasn't a rule in the Disciplinary Rule Book which forbad bonking! Jack was sent away to search the rules to see what the bloke could be charged with and found almost nothing. There was a rule that said behaviour likely to bring the employer into disrepute was unacceptable and subject to disciplinary action but as two MPs, very much in the public eye had just got away with being caught having affairs it didn't seem likely that anything more than a written warning could apply – certainly not dismissal as the OC wanted. There was also the problem of the woman, against whom the OC did not intend to take action. The Rep was most adamant that they should both be treated equally. Jack simply thought that the OC was too frightened to speak to the woman. In the event, it all became academic.

The Depot was a very noisy place with vehicles roaring and clanking past; lots of shouting going on, it being necessary to shout over the vehicle noise to be heard, so it wasn't unusual that there was a lot of noise outside whilst the meeting between the OC and the Rep was going on. What was unusual was the sound of cheering which gradually became apparent and that was unusual. Sent to discover what was going on, Jack discovered that the fornicating male had locked himself in a Centurion and was busily driving it through every door he could find. He had already smashed three hanger doors off their hinges and crumpled them into scrap metal and was heading for the fourth. As he drove through the door, the by now quite considerable, audience clapped and cheered. Instead of backing out this time, he continued on through the hangar and demolished the back door. He disappeared out of sight to the right with everyone chasing him to see what happened next. They ran around the corner to discover the Cent stopped – it turned out it had run out of petrol; only small amounts being kept in the vehicles whilst in storage – and no sight of the fornicator. A search quickly found him in his office in shed where he had originally been discovered fornicating, speaking on the telephone as though nothing had happened. Jack took the telephone from him and replaced it on its cradle. As he spoke to the fornicator, Jack became worried about his eyes; there was something wrong. Picking up the phone, he called the Guardroom and had two MOD Police attend at the double. He ordered them to escort the fornicator to the Guardroom and keep him in protective custody. He remembered a similar look in the eyes of a recruit who had attempted to commit suicide so he sent for the men in white coats who took him away never to be seen again. It made an interesting final visit for the Brigadier even if it didn't look too good on the OC's record.

The command structure was small and simple. The OC was the ex-para-Major, the 2i/c was also a Major but a long serving Ordnance Corps one who was on his last posting and three Captains. Two of them were also on their last posting and the last one was a 26-year-old with ambition. He was in charge of Tech Admin which functioned primarily as the production control office for the Depot. Made up of about 25 civil servants (it was difficult to know what the actual numbers were because they spent their time on leave, on courses on sick leave compulsory – Jack was astonished to catch the Whitley Council Rep talking to all the staff in Tech Admin on the first day back at work after Christmas. Talking during working hours was forbidden unless it was to do with work and Jack had returned after a pee to find them all assembled around the Rep. Investigating what was going on, Jack was totally amazed to discover that the Rep was handing out slips of paper to the named staff member listing how many sick days they had to take between then and the end of March when a new sick year began. The union was frightened that the number of days of sick pay would be reduced if the number used dropped). Jack was so incensed that he threw him out telling him that if he wanted to talk to his members, he could do so during their tea or lunch breaks not during working hours. The Rep claimed he could speak to his members whenever he liked but Jack didn't believe him nor did he care. Soldiers couldn't skive work like that and no bloody civvy was going to while Jack was around. Jack half expected to be hauled over the coals about that but nothing was said so he assumed the Rep had been trying it on.

The Captain in charge, Edward Barrington-Smythe told Jack that he would be a General in due course and his only concern was that Jack did not cock up in any way to reflect on him. Since he, too, spent time on training course after training course, visiting other units, visiting HQ Vehicle Org on any pretence and taking every single day of his annual leave, Jack hardly saw him during the 10 months or so he spent at the Depot. Having worked in each of the Departments, Jack then filled-in for each of the officers when they were absent. Since Barrington-Smythe was absent more than all the others combined, Jack almost naturally drifted in to the 2i/c position, the official 2i/c, on his last posting was not keen on taking responsibility for anything and was quite happy to let Jack run things even though he was the most junior officer there. Without knowing it, this in command role, when Barrington-Smythe was away, was to have relevance at the end of Jack's time there. When he was to go for an interview in the Civil Service Structure there was a Senior Executive Officer (SEO) in charge, several Executive Officers (EOs), six or so Clerical Officers (COs) and the rest were Clerical Assistants (CAs). Without exception, all of them were underworked. The staffing levels had originally been set during the war and had never been reduced. Much like the Fire Service which had been structured with the majority of staff on duty at night – to deal with the German bombers – and which had not been altered since. The CA who handled the mail would open the envelopes, stamp that day's date on every letter and then record in a book to which file the letter had been directed. Officially that was a 40-hour a week job but in reality it took little more than an hour each day so one hours work, eight hours pay. The rest of the time she read magazines, did the crossword in her paper, knitted or simply gazed out of the window. She could not be given any other work because of strict job demarcation. A problem was to arise a couple of months after Jack's arrival and his knowledge of just how underworked these civil servants were was to prove useful. Ironically, the only group who did work hard, for their full 40 hours and for whom Jack had the greatest respect were the Scrubbers!

Being such a small number of officers having a dining in Mess night every month was impractical so they dined with their wives at a decent restaurant in Andover more or less each month. Barrington-Smythe and his wife, she looked very much like the horse she spent most of her time riding, made it clear that she considered herself the equivalent of the Colonel's wife, especially as the OC wasn't married, or if he was he never mentioned her or attended with her, and the other wives were all the wives of officers who had started in the ranks obviously making her superior. Unfortunately for her, the other wives thought her horse was more intelligent, better looking and much better mannered so that they wished the horse attended. They were far too long in the tooth to be taken in by such snobby drips.

Chapter 29

Although Jack did not have an established post his role as 2i/c Tech Admin, filling in for the other officers when needed and his experience in working in all the departments proved surprisingly valuable in several unexpected ways.

One Monday, the OC said to Jack, on one of the rare occasions when Barrington-Smythe was present to do some actual work,

"Jack, this morning, I do not want you to attend the Planning Meeting." This took place at 10.00 hrs to go through the programme for the week. "I would like you to take a walk around the Depot and see just what goes on when all the bosses are not present; I suspect very little work goes on and it will be good for them to see that someone is watching them." So Jack did.

He made his way around the Depot starting at the back and working his way forward through the various departments. Each of the civilian manned ones he entered caused a stir and it was very evident that more talking than working was going on. In two of the sheds the workers were predominantly soldiers and they were in full flow. The final 'office' he entered was Reception. Since their office window viewed the path up to the office, by the time Jack arrived, all the heads were down and everyone was giving the appearance of working. Entering the office, Jack simply said,

"Good morning, carry on," and wandered around the office. Looking through the window in the back door, Jack knew all his Christmases had come at once. He could see a newly arrived Centurion with the engine covers open. Reaching into the engine bay was a soldier, Vehicle Specialist, working, and sitting on the cross section at the front of the engine bay was a civvy who was the bane of the OC's life. The unions had such a grip on the civilians' conditions of employment that it was almost impossible to dismiss a civil servant no matter how incompetent or worthless he or she was. The disciplinary system set a procedure of an informal verbal warning, then a formal verbal warning, then a first written warning and if that failed to achieve a change in the behaviour, a final written warning. Any sane person would then expect that a further misdemeanour would result in dismissal. Not so. The individual would then be transferred to another department with a clean record only to start all over. This particular individual, Tony Benn, had worked – make that been employed, work would be too strong a term, was now in a department for a second time. He was a complete waste of space but undismissable due to the strength of the unions. He caused problems in every department and by any sane judgement, he should have been got rid of, but he was a union member, paid his union dues and they were determined that he would not lose his job and them his dues. Although sitting and not apparently working which could not be remedied, Benn was smoking. Besides being an unbelievably stupid thing to do with petrol, diesel and other flammable lubricants around the place it was one of the only two or three offences which were subject to summary dismissal for a serious breach of health and safety. Picking up the telephone, Jack rang the Guardroom and ordered that two MOD Police be sent to Reception immediately. When Jack saw them arrive he walked through the door from the office, told them that Benn was smoking, witnessed by himself, and that the dog end was on the ground where Benn was standing and ordered them to arrest him and take him to the Guardroom where he was to be charged with a serious breach of health and safety and locked up until a disciplinary hearing could be convened.

Jack wasn't at all sure of how to proceed up to that point, let alone from there so he returned to the OC's Office where the meeting was just terminating.

"Well," said the OC, "find anything?"

"Not really, Sir, just Benn sitting on an opened engine deck of a Centurion and smoking. I've had him charged by the MOD Police, arrested and locked up in the Guardroom until I find out from you how to proceed from here." It took only a moment for what Jack had said to register before the OC's face split in a huge grin.

"Find that Whitley Council Rep bloke and bring him to the Guardroom immediately." Later developments ruled by tribunals laid out that in a gross misconduct situation and individual should be suspended, and investigation carried out, a disciplinary hearing set up, witnesses questioned etc., etc. On this occasion, the OC simply said to Benn,

"Do you deny that Lt Hughes saw you smoking on the back of a Cent?"

"No, not really."

"Good, you're fired for gross misconduct. A Policeman will escort you to collect any personal belongings and escort you from the Depot." And at that, he turned to the Whitley Council Rep and said, "I don't want to hear any nonsense about an appeal if you value your position as the Whitley Council Rep," and walked away.

On the way back to his office, he explained to Jack that although the Army had no say in who the civvies elected as their Rep, that appointment had to be recognised by the Army and life for the Rep could be all but impossible if that recognition was withheld. There never was an appeal but the OC was delighted with Jack catching him and subsequently being able to fire him. The following day the OC sent for Jack and when he entered the office, he pointed to something on his desk and said,

"Put them on, your promotion has just come through, nothing to do with me of course, it's based on service but I am delighted for you and I hope all the staff here will think it's because you caught that bastard in breach of health and safety and be a bit more careful themselves." Jack put them up, saluted and walked out. Walking around the Depot, the word soon got out that he had been promoted and it seemed to Jack, just a little seemed, that he was now a little bit more important.

Second Lieutenants were at the bottom of the ladder and now he was a little bit further up it.

The social side of the officers was very informal. Although technically they were all members of the Main Mess in Tidworth, having none of their own, they did not want a dining in night monthly when they would have to share the Mess with officers who lived in it. So on the dinning nights in Andover, previously mentioned, Jack became close to the two older Captains, ex-rankers like himself. One of them, Phil Townley, was very keen on fishing and was a member of a local fishing club. Jack went with him a few times but he wasn't keen on joining the club. He was astonished one lunchtime to find Phil sitting by one of the enormous water holes scattered around the Depot apparently fishing. When the air base had been built during the war, the supply of water was somewhat limited so, given the very inflammable nature of the planes, aviation gasoline tanks etc. the Yanks had dug holes, lined them with concrete, about 15 in all, and filled them up with water so that no matter where you were on the airfield, there was a handy water supply nearby. Much of the station had been demolished but the water ponds remained. So Phil, keen fisherman that he was, had been bringing fish back from his fishing trips and placing them in two of the ponds at the back of the depot which were isolated, near nothing, but great for an hour's fishing at lunchtime on a nice day. Jack did join him in that quite frequently.

The other older Captain, Ivan Novicoff, Jack came to know quite well because of the War Dogs. He had been the one to physically show Jack around the Depot when he arrived. Generally he was responsible for the administration of the Depot so the MOD Police answered to him in a peculiar way; he didn't command them as such, that was the responsibility of a branch of the civilian side of the MOD, he was responsible for the War dogs, of which there were six but they too came under the MOD Police and Ivan's command of them was sort of administrative, not military. When they arrived at the kennels on Jack's tour, all six of them started barking like mad, but one, a pure black enormous Alsatian bitch, was attacking the wire and trying really hard to get at them. Jack was concerned that she was doing herself damage as he could see blood appearing in her mouth from the bites of the wire. He was even more worried if she got through the wire.

"Watch this," said Ivan, and reaching into his pocket he took out a pipe and put it in his mouth. The bitch immediately stopped attacking the wire and shrunk back to the back of her kennel. It was amazing. "I think she must have been badly treated by someone who smoked a pipe when she was a pup because of the way she is frightened when one appears." Jack came to know her a little bit, not enough that he wasn't petrified in her presence but when he went to collect the soldiers' pay from the Command Pay Office every Thursday he did so in a Morris Mini Bus, a clapped out vehicle which should have gone to the great scrapyard in the sky years before, but it was totally enclosed, unlike the Landrovers, or the OC's Mini which he wouldn't let them use, and there was room for the two MOD Police, a Dog Handler, a driver and Jack in the front passenger seat as far from the dog as he could get. All six handlers bore the scars of the job. These were not like normal Police dogs, these were war dogs and trained to kill. But the bitch had one more peculiarity – being in a vehicle tamed her. Once she was in the vehicle, she could be stroked, her ears pulled or generally played with. But once she had got her two front feet out of the vehicle and onto the ground, she immediately reverted to killer mode so that she was always kept in the vehicle until last and until the escorts had got a clear distance from the vehicle. She had one more role to play for Jack but that was still some months away.

Chapter 30

A little into June, Jack received a letter from an Education Corps Colonel in Tidworth. It came as a shock. Although Jack knew that he was on a two-year short service commission, the two years still had the best part of six months to go, but it became apparent that the Army was looking six months ahead. The letter described that as at the date his commission was to end, 13 October 1969, he would have served for over six years, in fact six years and two weeks so that he had certain entitlements to a bonus (no pension with such short service), the right to attend a resettlement course of his choice (some were listed attached to the letter – mainly educational courses), the right to time off to attend training at his new employer, if he had one, before his service was up, and it described a number of other things like he could authorise Officers' Record to notify potential employers of whom they had many interested of his imminent leaving of the Army so that they could contact him if they were interested in him as a potential recruit. It was only when Jack turned the letter over, mainly to see the signature block, that he saw a final sentence that according to so and so regulations he was entitled to apply for an extension to his short service or even to apply for a regular commission. The writer, a Lt Col in the RAEC, finished by asking Jack to contact him ASAP with his choice(s).

Jack had not seriously thought about what he would do when his commission expired. Now he was forced into doing so before he really wanted to. He spoke to both Phil and Ivan as they were in a somewhat similar situation. They did not have the option of extending their service because they had just about reached the maximum age limit. They were intrigued by the courses on offer and the opportunity to finish their service a bit early. They had not known about the service to employers through Officers Records. Both of them, separately, had come to the conclusion that their pensions would not be enough to live on comfortably and had heard about other officers in their situation being employed by banks as cashiers. That attracted them, the money was good, the hours reasonable and some of the perks appealing. They would have no responsibility to speak of, something that attracted them after years of responsibility in the Army. Their advice was to suss out the courses and see if there was one that attracted Jack. They also told him about the 'bricks and mortar course'. It was designed for those who had spent their time in married quarters, or the Mess if single, and who therefore had never done any maintenance work on their property because it was always done by the property maintenance people. Even changing a blown lightbulb was done by them so that skills like plumbing, bricklaying, plastering, wall papering and decorating were unknown. The course, running for four weeks, remedied that.

Jack was not sure what he wanted to do. The Army, in one way or another, had been his life since he was 11 years old and he was now approaching 25, only 12 days after his potential demob. At 25, he would become entitled to Married Quarters and a higher rate of Marriage Allowance. Currently life was very expensive, paying rent for a private house and with the lower rate of Marriage Allowance they would not have been able to survive without Janet working.

Talking to her about his options the favoured one to emerge was to obtain an extension for at least another year, possibly two and save hard during that time ready for civilian life. So Jack wrote the required letter to the Commander of Vehicle Organisation requesting the extension. He received a letter a few days later to attend an interview with the Brigadier in Nottingham. He knew it was a new Brigadier but not who it was. The name on the letter meant nothing to him. Come the day, he dressed in his best bib and tucker and left early in the morning so that he would be in plenty of time for his 14.00 hrs appointment. Ushered in by a Staff Sergeant, he knew before he was asked to take a seat that his trip had been a complete waste of time. Sitting behind a huge desk was the same Brigadier who had torn up his letter at the Junior Leaders Regiment. Then, Jack had run a bluff and succeeded with a Lt Col, one of the jolly good chaps being crucified rather than a junior 2nd Lt who definitely was not one of us – good god he was from the ranks!

The Brigadier did not greet Jack but launched into why should the Army agree to extend his service? Jack had pre-prepared a selling pitch about how valuable he now was to the Army and how much he could contribute having had a long training – it was only proper that he now contribute at a higher level. He did not expect to be asked why he disagreed with his OC about the tradesmen doing so much PT. This told Jack that the Brigadier and his OC had had a very personal conversation about him. It was clear from the other questions he was asked that his career had been picked over to fault find even to asking him about the recruit who had attempted suicide when he commanded a Recruit Platoon at the Depot. The Brigadier told him that he would hear in the next few days and Jack was dismissed. He knew as he drove back that his time in the Army was over; the old boys' network did not like him – he had bested one of their own– so his career was finished.

He told Janet that night what had happened and she surprised him by saying that she was glad; she had never really wanted to be an officer's wife and she was looking forward to not being one as soon as possible. A couple of days later, the OC sent for Jack. He had a letter in his hand and he said,

"Mr Hughes, I have here an answer to your request to extend your commission—"

Jack interrupted and said, "I know what the answer is, my face doesn't fit so on 14 October, I will be a civilian." Jack simply looked at the OC. He tried to put into the look all the contempt that he could for the prat sitting in front of him but it probably didn't work.

"Well, yes, that's right," he said. Jack simply turned around and walked out – if he thought he was going to get a salute, there was more chance of him flying upwards with his parachute to the planes that he was so fond of jumping out of than that; after all, what could he do?

Phil and Ivan were probably more upset than Jack was. Jack had had the time from the interview to adjust to the fact that he was a persona non grata; in many ways, he had felt that since the Junior Leaders. Driving back from Nottingham, it was a long way and he didn't push his Viva to more than 50 mph, he had considered his situation which he then discussed with Janet when he got back home. He would be 25 a few days after his demob. If he were to stay in what extra skills would he learn that would help in civilian life? In an extra year, he would have not have learned any more valued by civilian skills; maybe at 25, he was getting a bit old to become a trainee for some new skill. Phil and Ivan would be 55 when they left and they would not really have a much greater skill set then than Jack had at this moment. Their intention to get a little dead-end job that carried little or no responsibility was fine for them because they had their pension to boost any earned income. Jack would not have a pension nor, of course, was the option to extend now open. So the big job now was to find a worthwhile career outside the Army and that meant going to see the Education Corps Lt Col and discuss the courses open to him and their merits and demerits.

The guy was a nice bloke, put all rank away and just went through the options. It didn't help that every now and again he kept bringing up the issue of extending his short service commission or changing to a regular one. At first Jack just ignored it but it became obvious that he saw his job as being one to keep young officers in the Army that Jack had to tell him that he did not have that option. He was quite thrown by that, he quite quickly changed his attitude and swept through the interview at quite a pace. Jack didn't mind, the sooner he was out the better but he did need to know the options open to him and in that respect he did get copious details of courses available to him.

Study over the following days eliminated most of the courses. Jack didn't have a job to go to and until he did, he could not select any of the specialist educational/specific skill type courses. He did find letters starting to arrive from potential employers routed through Officers' Records. Some simply told him about themselves and left it to Jack to apply to them. Some were more forward and contained invitations to interviews. One from an industrial gas company contained a professional brochure listing all the different careers they had and invited Jack to apply. The problem as far as Jack was concerned was that the brochure stressed, for every section, the requirement of having a degree. Jack didn't have one but one of the specialisms, in Personnel, attracted him so he replied pointing out that although he didn't have a degree, he was interested in the Personnel specialisation. He received a letter by return inviting him to an interview in Hammersmith, just off the A4. The Head Office was a massive tower block and it was obvious that it was a first-class company of enormous size.

Jack was ushered into a palatial office on the top floor to meet the person responsible for Graduate Recruitment. After the rather banal pleasantries, the first thing Jack said was,

"I feel I must point out that I do not have a degree and I feel like rather a fraud being here."

"We certainly do concentrate on graduate recruitment here but we have found over the last few years that the intake into Personnel has been somewhat lacking. Graduates from universities are supposed to be well-rounded individuals having completed their degree. And this is mainly true of the academic streams, chemistry, physics and similar. However in Personnel, the graduates we have interviewed are too young, immature and inexperienced to deal with personal issues which they face in that role and it is not until they've got a few years under their belts that they have become fully effective. Three years ago, we recruited a chap in the same position as yourself, ex-short service, not so very different in age from the graduates but a world away from them in experience of life, maturity and understanding of people and their problems. He and the three we have subsequently employed have proved exceptional in almost every way so please do not feel a fraud or inadequate you are very qualified for the role we are seeking to fill."

He went on to describe the training programme, which would last six to 12 months depending on the department he would eventually be employed in. Whilst training, he would be based at the HQ they were currently in but once trained, he could find himself working anywhere from the far north of Scotland to a unit in Bournemouth on the south coast. He asked many questions which Jack had no trouble answering and when he left he felt he had done well. The interviewer explained that the training courses commenced at the start of October and they would be in touch with Jack within the next three weeks to invite him to a final interview if he had been successful in this one. Jack returned to Kimpton confident that he would be asked to the second interview but he was going to have to discuss with Janet a job where they could be posted anywhere in the UK and moved at relatively short notice to another site.

Chapter 31

At the Monday production meeting, there was a surprise. The Veh Org Commander, Brigadier Champion, he of the torn-up letter fame, came in with the OC. All the civilian heads of departments were excused and just the seven officers sat down. It was clear from his first word that he was in a bit of a funk.

"You will be aware that negotiations have been going on with the MOD civil servants about their claim for a substantial pay rise, a reduction in the working week, an increase in holidays and an increase in sick pay and sick days. I can tell you that the Government has been negotiating for several weeks and it looks like, because they are not going to agree in any significant way with the union claims that the civvies will be going on strike next week. Even without them, you still have to get all your deliveries out in that week, some of them are extremely important, and you will have to achieve it with the 85 soldiers you have. You will have to break the strike, unpopular as it will make you, because those deliveries will have to go out. Clearly 85 soldiers cannot match the output of 250 civil servants so I need you to come up with a plan of how you intend to achieve this." Jack thought, *There's a lot of 'you' in all that and not one 'we', typical.* Jack sat still as it was for the OC to speak, he was after all in charge and got the mega bucks for it. However, as the silence extended, Jack started to think he hadn't got any idea. Clearly as the Brigadier had put it, 85 men couldn't do the work of 250. Or could they? As the most junior officer there, he waited for any of the others to speak but neither the 2i/c or any of the three captains said a word so Jack thought, right time for some fun.

"If I may, Sir, it is true that there are nominally 250 civvies but that doesn't mean that we get 250 X 40 hrs work a week from them." As he spoke, Jack got up and walked to the flip chart stand just to the left of the chair at the head of the table. Adjusting it to suit what he was going to do, he forced the Brigadier and the OC to move down the table. Picking up a red marker pen, he wrote,

250 X 40 = 10,000 man hours.

"However, no one works 40 hours, they lose hours for:
1 hour for lunch = 1 hour
2 X ½-hour tea breaks = 1 hour plus 1 hour lunch =2 hours total per day lost therefore multiplied by 5 days = 10 hours per week lost per individual.
Therefore 30 hours X 250 = 7,500 hours at 100% efficiency.

"One cannot assume that they actually work all those hours at 100% efficiency. For example, the mail girl in Tech Admin actually works 1 hour per day = 5 hours per week. That is 5/35 = about 15% efficiency.

"Applying 15% efficiency to the whole depot means 15% x 7,500 hours = 1,125 hours generated. Clearly that is an unrealistic low but if we applied 50% to 7,500 hours = 3,370 hours of work generated. Probably quite accurate but if you wanted to try 75% efficiency that would be 5,625 hours. The Scrubbers are probably the closest to 100% but there are only five of them so their total hours are unlikely to affect the grand total very much. I favour the 50% having worked amongst the civvies in each department. However, whichever is the most accurate, we need to look at what the soldiers produce.

"To match the civvy output then, 85 soldiers have to generate about 3,500-3750 hours. What do they do now?

"85 soldiers X 40 hours = 3,400 nominal hours, not too far short of the civvies' total! However they too, do not actually work 40 hours.

"The same as the civvies, they lose 2 hours per day lunch and tea breaks. Further they lose 1 and 1/2 hours per Tuesday and Thursday for PT. Nominally, the PT is before work but with showering, dressing and moving to their places of work, they ensure they get their hour or so back. They also lose 3 and a ½ hours for Wednesday sports afternoon. That means:

Total	*40*
Less tea/lunch	*10*
	= 30pw
Less pt+	*6.5*
Equals	*=23.5 hrs pw generated hours.*

Not a very impressive efficiency."

Jack thought he would not have a better chance to put the boot in so he said,

"That is, of course why we have so much overtime, especially as the civvies work slowly to spin it out, roughly two hours for everyone a soldier would take to do the task at time and a third or time and a half and even double time if they work on a Sunday – wonderful for them! No wonder the overtime is so high and the civvies love it." The Brigadier gave the OC a look which meant they would be having a meeting later that the OC would not enjoy.

"Of course with just 23.5 X 85 = 1,997.5 soldier hours we will still be:

Civvies	*3,500*
Soldiers	*-1,997*
	=1,553 short.

"But there is a way that we could get closer.

"Scrap the PT and sport for the one week = 6.5 hrs saved per soldier.

"That generates a 30-hour week X 85 = 2,550 hours.

"Then start them at 08.00 hrs, only half an hour earlier than normal. Then move the finish time to 18.00 hrs. Obviously a longer day but hardly one that compares to jumping out of an aeroplane for a five-day exercise where the hours can be 24 per day. That increases the day to 10 hours, less half an hour for lunch and a half hour tea break at 16.00 hours making a nine-hour day. In the morning, they'll get their tea brought to them by those old tea trolleys stored in shed three, so no tea break as such in the morning. The SLALs (sick, lame and lazy), three of them, who are only on the sick because they are determined not to do all that PT and sports, will agree that it would be much better for them to do this than find that they will have terrible problems getting their pensions paid to them when they are demobbed which might mean they would have to wait six or even 12 months for them to come through because I had to go around with the tea wagon and didn't have time to do their pension admin."

The Brigadier interrupted,

"How do you know they will?"

"Because I'll back the hearse up to the door and let them smell the flowers, and besides, I asked them on Friday afternoon when they came in for a meeting with me and faced with the option they agreed. They also will be coming off the sick to contribute their hours to the schedule otherwise the calculation is x 83 not 85."

"How on earth did you know what I would be saying today?"

"Easily guessable, I have thought about this since last week when it became clear that there would probably be a strike. May I continue?" Without waiting for an answer, Jack carried on. "I propose an extended half hour's break at 16.00 hrs to revitalise them ready for the final one and a half hours of the day.

"This means:

85 soldiers X 9 hours X 5 days = 3,825 man hours of actual work. We would therefore generate more work than the civvies do but of course, normally there would be the soldiers' contribution of 1,997 hours which we cannot count twice I am not totally sure of my efficiency figures for obvious reasons because they are based on guesses of performance but I believe we would still come up short of a normal week. Also, I know that there are a number of soldiers at Nottingham who could contribute to the work hours here. They are the Corps football and rugby teams and they spend all their time just playing games. There are more than 40 of them and they could easily be temporarily transferred here for the week, possibly a few days before for some training. With those 40x9x5= 1,800 additional hours. We could also look at seven-day working – a not unusual situation for soldiers but I would keep that in reserve for now. We could perhaps think about introducing a 'job and knock' system which would generate a lot more work in the same hours and maybe even exceed the civvy total."

The Brigadier and the OC looked as though they were about to explode. The Brigadier was the first to speak,

"They are approaching the championships and it would damage, even cripple their chances if they stopped their training now, no, no, that can't be done."

Jack said,

"I thought oh so important sport would be more important than these oh so important deliveries, so it might be appropriate to consider that, two of the new vehicle suppliers are on their Wakes' Weeks shut down next week and that will reduce the vehicle inputs here next week by about 15%. In addition, 25% are

returns for disposal so that we could just run them into Reception for the safety checks and then run them around to Shed 5 which is pretty well empty. They can just stand there until we can get around to them some time in the future. We are going to be about 19% short on manpower but the workload is going to be reduced by at least 40% so operating my proposals will probably mean that we can exceed the expected workload and make a dent in the following week, especially if you two," looking at Ivan and Phil, "could do a bit of vehicle shifting in the afternoons." Looking at Darby-Smith he said, "You, of course cannot drive or do any of the work of the other departments because you have never worked in them, so perhaps you could do all the Tech Admin work necessary to keep vehicles moving and if there is any time left over you could go on a course or something to impress your superior officers." Darby-Smith looked daggers at him. Jack walked over to his seat and sat down. He had not invited questions and indeed he didn't get any bar two from Darby-Smith.
"What's job and knock?"
"It's where once the allocated work has been completed the individuals can knock off and go home. It encourages the work to be done quicker. It generates a lot of work fast but you have to watch the quality especially." Darby-Smith then asked his killer question,

"What are you going to be doing whilst the rest of us are working?"

"I'll be leading a team of three scrubbing those vehicles which need to be done now."

Nobody spoke. Then Ivan Novicoff stood up, put on his hat and placed his cane under his arm. Stamping to attention as only an ex-CSM can, he said,

"I'm going off and get some refresher training on driving to help move vehicles. How you two numpties can sit there with the view that this man's Army can do without a young officer like Mr Hughes I do not know," and with that he turned more towards Jack, threw up a tremendous salute and walked out. No one knew that Ivan had received his demob date that morning and thus could not care less what the two senior officers thought. Phil saluted and left saying nothing. Jack thought of staying just to force the Brigadier or the OC to dismiss him but thought better of it and simply left.

The OC adopted Jack's suggestion with almost no alterations other than the sports teams skivers did not appear and the week progressed very well as Jack had forecast. Indeed by Thursday afternoon, they were so well ahead that they could have finished for the week if it wasn't for the vehicles coming in the next day. These were completed by lunchtime and so Jack asked the OC if the soldiers could be dismissed for the day. Jack also said,

"I'm also thinking of saying to the parade when I dismiss them that I am going to suggest to you that it is clear from how well we've done this week that it is clear that we do not really need the civvies at all and they can stay on strike forever. I am sure that will soon spread to the civvies and if they think they'll lose their cushy little numbers, they'll all be back on Monday." The OC smiled for the first time in the week and replied,

"Excellent idea, Mr Hughes, do it." So Jack did and the civvies came back on Monday. Whether it was because of what Jack had said, they never found out. Jack, of course, was given no credit whatsoever for his plan but the OC did receive a 'well done' letter from the Brigadier which he showed to no one. But Jack knew about it because the Mail girl opened it and told him.

The following Friday not only did they not get away on time, but they found themselves working over. Just as Jack was heading for the gate at 16.30 hrs, the OC stuck his head out of his office window and shouted at Jack to "shut the gate because we've got a job on". The soldiers were not happy, for it was they who would have to do the work, the civvies could not be ordered to do overtime, only asked. And following the conversation the OC had had with the Brigadier, overtime had been reduced considerably.

An emergency order had come in from the MOD to get six of latest mark Saladins, with all their kit, ready for loading to RAF Brize Norton to be there by 09.00 hrs on the Sunday to be flown to Nigeria for use in Biafra where the Nigerian army was getting a bit of a kicking by the Biafran militia. In the event, it wasn't much of a job and they were ready for collecting by the RCT by 12.00 hrs on the Saturday. Watching them leave Jack did not know that they would reappear, if briefly, in his life almost 50yrs later.

(In 2015 Frederick Forsyth was to publish a book 'The Outsider' in which he describes being chased down the backstreets of a town in Biafra by a Saladin firing its machine gun at him. Jack, fascinated by the book and enthralled by the story, wrote to Mr Forsyth telling him of his role in getting those Saladins to Biafra and that they were armed with medium machine guns not heavy as Mr Forsyth described. Being very much a gentleman of the old school he wrote back politely to Jack thanking him for the information pointing out that they certainly seemed to be heavy machine gun bullets when they were being fired at him and wishing Jack well with his attempts to get his own book published. It is a small world this global one)

Chapter 32

Most of the rest of his time at Ludgershall, Jack spent preparing for a civilian life. Besides the job with the gases company, he attended an interview with a company providing repair and replacement part, radiators, silencers etc. to motor repair garages. The interview was conducted in Reading by their Personnel Director. Shown in the first thing Jack noticed was a little name display which said, 'Lt Col J Hythe (ret'd) on the front of the desk. He looked like a Colonel and he spoke like one. After the introductions he started with,

"Played rugger of course?"

"Yes, Sir."

"First fifteen?"

"At school and for the 6th Training Bn RASC in Yeovil."

"Any other sports?"

"Cross country, school cross country champion five years running and Wessex Division cross country champions 1964."

"You're just the sort of young chap we need. I'll write to you with an offer. Any questions?"

"Not at the moment, Sir."

"Good chap, on your way."

Jack couldn't salute but he did sort of draw himself to attention before walking smartly out. Nice to know he had a job if nothing better came up but the last thing he wanted to do was to join a civvy army where the interviewing was a joke and almost certainly the Colonel would want to continue as a Colonel.

He also received a letter from a Senior Inspector of Taxes who turned out to be the recruiter for the southern part of England. It invited him to a preliminary interview in Southampton if he might be interested in joining the Civil Service. As it meant time out of the depot and a pleasant drive to Southampton, and as he hadn't as yet found a job that attracted him above all others, he wrote accepting the invitation. Turning up on the due date, he wore his uniform to show off his medal ribbon and his new seniority as a Lieutenant. He was shown into quite a large office, he was shortly due to discover what size meant in the Civil Service, and after the normal pleasantries, the interview started with an explanation of the Senior Inspectors role in recruitment and then his first question was,

"What educational qualifications do you have?"

"Eight 'O' levels, the equivalent of five 'A' levels and, of course, my commission."

"What do you mean by the equivalent of five 'A' levels?"

"I had to take the Civil Service Commission entrance examination for RMA Sandhurst. It's a matriculation type exam where you take five subjects and have to pass in all five. I did." The guy looked at Jack.

"Well, we don't actually recognise that exam so as far as we would be concerned, your educational qualifications would be eight 'O' levels." Jack sat there astonished. Drawing himself together he said,

"But it's your exam; you set it and you mark it. The Army accepts it, why don't you?"

"We simply don't, but I wouldn't worry about it after one year; you would be able to take the exam for Executive Officer and I'm sure a clever chap like you would pass with flying colours."

"Does that mean I would join as a Clerical Officer?"

"Yes."

"I will have to think about that. What would be the pay, holidays etc.?"

"I would go through all those things plus where you would be working. Of course, like the Army we do move people around, especially on promotion – we don't normally like promoting someone to EO in the department in which they were a CO and probably friendly with all the other COs. Giving orders to recent, even current friends, can be quite difficult so our policy in such circumstances is to move the CO when they are promoted." Jack thought that as a policy that was quite sensible. When he had been promoted to Lance Corporal, and still shared the same room with the three other Privates who had been there with him as a Private, it could have been very difficult apart from him charging his best mate when the RSM was with him in Aden, which did definitely make life easier. However, Jack was to witness this policy falling apart. Traditionally not many women had applied for promotion to the EO levels and above. Most that did were single. The married women were mainly a lower wage earner than their husband so that the idea they would have to move and take their husband away from his current job to a who knows what job somewhere else was a no, no, for them and they therefore, often, did not apply for promotion. However, the world was changing and women were demanding to be promoted and to be allowed to stay where they were. The management started allowing this and the policy simply fell apart. It meant that Jack could probably refuse to move on promotion to an EO in a year's time if that was what he wanted. The interview ended with the Senior Inspector of Taxes, an SEO, saying that he would be writing to Jack following the interview and although he probably should not say it, that letter would be offering him a post.

Jack was to experience one of the stupidities rife in the Civil Service shortly before he was demobbed. The Army was seeking to modernise, streamline and improve its admin systems. A Vehicle Specialist working on a tank might require a new nut or bolt, the old one being too rusty to be used again. To obtain the nut or bolt, he would go to the stores and fill in a form in triplicate and the item would then be forthcoming. Someone had recognised that this was stupid. The nut only cost a couple of pennies, if that, but the system required a considerable expense in the paperwork. A figure was becoming standard that 20% of the materials represented 80% of the costs. So 80% of the materials represented 20% of the costs. So the decisions was taken that supplies of the cheap, 80% items, like nuts and bolts would be put out on trays and anyone needing one would simply pick it up and use it, no paperwork needed or produced. As an idea, it was brilliant but no one knew exactly which items fell into the 20% category and which fell into the 80% which would not need accounting for. So a Cost Accountant, an SEO, would be coming to the Depot for three months or so to do the work of placing each item into the 20% or 80% category. Once that had been done he would move on to the next Depot and an Accountant, an EO, would be based in the Depot to run the system. So far so good.

The problems arose as to where the Accountant would be located. Although the Depot had loads of space in the huge hangers, what they didn't have was lots of office space. The Americans had built the airfield and hangars in no time flat. The offices were wood or plasterboard built in a couple of the hangars. All were occupied. Eventually an office, currently full of builder materials was identified and cleared out. It was outfitted with a desk, a couple of chairs, wire coat stand and a couple of filing cabinets. The Whitley Council Rep took one look at it, took out his tape measure and declared the office, having measured it, to be nine inches too small in width and 10 inches too short in length. It did not have the right sized carpet and the coat stand should be wood not wire work. The filing cabinets were basic, rather than wood appearance and they would have to be changed. The desk was inadequate and would have to be replaced with a larger, more expensive one. The whole office was entirely inappropriate for such a senior post. The OC looked at him as though he was about to practice his silent killing on him but eventually had to agree and the changes were made.

A bit pathetic, especially as this SEO, whoever he was to be, would have a bigger and better fitted out office than the OC and he would only be there for three months or so. Jack wasn't there when the SEO finished setting up the system but he heard about it. The SEO having finished, the Whitley Council Rep reappeared with his tape measure, measured and then declared that this office was too large for an EO and was fitted out to a standard higher than the entitlement of that rank. The walls had to be put back to their original positions and all the furniture changed. It was unbelievable, especially as the SEO was a Cost Accountant sent there to save money! The Civil Service proved by its every action that it was peopled by dopes.

Besides the information coming to him via Officers' Records Jack was scouring the papers for job adverts. In terms of numbers the Daily Telegraph and the Guardian were the best. However those in the Guardian were nearly all Civil Service or Government-sponsored jobs requiring qualifications Jack did not have but more importantly didn't fancy. The Daily Telegraph had several that caught his eye, of ten demanding qualifications, usually academic, that he did not have but that did not stop him applying using the experience of the gasses company as a starter. The Sunday Times also carried quite a few vacancies, but Jack hadn't seen any to attract him.

One of them in the Daily Telegraph particularly caught his eye. The job title was Training Development Officer for the Clothing and Footwear Industry Training Board in Northern Ireland. The detail described that they were particularly looking for someone with expertise/experience of training instructors. Three things pulled him to this job. He had been sent on the 'How to Train Instructors Course' at the Army School of Education when he was stationed at the Junior Leaders Regiment in Deepcut, so he could legitimately claim to have considerable experience in this field even if he did not possess a degree which was also listed as a requirement.

Secondly, he was remembering when he was sort of dragooned into going into the Spiritualist Church in Colchester. The medium there had said that she could see him with two things (she didn't know the proper name!) on his shoulder showing his rank and that he was in Ireland. At the time, it meant nothing, he had just failed the Regular Commissions Board and there was therefore no prospect of him becoming an officer, nor was there much chance of him being posted to Ireland. Over the years since then he had attended, with Janet, a few services in the Spiritualist Church but the forecast of him being in Ireland had been entirely forgotten till now.

Finally, the money and terms and conditions were better than any others he had seen.

So he applied and was not too surprised to receive an invitation to an interview in Belfast. Flying from Gatwick to Belfast was an experience; it was a foggy morning and he dreaded the flight being cancelled or delayed as all his timings were a bit tight. In the event, the BAC 111 was fitted with foggy conditions equipment enabling them to fly when many others couldn't. They even surprised all the rabbits at Aldergrove Airport – there were hundreds of them along the side of the runway on the grass, Jack had never seen so many. Amazingly when the airport was moved a year or two later, the rabbits moved with it! The interview was a group one, a surprise to Jack, but it at least allowed him to see and measure up the opposition. There were private interviews with three people there asking the questions, one of them the guy who would be his boss if he were successful, one who was the Secretary to three of the Training Boards and one, a woman, who said not a word during the whole day. One group task involved discussing how to solve a problem in a company where the Cutter, the only one in the Company, was nearing retirement and there did not exist anyone else in the company who could do that job. He had, for a couple of years, point blank, refused to show anyone else how to do it and now they were looking at a problem. What could be done about it?

Jack's first thought was, as he had done over the years, find a replacement who was a qualified Cutter by advertising in the paper using an Agency and once the replacement had been found fire the awkward sod. However this was a Training Board and the answer they would regard as the best one would probably be one involving training. As the conversation in the group of six developed, Jack started to feel that the competition was between him and a middle-aged man who had told them he had worked in the industry in a management position for many years and he was starting to suggest going down the disciplinary road with this Cutter. Jack came out with asking why the Cutter would not help with training his replacement as he would have to retire anyway, was there a problem with him regarding the retirement? They had been told that they could ask any questions they wanted and when Jack asked this they were told that he had a problem that his mortgage would not be paid off until seven months after his retirement date and if he was forced to retire at 65, then he could not afford to pay the mortgage on his pension. In that case, Jack suggested there were two ways to go, find a replacement and retire him at the due date or, if his knowledge of the idiosyncrasies of the cutting role were so complicated and important to get him in and agree that he could retire at 65 but he would then be employed as a consultant to train his replacement, thus transferring the needed knowledge whilst not breaking their policy that everyone retire at 65. Others came out with other suggestions and the interview concluded with them all being asked to follow the Board Secretary apart from Jack who was asked to wait behind.

The Board Secretary soon returned and when he did, he offered Jack the job. They had a conversation regarding the pay, terms and conditions, removal expenses etc. Jack asked when they would need an answer which rather threw them back. Jack explained that besides talking it over with his wife, he would, after their meeting, visit some estate agents to get an idea of what rental accommodation was available and how much it would cost both in Belfast and Londonderry, where he would be based after his six-month induction training – something that had not been clear from the advert and he did not know how his wife would react to moving and then moving again. He made all sorts of reassuring noises that he was sure it would be alright, how much he wanted the job etc. but he also needed some time before he committed himself as he had a couple of other interviews to attend for other jobs which had already been set up. They said that they would be putting the job offer in writing, containing all the relevant terms and conditions and they agreed that Jack would respond to that within seven days. As the interview had taken place in the Board's offices in the city centre, there were plenty of estate agents within a few hundred yards and Jack eventually caught the flight back having arranged to receive copies of the property newspapers each week and details of properties coming up for rent. They had provisionally agreed that, subject to him being able to find a property, his likely commencement date would be around the beginning of November, two weeks or so after his demob date.

He was a little surprised to find the job offer in the mail the following day! One of the jobs he went for an interview for was a bit of an unknown. Described as a Management Assistant to the Managing Director it sounded a bit like a Chief Clerk's role but at a higher level. Foreign travel was involved assisting at conferences and acting a bit like an Aide de Camp. Jack arrived at the very plush offices in Mayfair five minutes before the appointed time. He was made to wait for almost an hour before being shown into a palatial office where the MD, he assumed, no introductions were made, was sitting behind a huge desk. There was one chair in front of it and it had been placed in such a way that the sun, which was streaming in, shined right into Jack's eyes as he sat down. Realising how uncomfortable it would be, Jack stood up and moved it to the other end of the desk not in the direct sunlight. He was about to say,

"I hope you don't mind but that sun was bothering me," when the MD spoke,

"That's a bloody awful suit you are wearing." The suit was brand new, he had only worn it once, to the interview in Belfast and the comment was a bit one step too far. He had been made to wait for so long with no explanation or apology; the placing of the chair in the sun was obviously deliberate and now the insult regarding his suit. Looking at the guy, he said,

"I don't go a bundle on yours either, I don't like being kept waiting for an hour without any sort of apology and I certainly don't like playing games with chairs." And with that, he stood up and started for the door. The MD said,

"No, stop. Your reaction is absolutely excellent and just what I'm looking for in an assistant. No questions can deliver the knowledge of your character that your behaviour has just demonstrated so I am sure we will be able to get along just fine." Jack thought about his answer, the fact that he had already been offered a job he quite fancied and he said,

"I don't think I want to work for someone who believes that behaviour like that is acceptable. Good day to you," and walked out. It was to be several years before he came across a description of stress interviewing, being advocated by the Yanks of course, which that interview had clearly been. He didn't agree with it at the time nor did he later – it pissed him off and so he walked away; how many other suitable candidates did the same thing?

Chapter 33

The Education Corps Colonel had been quite uncomfortable when Jack said he wanted to take advantage of his right to a resettlement course. Jack was entitled to one because he had been in the Army for more than six years – the fact that he had only been in for six years and two weeks was neither here nor there, it was more than six years and thus he was entitled. From the list on offer, he had chosen the 'bricks and mortar' one. The information and skills gained would be useful, none of the other courses would help with his work for the Training Board and it would get him away from the Depot and any soldiering work for four weeks. The Colonel had delayed everything, hoping that Jack would change his mind and stay in the Army and he had to be reminded a second time that the Army did not want Jack before he stirred himself. The course started five weeks before Jack was due to be demobbed so he would only have one week left when he returned from Aldershot – absolutely bang on as far as Jack was concerned.

Jack travelled to Aldershot on the Sunday night; for the rest of the course, he would travel early on the Monday morning but he wanted time to settle in, find his way around etc. before the course started. On Monday morning, a group of about 40 people were milling about the enclosed sheds where the course was to be run. Jack was the only young man there. Unexpectedly, there were RAF and two Navy men there in the mix. The Major running the course called them to order and told them to pair off as some of the work they would be doing needed two people. Most of them were wearing overalls and most of them had badges of rank of some sort or other attached to them. Jack hadn't bothered, the Army didn't want him and he therefore did not want the Army and he certainly wasn't going to expend the cost in buying rank badges and sewing them on himself. Most of the Army officers were Majors or Captains, the Airforce were Flight Lieutenants or Squadron Leaders and both the Navy men were Lieutenants, as, of course, was Jack but a Navy Lieutenant was roughly equivalent to an Army Captain, which left Jack as the youngest and most junior and a much older man wearing no badges of rank as his pair. When the Major approached Jack's pair, saluted, and said,

"General Sir Adam Solly, a pleasure to meet you, Sir. I hope this course will provide what you are looking for and it there is anything you need please do not hesitate to bring it to my attention, Sir."

"Thank you I certainly will," said the General. Jack was the only one close enough to hear the "Creep," which followed and see the twinkle in his eye. Looking at the General, Jack thought, *I am going to enjoy this.*

The course was programmed to cover woodworking/carpentry, plumbing, decorating, plastering, bricklaying as the main subjects but there were gaps in the programme to include any subjects the attendees wanted regarding household maintenance. The one subject they were not going to cover was electricity other that the most basic how to change a fuse, change/wire a plug. It was thought too dangerous for the short time available. They were split into two groups and Jack's started with woodworking/carpentry. It was mainly to teach measuring cutting and jointing pieces of wood to form simple items like toolboxes, stools etc. Once those fundamentals had been learned, then the students could make whatever they wanted to back home.

The first item they started on, as individuals, was to make a simple toolbox. About 15 inches square and divided into four quarters with a simple carrying handle it would teach measuring, planning, smoothing, corner joints, a flat base producing a useful little bits and pieces carrier. Jack still had his 50 years later and it was packed with fuses, plugs, insulating tape, odd screws, washers and thingummy bobs. The Generals was probably consigned to the dustbin within a few days. None of the corners were square, it wasn't flat, there were gaps through which quite large items could fall and all told it was a disaster. The biggest disaster though was the General used up all the plasters in the first aid kit patching up his cuts. The Major took Jack aside and said,

"The General is clearly not a man of manual techniques. I would like you to work with him as a pair as much as possible. Alright?" Jack could only agree.

The third morning of the course, there was a tap at Jack's door in the Mess. When he opened it, the General's driver was standing there.

"The General was wondering if you would like a lift to the Centre, Sir." Jack was surprised. Generals, especially full Generals, did not normally offer lifts to Lieutenants. Jack had already formed the opinion that it was a bit funny, a bit ironic that as a pair he was the second most junior officer rank in the Army and the General was the second most senior. They had 'second' in common but that was all. Jack said,

"That's very kind of the General but I thought a walk in the fresh air would just set me up right for the day, so, thank you but no thanks."

"You don't quite understand, Sir, the General wonders if you would like a lift." Even though he did not have much longer in the Army, Jack knew enough from the tone of the way it was said the second time that he was expected to accept the lift so he did. Jack rode with the General, mornings and evenings for the rest of the course. Their conversation, led by the General covered all sorts of subjects but Jack began to suspect that the General had had access to his records because odd comments seemed to indicate he knew far more about Jack than Jack had let on. On Thursday before the end of the course on the Friday, he came right out and asked Jack if he would like to stay in the Army because if he would that could be arranged. Jack explained that he had been refused an extension to his short service commission and that had caused him to take stock of himself and what he would have to offer a potential employer. He had now also had the experience of applying for jobs in Civvy Street and that now held no fears. He concluded that he would not increase his employability very much for each year he stayed in because he would obviously be doing Army-type things for the main part. Crucially, he would be getting older and would find it more and more difficult to start a new, worthwhile career in Civvy Street. He quoted several of the officers on the course who had all said, as had officers at the Depot that the pension was inadequate to live on in retirement and they were all seeking little top up jobs, none of them wanted to get jobs which carried responsibility having had enough of that in the Army or the RAF. In his case he wouldn't receive a pension and could not rely on obtaining a long enough extension to get one so he had to go now to start the new career. Consequently, although it was the Army throwing him out, he now believed that was for the better for him personally and if the Army suffered by it well that was their fault for throwing him out in the first place.

"What a real pity," said the General and didn't raise the matter again. Jack did think about it again over the years and wondered what had set the General off in the first place; he was never to find out, but both of the Captains in Ludgershall had been Chief Clerks earlier in their careers and could well have served under the General and, perhaps, had approached him on Jack's behalf.

The General had proved to be a disaster throughout the course and it was just as well he would have a substantial pension to be able to afford to employ tradesmen when he retired. When they covered plumbing, they were using a newly invented system which just involved pushing plastic pipes together. The old way of soldering copper pipes was being replaced by plastic compression joints. Jack's, and all the other course members' joints, were watertight – not the Generals, they managed to flood the floor before they could get the water turned off. His wall papering was awful; the paper peeled off the wall, where there were two pieces touching the pattern did not match by a considerable length. His painting overlapped the glass and the wood to wall joints. Finally, the wall he built stood up! It had small buttresses at the back to help it to stand up – they weren't allowed to dig foundation trenches through the floor of the classrooms – and they then rough plastered the wall, about 2' 6" wide and 5' high. On top of the rough plaster went a smooth plaster which could then be the base for a painted or papered wall.

The Major had been unable to call the class around to admire the General's work, as he had done several times with all the other attendees, because it was so awful but looking at the wall, he seized his chance and called everyone around to admire it. He started with his, "I would like you to gather around and look at this wall…" As they all arrived, someone came in through the door slamming it behind them at which the General's plastering slid down the wall and onto the floor to be followed immediately by the bricks tumbling down in an untidy heap. From the back of the assembly came a voice,

"Christ, I hope he was a better General than he was a brickie," and the class dissolved in laughter, all bar the Major who wished there was a substantial foundation trench into which he could disappear.

The General laughed.

Chapter 34

Jack enjoyed the course and the company of the General; it was a rather unusual paring but they had got on well together. When Jack returned home on the Friday night it was to find a letter from the Civil Service recruiter waiting for him inviting him to an interview, at which an offer of employment would be made, on the following Tuesday. By this time Jack had made up his mind that he was going to accept the job in Northern Ireland and had written to accept it; the gasses job was the best of the others but working in London, expensive as it was – they had offered to match his Lieutenant's pay but he wouldn't get a pay rise for a few years until their pay structure caught up and gave him one, but the uncertainty of not knowing where he would be going at the end of an unknown training time all put him off. If he had not received the Irish job offer, he would probably have accepted it, but he had and Ireland it was. Still he would go on the Tuesday, the SEO had said he would check about the acceptability of the RMA Sandhurst exam and if he had found out that it was then there might be a decent offer coming and besides, it would get him out of the Depot for the day.

When he arrived at the Depot on Monday morning, it was to find a 2nd Lieutenant at the Guardhouse looking somewhat lost. There was something familiar about him and it was only when he got up close, he recognised him. Solomon Terence-Darby had been on the Young Officers Course with Jack nearly two years previously. A very considerable Hooray Henry, Jack and he had clashed almost immediately. Jack had been put in charge of ensuring that they all got to where they had to go and did what they had to do. Terence-Darby had resented that an ex-ranker should be giving him orders. Jack's commission predated Terence-Darby's which automatically made him the senior anyway, (Zulu with Michael Caine and Stanley Baker had shown the importance of seniority with Baker as Chard pulling rank on Caine as Bromhead by virtue of his earlier commission, which had come out a few years before) but the Adjutant specifically put Jack in charge even over two full Lieutenants and the 2nd Lieutenants but Terence-Darby tended to ignore this whenever he could. When Jack's resentment finally boiled over, at the constant superiority signalling by Terence-Darby and his spineless followers, it had resulted in Jack giving him a severe beating after a particularly tiresome and typical show by him, which resolved the matter at the time but now Jack was thinking was it about to start all over.

By now, Jack was, of course, a full Lieutenant having been promoted about four months previously. Jack not only wore the two stars on each shoulder, but in the two years had matured and become far more senior in manner and appearance. Terence-Darby recognised Jack at almost the same moment. He made no attempt to salute Jack. Saluting between 2nd Lieutenants and Lieutenants did not normally happen during the day, when they might meet one another frequently, but it was expected to happen on first meeting in the morning. Seeing that Terence-Darby had resumed his old tricks and seemed to be indicating no intention of saluting Jack, no matter how senior an ex-ranker he might have become, Jack said,

"You have ten seconds to salute me before I order Sergeant Rota here to lock you up in his Guardroom – you have room, don't you, Sergeant?"

"Yes indeed I do, Sir." Jack could tell by the alacrity of his reply that Terence-Darby had already been making himself unpopular with mere soldiers which Stan confirmed later in private. Terence-Darby saluted.

"Now, why are you here?" Jack asked, returning the salute in the most casual way possible.

"I have been posted here and am reporting in." Jack was surprised. There had been no talk of a replacement for himself before he left to go on the course four weeks before and given the OC's opening words when he, Jack, had arrived 10 months before, that there was no place for a junior officer, it was a bit of a surprise to find his replacement standing in front of him.

"You'd better come along then," said Jack and led off to the OC's office. Walking in, Jack saluted and said, "Look what I found, my replacement." Jack was to discover, again from the OC's Secretary that the OC had written to the Personnel Department saying how useful Jack had been and could he have another one. *Good luck with that,* thought Jack when he found out about it later in the week – he didn't believe that Terence-Darby would be anything like a good replacement for himself but you never know. He didn't care either.

He told the OC that he had an interview with the Civil Service the following day, so would not be in and also that he had managed to sell most of his uniforms and stuff to a Lieutenant Mike Huss who would meet him in the Officers' Mess on the Friday to take them away. Consequently, he, Jack, would not be in uniform on the Friday because he wouldn't have any. Although Jack delivered it as 'I am going to' rather than a request, the OC said,

"That's OK and come back in ten minutes and collect Mr Terence-Darby. I'd like you to manage his training, for this week at least, the same one as you went through." It took a moment for Jack to take in what the OC had just said and he replied,

"Yes, indeed, Sir." Scrubbers, here he comes!

When they got to the Reception bit and Jack introduced Terence-Darby to the Forewoman, he wished he'd had a camera to take his picture. Walking around the Depot on the tour before arriving at Reception, Terence-Darby had been pissed off at the reception accorded to Jack. "Welcome back, Sir" accompanied by a smart salute and a big smile had been the actions of most of the soldiers they had come across and it was obvious that Jack was well regarded. Even the civvies had started talking to him again since the strike. The Forewoman in Reception asked,

"Is it true that Friday is your last day in the Army, Sir?"

"Yes it is."

"Well, don't you forget to come and say goodbye to us, we've heard what you said about us when you presented your plan to break the strike and would like to say thank you for it." Jack wasn't sure if she meant they wanted to thank him for saying what hard workers they were or to speak to him about his role in breaking the strike.

"Well, I'll have to come back to collect Mr Terence-Darby here on Friday, if there's anything of him left." And with that, he turned to Terence-Darby and said, "I'd put some overalls on if I were you and you don't want to ruin your l-u-v-e-r-l-y SD." Terence-Derby's mouth dropped open.

"You don't mean that I am expected to get down there with these Scrubbers?" The tone of 'Scrubbers' clearly registered with the Forewoman whose face opened in a smile when Jack said,

"Not only do I expect you to get under there and scrub the vehicles but, being such a posh officer, I expect you to do a better job of it than they do." At that, Jack waived a salute in the general direction of the Forewoman and walked off.

As he walked away, Stan Rota caught up with him and said,

"The OC sends his apologies but he forgot to tell you that you are Duty Officer this week." Stan could see what Jack thought of that message by the look on his face. As they walked back to Tech Admin, Jack said,

"Strictly between you and me, watch out for that one, he's a wrong 'un." Just how wrong was to be proved much quicker than he thought.

The following day, Jack arrived five minutes before his appointment time but was kept waiting a good 15 mins. The SEO did at least have the courtesy to apologise profusely for doing so and he then followed that with another apology that he had checked the rules and the entrance exam for Sandhurst was not recognised by the Civil Service. Before Jack could say anything, he rushed on to say that nevertheless he did have some good news that he was able to offer Jack a job which he felt was right up his street and which was something with which Jack would already be au fait which would be a help when he took the EO's exam in a year's time. Handing Jack a letter, he said,

"You will obviously be more familiar with these Army terms, such as CVD Ludgershall, than am I but what do you think?" As Jack read it, he could not believe what he was reading. The letter was offering him a Clerical Officer post in Tech Admin at CVD Ludgershall!

"You are right that I do understand CVD etc. That department is currently made up of about 25 Civil Servants, the normal Clerical Assistants with Clerical Officers over them, three or four Executive Officers over them and a Senior Executive Officer over all of them. The Army command of that office is a Captain's post and under him, but overall the Civil Servants, is a full Lieutenant that is, me. You are offering me the most junior CO post, at a salary currently half my own, in an office in which I am already in charge most of the time when the Captain is away. Is this some kind of joke?" As the import of what Jack had been saying sunk in, so the blood slowly drained out of the tax guy's face.

"No, no, not at all." Snatching back the letter, he read it through. "There must be some kind of mistake. Still we do have other posts." Scrabbling around on his desk, he picked up another piece of paper and said, "Look we have a CO post in the Command Pay Office in Tidworth which I could offer you."

"You mean the one I go to every week, with armed guards and a dog, to collect the pay for the soldiers at Ludgershall and where the staff customarily stand up when I enter the room and where I would have to stand up when the 2nd Lieutenant, who has replaced me at the Depot, comes to collect the pay every week?" Jack wasn't too sure that his English was very good at this point but the SEO certainly understood. Before he could say anymore Jack said,

"No, I'm not going to waste your time anymore. I only came in the hope that you would say my exam qualification was accepted and you were going to offer me an EO post in which case the salary might have been somewhere acceptable but £750pa is not anywhere near acceptable. I have been offered a job at a Training Board in Northern Ireland, which is a Government, i.e. civil service type post at £1,750pa and I am going to accept it." (He didn't want to reveal he had already accepted it and coming today was therefore a complete waste of time for the SEO; but it wasn't a waste for Jack; it was a day out of the depot and the Army.)

"But that's more than I'm getting and you don't have any qualifications," spluttered the SEO. Jack laughed.

"Tough," he said and walked out. It was ironic that the Civil Service, many years later was to do away with the minimum of five GCE 'O' levels as the qualification for entry, as it was said to restrict minority, ethnic groups etc. from entering the Civil Service. It certainly led to a huge increase in numbers being recruited and an identifiable point at which the standard of work produced in the Civil Service fell apart.

Jack conducted the inspection he was required to carry out once per week of the soldiers as Duty Officer, with Terence-Darby in attendance, and was very moved that when he dismissed them to their duties they all clapped him.

On Wednesday, they took stock of the Depot. It was for the Annual Admin Inspection which was due the following week. Every commanding officer hated them as they effectively tested the commander's quality of managing the unit. In Ludgershall, everything to be counted was a problem because the vehicles were constantly on the move and counting them therefore became very difficult. The first count showed that they had one Chieftain tank too many in the Depot. That seemed impossible so they had to count the moving vehicles all over again. Again they came up with one too many. So they had to count them again but this time all the vehicles were stopped and not allowed to move until the count was over. The problem was that count threw up one too many Chieftains! The only way to determine which one it was, was to note the number plates and then compare them to the vehicle receipt records to find out which one it was. It was finally identified late in the evening. An armoured regiment had moved back from BAOR to the UK and been issued with all their armoured vehicles having left theirs in Germany for the Regiment taking over from them. This was the first Regiment to be issued with the Chieftain as the numbers coming off the production line had been issued abroad first and lastly to UK-based units. The Regiment concerned had come in to the Depot to collect their vehicles and drive/transport them to Tidworth where they were based. Most were transported on RCT Transporters but a few had elected to drive them back by exiting the Depot back gate and driving them cross-country. One of them had been collected by a 2nd Lieutenant who had been on the course ahead of Jack's at Mons. The progeny of a very, very important family, ADC to a Royal, scheduled for great things in the City, Parliament and a post as a Minister of the Crown, he had failed to listen to the instructions of how his Chieftain should be driven, had elected to drive it himself rather than sit up in the turret and had wrecked the gearbox inside of 300 yards and 100 yards before the back gate. Considering that the tank was designed to stand up to shot and shell, mines and clumsy soldiery to wreck it so comprehensively so quickly was quite in keeping with his normal standard of performance. As, unfortunately for him, he had signed for the tank as being A1, properly kitted, full of fuel etc. etc. The tank belonged to him and no longer to CVD Ludgershall. It was therefore his responsibility to get it repaired. He had left the Depot saying that he would arrange for it to be collected that afternoon and that was two months ago. In fact, the tank had stood there so long that weeds and flowers were growing up through the tracks. Captain Ivan Novicoff, due out of the Army shortly himself decided to telephone the Israeli Colonel responsible for buying tanks for Israel and asked him if he would like to buy a Chieftain going very cheap as it had a buggered gearbox. Negotiations were progressing slowly and carefully but unfortunately the Regiment with a history going back to the Charge of the Light Brigade and before had their annual admin inspection coming up and had discovered that they were one Chieftain short. Phone calls to Ludgershall were answered with a "Sorry, mate, we haven't got it, we have a piece of paper here signed saying that you took it from us so you have it". But unfortunately the Chieftain could be seen from the road to the back gate and the Regiment appeared with a transporter, loaded it on to it and disappeared before anyone in the Depot could stop them. It cost Ivan a slap-up lunch for the Israeli Colonel who wasn't too pleased to travel all the way to Ludgershall from London for nothing! Just quite how Novicoff was going to sell it to the Israeli Colonel and divide the money amongst the officers was unknown to Jack and he never did find out!

Jack was also required to check on the Guard at night once in the week. It was entirely up to him what time he did it at, not like the machinations created by that prat at the Depot but it was impossible to catch them out sleeping on duty or similar because of the way the Depot was set up. The Guard was provided by Ministry of Defence Police and once everyone had gone home for the night the gates, front only because the gates at the back were only unlocked on special occasions, were locked and the six war dogs let loose. To obtain access at night, one had to drive up to the front gate and ring the bell. That activity would normally attract the attention of the dogs who would look upon the caller as supper and indeed would enjoy them as such if it were not for the handlers calling them in. If they were asleep in the Guardroom, it would never be possible to catch them at it because no one in their right mind would enter the Depot whilst the dogs were loose. The time taken to round them up was always long enough to allow the Guards and the Duty Driver to remove all evidence of sleeping. The only other one in the Guardroom was the Duty Sergeant, in charge of the military element of the Guard. He was a bit of an anachronism as there were no soldiers on guard so no one for him to command but no one was prepared to do away with the duty.

When Jack described the duty to Terence-Darby and that he thought they were probably, regularly, sleeping on duty and relying on the dogs to keep the Depot safe, Terence-Darby said,

"What would happen if someone fed poisoned meat to the dogs?"

"Indeed," said Jack, "but it's difficult to imagine what they would want to steal. Any vehicle starting up would create so much noise, it would be bound to wake everyone. Anyway, the keys are kept locked in a safe in one of the hangars so it would have to be something fairly small. There are no weapons on site so anyone wanting to steal easily portable stuff from the stores would have to break in there, so overall I don't think there is too much to worry about, especially as Phil Townley told me the dogs have been trained not to eat anything that is not fed to them by their handlers." Later that day, Terence-Darby came to Jack and said,

"I've thought of a way to creep up on the Guards and catch them asleep." Jack looked at him.

"How?"

"We could park a Ferret with a turret by the back gate just before finishing time. No one uses that gate so it would not be noticed. You could drive me to the back gate when we come in to inspect the Guard and leave me there, then drive back to the front gate. Don't ring the bell which would warn the Guard but your presence at the gate with your lights on will attract the dogs. When I see the way's clear, I'll climb the fence and jump in the Ferret before the dogs can get to me. I can then drive to the Guardroom, nip out and catch them." Jack looked at him.

"You're bloody mad, but on your head, be it." So that's what they did. There was no sign of the dogs at the back gate, it was after all a good 400 yards away so Jack drove back to the front gate and stopped. As he had guessed, the dogs were hanging around there and all congregated at the gate barking like mad; so much so that Jack only just heard the Ferret starting up. Ferrets were not easy vehicles to drive and they certainly weren't like an ordinary car. Terence-Darby must have had someone show him how to do it because it did start alright but almost immediately, it spluttered and died. The plan, however, had failed before that point. The dogs barking at Jack made so much noise that they woke the Guard anyway, if indeed they had been asleep. Also Terence-Darby hadn't worked out that if he had been able to drive to the Guardroom, then the dogs were there, or very soon would be drawn by the moving Ferret and he would not have been able to get out and reach the Guardroom without the dogs getting him. As it was, Jack inspected the Guard, signed the Duty Book as everything all right and said goodnight to Stan Rota, who was the Duty Sergeant that night. He then drove home leaving Terence-Darby sitting up in the Ferret turret with the dogs sitting all around it looking up at him. Jack discovered later that someone had drained all the petrol out of the Ferret leaving just enough in the carburettor to start it up and get it 20 or 30 yds from the back gate. Perhaps if Terence-Darby had carried out a proper reconnaissance, he would have discovered that Jack had shared a room with Stan Rota, the Duty Sergeant, in Aden, and their wives were still good friends even if Jack and Stan were not able to mix so freely anymore. Jack often wondered in future years whether he would have made that phone call to the Guardroom if it had not been Stan on duty.

The Friday passed very quickly. He arrived in civilian clothes even though technically he was a commissioned officer until midnight. For most of the morning, he was finishing off a report and then he drove down to the Mess at lunchtime where he handed almost all his uniforms over to the Lieutenant there, Mike Huss, who was exactly the same size and shape as Jack and who was delighted to enlarge his wardrobe with the kit. Jack did very little in the afternoon, he had no intention of going around all the departments to say goodbye that he felt would be too stressful, but some of the staff had other ideas. The Scrubber Forewoman arrived and dragged him to Reception. There she made a little speech thanking him for the respect and kind comments he had made about them and handed him a card and a Pewter Tankard as a gift. Terence-Darby was under one of the vehicles and he ignored Jack who was equally happy to ignore him. As he really had nothing to do, he stopped by the OC's office; he wasn't there which Jack knew, but he wanted to say goodbye to his Secretary, which he did and then he was staggered to find as he drove past the Guardroom that the two Captains, Phil Townley and Ivan Novicoff, were lined up, along with Stan Rota, two of the Corporals, the one who had guided him over the OC's Mini and the one who had moved the railway line, who were all called to attention by Phil and they all saluted as he drove past. The Army wasn't quite finished with Jack but for now that was his career over.

Epilogue

The second book is real and set in an even smaller area and time than the first so some people would appear to be easily identifiable, they are not! It is a work of faction with real settings and times but the author has created his own world in this time and place so although you may think you can identify yourself, you can't!